# *My* BROTHER THEMBA

## MICHELE VAN RENSBURG

For my sons

*"Unless we learn to live together as brothers,
we will die together as fools."* —Martin Luther King Jr

Cover art by JRM Creative
Edited by Nancy Haight

Cover design copyright © Michele van Rensburg

Paperback ISBN: 978-1-09835-730-6
ebook ISBN: 978-1-09835-731-3

Printed in the United States of America

# PROLOGUE

ALEX AND THEMBA FORMED A sibling relationship in the late 1970s when South Africa was still in the steely grip of Apartheid. The years leading up to 1989 were turbulent. Finally, President FW de Klerk recognised that minority rule was no longer viable, and a period of hope was born, when he and Nelson Mandela negotiated the transition of power, culminating in a free and fair election for all.

Alex and Themba's lives are affected by their early foundations in brotherhood and friendships. The bonds they form will last a lifetime and become integral to the men they become.

This story is about the macro environment's influences on individual's lives. The micro-environment responds to these external influences, sweeping along the characters, mostly against their control. The characters try and negotiate their lives, make allowances and mediate against external control mechanisms like segregation as a policy of the apartheid government.

# Table of Contents

Prologue vii

Glossary xi

Chapter 1 1

Chapter 2 6

Chapter 3 13

Chapter 4 21

Chapter 5 44

Chapter 6 59

Chapter 7 72

Chapter 8 81

Chapter 9 83

Chapter 10 89

Chapter 11 98

Chapter 12 107

Chapter 13 111

Chapter 14 119

Chapter 15 131

Chapter 16 150

Chapter 17 155

Chapter 18 167

Chapter 19 173

Chapter 20 177

Chapter 21 182

Chapter 22                                        184

Chapter 23                                        193

Chapter 24                                        203

Chapter 25                                        210

Chapter 26                                        217

Chapter 27                                        224

Chapter 28                                        230

Chapter 29                                        239

Chapter 30                                        241

Chapter 31                                        254

Chapter 32                                        258

Chapter 33                                        260

Chapter 34                                        262

Chapter 35                                        268

Epilogue                                          273

Acknowledgements                                  276

# GLOSSARY

| | |
|---|---|
| Alexander | Strength, protection |
| Themba | Trusted, faithful, hope |
| Soetewater | Sweet Water |
| Kasteel | Castle |
| Braai | Barbeque, a type of social gathering |
| Gogo | Grandmother, or granny |
| Veld | Field |
| Baas | Master or boss |
| Pap | Maizemeal porridge as a breakfast |
| Stywe pap | Maizemeal porridge, with a thick consistency, used alongside savoury meals or barbeque |
| Afkak | Afrikaans word which relates to a form of physical punishment used in schools, usually by an older child on a younger child |
| Snoek | Cod |
| Kaffir | Derogatory term used to describe a black person |
| Bakkie | Pickup truck |
| Stoep | Veranda or porch |
| Bobotie | Mild oven-baked beef curry of Malaysian origin |
| Umntwana | Child |

# CHAPTER 1

*December 1977,*
*Soetewater Farm, Karoo, South Africa*

THE EARLY MORNING SUN PEEKED over the hilltop, which was still a dark silhouette against the pale blue skyline. The golden grass swayed in the tender breeze as if dancing to a rhythm of African music. The heat rose with the *tjir-tjir* sound of the sun beetles heralding the start of the day. A persistent murmur announcing that summer had arrived.

Amongst the bushes, rocks and thorn trees, Alex could see a zebra standing alone as if watching him sitting on the top step of the *stoep*. He lifted his binoculars, saw the zebra's dark eyes, with the long eyelashes, blinking. He panned his view to the right and the left but did not see any others. Alex thought he must be a young zebra, as he did not have much height to him. It was all alone in the *veld*.

Alex continued sitting on the *stoep* step, looking at the dusty yard and his mother's attempts at a garden. Each fruit tree stood in its own square bit of tilled brown soil. They had yellow cling peaches, mulberries, quince and fig trees. Alex's mother made jams or preserved the fruit in some way every season. Alex's favourite was the whole preserved green fig, which he would hold by the stem and bite into, the sweet syrup running down his chin.

Soon he'd have to go and water each plant. Alex placed his binoculars on the stone step and wondered what his classmate, Klaas, was doing today. Klaas lived on a neighbouring farm, Kasteel. School had just broken up for the summer holidays, and he would not see his school friends for six weeks. Alex hoped his mother would let him phone his friend in a few days to see if they could arrange to visit each other. He knew this would mean asking his father to take him to Klaas's home in the farm *bakkie*, which was about an hour's drive away, on a bumpy dirt track. His heart sank as he realised his father was unlikely to do this, as it was a long trip to undertake when his father was usually out at dawn and only returned home by sunset. A whole day's work would be lost.

An added problem was that his parents were not going to the beach cabins in Port Alfred this year. They usually went every Christmas summer holiday to meet up with aunties, uncles and cousins. His father had explained that he needed to do significant refurbishments of the farm's water reservoir pumps, or they would not have enough throughput of water during the dry winter. Ever since the drought five years ago, his father was fastidious about ensuring the borehole and pumps were in working order at all times. The cattle and sheep needed a constant supply of water, while they foraged for food. The Karoo was a dry and unforgiving environment. You could not let your guard down.

The long, hot, summer lay ahead of him. No friends, no brothers. The only time he might get to see his friends was during a trip to town with his parents to church on a Sunday. He enjoyed going to Sunday school with the other children, while the grownups attended the service. Sunday school did not take place during school holidays, but at least he would get to hang out with his friends while his parents drank coffee and ate cake after the service.

He could also go with his father when he took the farmworkers into Cradock once a month so they could buy supplies. He might bump into a friend then, and go for ice cream or a Coca Cola at the café. There were possibilities, but not many. Alex felt glum and lonely. He sat with his chin in his hand, thinking about all his options. But he kept coming back to the beginning, which lay like a blank canvas on his mind.

The *stoep* step was still cold, but Alex knew that once the sun was up, the heat would slowly increase, like an oven warming up just before his mother baked bread. He'd best get going while the morning was still crisp. Putting his daydreaming aside, he stood up and made his way to water the plants, then to feed the chickens and collect any eggs that they had laid since yesterday.

Even though he was only eight, Alex was tall and strong for his age and able to carry a full watering can to each plant. He liked to accidentally splash himself at the same time; the cold water trickled down between his toes, washing the dry brown dust off his bare feet. Alex, like his friends, never wore shoes unless it was to church.

He went to the storeroom and collected a tub of chicken feed. As he walked to the hen house, he could see in the distance two figures walking down the dirt track from the main tarred road. One was much smaller than the other. He ducked his head and went into the chicken coup to feed the hens and collected the eggs.

He placed the tub of eggs at the back door; they were ready for his mother to use for cooking or baking. He deliberately walked around to the front *stoep* where he had been sitting earlier and sat down on the step waiting. The two figures slowly got bigger and bigger. They were less of a silhouette now, as he could begin to see who they may be. A woman was carrying a suitcase, and a child was walking next to her.

The woman approached the house at the front steps where Alex was sitting. They greeted each other in isiXhosa. Alex knew the basic greetings but was not fluent. The woman picked up on this and switched to speaking broken English.

"I've come for the job," she said. Alex assumed it would be something his mother was aware of, and he asked her to wait while he called his mother. The child stood behind the woman, peering at Alex from the side. He had big brown eyes and short, curly black hair on a brown face with two dimples next to a smile of gleaming white teeth. Alex cocked his head at the child, then jumped up and went into the house to search for his mother.

"Mum," he called, walking into the kitchen. His mother's hands were full of flour, which she wiped on her apron as he told her about the visitor.

"Ah, yes," she said, "she's called Beauty and is coming to work for me in the house." Alex followed his mother out front.

4

While his mother and Beauty were talking, Alex tried to catch the eye of the child. He went behind Beauty and said hello to the child. "My name is Alex, what's yours?"

Beauty broke off speaking to his mother and talked to the child in isiXhosa.

The child then said, "Themba."

"Alex," his mother caught his attention, "will you take Beauty and Themba down to Gogo's hut. Gogo is expecting them. They are going to stay with her." Alex started walking, motioning for the mother and son to follow him.

# CHAPTER 2

*November 1977,*
*Kasteel Farm, Karoo*

SARA DROVE HER LITTLE VOLKSWAGEN Beetle slowly and gingerly down the winding dirt road that led to the Kasteel Farm homestead. The track was dry, and the car kicked up more and more dust the further she went. She had to keep the windows shut, but the vehicle soon heated up, and a glistening film of sweat covered Sara's body. She drove carefully, as there were potholes everywhere and the road was like an uneven corrugated iron surface. She would rather be late for her visit than break down on a deserted farm road.

Although the two farms were adjacent to each other, the Fish River bordered Kasteel on the western side and the rolling blue mountains on the other. Sara had to make a round trip as the entrance to the 3,000-hectare farm was on the opposite side. The family were one of the wealthiest and most successful farmers in the Eastern Cape dating back to the 1800s.

The farmer's wife, Karen, had invited her to come for coffee while their sons were at school and their husbands were out working on their farms. Sara did not know Karen very well. They only met on rare occasions at church on a Sunday. They usually chatted over a cup of coffee while serving the congregation from the kitchen after the service. Karen's husband was a highly respected deacon in the church and would often lead the service when their minister was away.

A few weeks ago, Karen had invited her to Kasteel, as she knew Sara was looking for a domestic worker. Sara had mentioned that she was teaching part-time at the children's school and that she needed some help at home. Karen had a worker called Beauty, who was looking for alternative employment, so they agreed to meet up.

Transferring staff between farms was common and usually came with a recommendation and a clear understanding of the worker's skills.

Eventually, Sara arrived at the main entrance to the farmhouse and parked near the house. The traditional, white-washed farmhouse had two white front-facing Cape Dutch style gables on each side of a deep *stoep*. There was a sweeping set of stairs to the double-fronted glass doors. The lawns to the front of the house were immaculate, with two large acacia trees giving the garden and flower beds much-needed shade. Water to keep this garden looking so green and fertile would be from a borehole or the river, Sara thought. She was impressed. This magnificent property was a far cry from their homestead, which was a simple two-bedroomed house, with a covered *stoep* running along the front.

Karen was waiting at the entrance and welcomed her inside. Sara noted that the house's interior style was in traditional South African yellow wood furniture, and spotlessly tidy, with glossy polished wooden floors and a pair of Gemsbok horns mounted on the wall on either side of the front doors. The house felt fresh and crisp, despite the bright and harsh Karoo sunshine. They went into the living room, and Karen called out to Beauty to bring coffee and rusks for their guest.

Sara wondered why Karen had wanted to discuss the arrangements in her home instead of at their church meeting. Karen launched straight into the purpose of their meeting in hurried and hushed tones, telling Sara why she needed to explain the agreement in confidence, away from church.

"Sara, I know I can trust you. You are a teacher and used to keeping pupils' home circumstances confidential," Karen whispered like they were co-conspirators in some elaborate plan.

With a sigh, Karen continued to tell her that her husband had a sexual relationship with Beauty some years ago, and there was a child. This child was therefore of mixed race or Coloured, and she was worried that her husband would get in to trouble as it was against the apartheid laws for there to be relations between a black person and a white person.

"You know it is illegal, and my husband could go to prison if the authorities became aware of the child. I can't have a scandal in this close-knit community where everyone knows your business. You know my husband is a deacon as well," she continued.

Their family life and status in the town would be open to public ridicule. This child was evidence that such relations had occurred. When he was young, they could hide the child amongst the other farmworkers and their families in the compound, which was away from the main house, but now that he was nearing seven, it had become challenging as he was more difficult to contain and control. Karen sighed with relief, the circumstances and burden finally shared with someone she felt she could trust.

Sara looked aghast at Karen, who appeared anxious, holding her breath and speaking in soft staccato tones, explaining this was why she had wanted her to visit her at home while her husband was out in the fields working. Beauty came in with a tray with cups of coffee and rusks. Sara spoke briefly to her, and they agreed that she would move across to Soetewater in December.

"Please," Karen said, "don't mention our agreement to my husband; he knows nothing about this. When Beauty is gone, I'll tell him she ran away. He won't be bothered, as it's happened before. Our husbands only really talk to each other at church and don't visit each other, which means that she will be safe with you. I needed someone to help me that didn't have any links to my family and was someone I could trust. You're not from here, are you, and your family live in Cape Town, yes?"

"Yes, you're right, I come from Cape Town where my family still live. I came here about ten years ago, as a newly qualified teacher, and I met my husband and stayed in Cradock. What do you mean by me being able to keep Beauty and her son safe?" Sara was puzzled.

After some hesitation, Karen replied, "Well, he won't beat her anymore, or threaten to kill her if she told anyone who the father of her child is. I'm also worried she'll have another baby." Sara didn't know what to say, so she nodded that she understood that she had to keep this a secret. Sara wondered whether Beauty had any say in any of this. Had Karen challenged her husband about this? Most likely not. Families in this farming area were mostly patriarchal, with women having little say in their private affairs and having to resort to covert manipulation to regain some control.

Karen sat with her hands in her lap, wringing her fingers, knotting and unknotting them. Sara then noticed bruising on Karen's inner arms. She was about to ask her what these were and whether she was okay when they both heard a *bakkie* screech to a halt outside.

Sara recognised Karen's husband Klaas Senior, as he came storming through the doorway speaking in a booming voice. "And what do we have here, a bunch of cackling hens?" Klaas Senior was tall and weighed at least 115 kilograms. His bulk dominated the doorway and blocked out the sunlight.

Karen began to stutter, saying, "I … I knew you were out in the fields all day, and I felt like some company. I had asked Sara to come and visit as we've only recently chatted at church. We also need to work out the coffee rota for the ladies serving after the service on Sundays."

The man's towering presence was intimidating, and by Karen's behaviour, Sara could see she was anxious and guilty that her husband had walked in on her visit, which he was oblivious to. His towering bulk was blocking the doorway. Sara began to feel very uncomfortable, and she had an overwhelming need to get out of the house as fast as she could.

"I, um, I was about to leave. We were chatting about our boys and how they are doing at school this year." Sara turned to Karen, saying, "Thanks for the hospitality, but I really must go home as my husband will be expecting his lunch. I'll draw up the rota of ladies to do the serving, and we can finalise it at church."

"Yes, you women must make sure that hungry, hard-working farmer husbands are well-fed," Klaas grunted, standing with his feet apart and hands on his hips. Sara thought to herself, well that's not what my husband says. He often made his own lunch, especially when it was one of the days she was teaching at school. Her instinct was that it was best not to challenge this large and intimidating man. His physical presence and brusque demeanour made her feel uneasy. Her instinct was giving her brain the message that the underlying threat would be physical. She stood and picked up her handbag to go.

Klaas Senior did not move from the front door until she got right up to him and she had to prompt him to make way for her by saying, "Excuse me, I need to go now." He slowly moved out of her way, keeping a fixed smile with his piercing gaze directed at her, his hands still on his hips. She had to squeeze past him through the doorway.

Outside, Sara fumbled with her keys. Her hands were shaking so much that they rattled in her hand. She dropped them, picked them up, and got back in her car, relieved, and set off back home. Her heart was pounding, and sweat was running off her forehead. She held on tightly to the steering wheel, again slowly and carefully navigating the many pot-holes in the dirt road. She was petrified of hitting one and having to go back to Kasteel homestead and asking for help.

Once she reached the main road, she let out a sigh of relief, breathed deeply and slowly, dropped her hunched up shoulders, changed gears and turned on to the tarred road. With some clarity in her mind, and with her breathing steady again, she wondered why a wealthy farmer would not resurface the access road to the farm. Was it a way of keeping people out? Was it a way of keeping people at a distance and nurturing secrets? Was the consequent dust storm from a vehicle a warning signal to Klaas?

She promised herself she would never go back to Kasteel again. Any socialising with Karen would have to be at church gatherings.

# CHAPTER 3

*December 1977,*
*Soetewater Farm, Karoo*

SARA WATCHED FROM THE FRONT door as Alex knocked and entered Gogo's hut, followed by Beauty and Themba. She felt nervous and relieved that mother and son were finally safe, but she was not sure what the future would bring. Sara wanted to avoid talking to Klaas Senior at church or being forced to answer any questions about what had happened regarding Beauty's disappearance. Thinking it through, she doubted he would speak to her about this. He would most probably brush it under the carpet to keep this child's existence a secret. Maybe he would even be relieved that they had run away or disappeared.

To be on the safe side, she would make excuses for them not to go to church for a few Sundays. Her husband was so busy servicing the borehole pumps, she knew he would prefer to stay home to finish the work. That would be a good excuse all round.

Sara thought about how best to keep Beauty and Themba safe. She was worried that Alex would inadvertently blurt out at school that they had a new housemaid and her son living with them. Perhaps it would as a start be best to use Beauty's isiXhosa name, Buhle. She shook her head, still struggling to understand why people insisted on changing worker's traditional names, perhaps because they struggled to pronounce them? Or was it a way of denying their traditional heritage? Sara knew her views were considered liberal and in the minority in this rural area, and she had to be careful with what she said. She and her husband shared their ideas, but always in private. Being a dissenting voice would not go down well, and some may even feel the need to report them to the authorities.

Alex knocked and entered Gogo's home. He greeted her warmly and introduced Beauty and Themba. While the two women spoke and settled in, Alex motioned to Themba to go outside with him. Alex walked around the farmyard, showing Themba where the chickens were, where his father's workshop was, and the garden that he looked after.

"Themba, all the farmworkers have their own chickens and that vegetable garden," Alex said, pointing towards the open area encircled by the workers' huts. There was a large patch for growing vegetables with a chicken coup next to it.

"I'll let Gogo show you around. She's in charge of it all."

No doubt, Themba would be expected to help her look after the chickens and water the vegetable patch like he did for his parents, but Alex felt that was best explained by Gogo in isiXhosa. Alex wasn't quite sure whether Themba understood him, but he thought to carry on talking in English anyway.

Gogo's husband had been a farm labourer all his life. When her husband died, Alex's parents kept Gogo on to look after the vegetable garden and chickens to feed the other workers and to give her a roof over her head.

Alex led Themba towards the back of the farmhouse. Alex showed him his workbench in his father's workshop. He explained to Themba how he had been making the wire-frame cars with which all the local children played. Themba nodded that he understood.

Alex used pieces of thick wire his father no longer needed to fix the fences on the farm. He twisted the wire with his father's fencing pliers, using a thinner wire to bind the various parts into making the shape of a car, with wheels that turned. The steering mechanism was a rudimentary axle fixed to the steering column. Alex also shaped the wheels from the wire.

Making sure they were round and could run smoothly required skill. Alex steered the car with an extended cable attached to an oversized steering wheel at child height so he could run behind it, pushing it. He could walk or run behind the vehicle, turning the wheel left or right, pretending he was driving. Alex loved this game and had made quite a few cars. A few months ago he had bought a car from an older boy when he was in town with his parents and copied it. It was trial and error, but eventually, it worked, with a bit of help from his father. He tried to explain to Themba that he would make him one if he wanted. Themba nodded his head, smiling up at him.

Alex took Themba back to Gogo's hut and explained he'd come and fetch him in the morning, and they would work on a car for him. Themba nodded and grinned. Beauty put her arm around

Themba, smiled and asked Alex if he could try and speak as much English to Themba as he could, as she wanted him to become fluent. He promised he would.

Alex ran back to the house, arms pumping the air, thinking, *Wow, I've got a friend now, no more lonely summer ahead.*

Alex ran into the kitchen, breathless, asking his mother, "Are Themba and his mum staying with us forever?"

"Well, I don't know about forever, Alex," she replied. "Perhaps for a long time. I was thinking, Alex. It's always best or more respectful to call someone by their given name. I think we need to call Beauty, Buhle, which is her real name. What do you think?"

Alex nodded his head. "Yes, that's a nicer name, really; it's more like a real name. Beauty isn't an isiXhosa name, is it?"

"No," his mother said. "We'll only call her Buhle from now on. Alex, you say it properly by pronouncing *Bu..gggh..le.*" Sara modelled the sound with her tongue on the roof of her mouth, blowing out the *gh* sound.

"Will you lay the table now, Alex? Your Pa will be home soon, and I'm sure he'll be hungry. I've cooked his favourite mutton and tomato stew."

"Yum, I am hungry, Mum," Alex said, taking three plates and cutlery out of the cupboard, and setting the table in the kitchen.

Sara could hear her husband, Dan, coming into the back yard in his *bakkie*. Brown dust flew across the yard. He went straight to the outdoor shower behind the workshop to clean up and change.

Dan was a soft-spoken man who was both fair and firm with his workers. Sara knew their workers were loyal to him, and they always went to him with any disputes or troubles they had. He worked as hard as any of them and was still the last to come home after a day's work. Their marriage was stable and resilient, and they worked well together as a team. She managed the household and Alex's schooling as well as the farm's accounts. Dan was practical and supervised the workers, the farm livestock and crops.

She taught part-time at Alex's small bilingual school. Cradock was a rural town, traditionally Afrikaans-speaking with the matching culture. The Eastern Cape towns of Port Alfred were mostly English-speaking, so there tended to be a crossover in languages. IsiXhosa was the language spoken by most Black people in the area, but they spoke Afrikaans on the farms as well. Dan spoke isiXhosa and Afrikaans fluently, but he was not as fluent in English with a heavy Afrikaans accent. They spoke mostly English in their home.

Dan walked through the back door, his dark brown hair still wet from his shower. He kissed his wife on the cheek. Alex smiled at his father, who ruffled his hair, which was the same colour and short. Dan was not a man of many words, but Alex usually babbled away, making up for his father's shortcoming.

"I've got a new friend, Pa," Alex said. "His name's Themba, and he's seven years old."

Dan looked confused, "I didn't know we had any children on the farm called Themba."

Sara went on to explain the basic circumstances of Buhle and Themba joining them. She left out the bit of Themba's paternity. She knew Dan wouldn't be interested anyway.

"Oh," said Dan, "that's alright then. I need you to keep helping me with the farm accounts, Sara, and of course, your teaching. I'm

17

glad you've got a friend, son. At least you won't get lonely during the holidays. I know the other farm children are a lot younger than you, so they aren't regular playmates."

With that, the family tucked into their meal, with Alex chatting about what he and Themba would be doing the next day. Dan just nodded and smiled at his son.

~

As the morning sun began to shine through his bedroom curtains, Alex stretched and started to wake up. He peeked through the window and saw Themba sitting on the steps of the *stoep* waiting for him. He wondered if Buhle was already in the kitchen getting breakfast prepared.

He pulled on his shorts and t-shirt and went into the kitchen. His mother was talking while showing Buhle the cooking area, stove and scullery. Soon, Buhle was putting on the breakfast *pap,* which needed cooking for a while. Alex went through to the *stoep* and sat next to Themba. Alex chatted to him, assuming Themba understood everything he was saying. Themba would smile, looking at Alex, pulling funny faces and nodding. Alex laughed and carried on babbling away in English.

Dan was always up at sunrise and was busy in his workshop until breakfast was ready. Today, he would be going out with some workers to fix posts and fencing before moving on to servicing the borehole pumps.

He had been feeling guilty that they were not going to Port Alfred this year. Alex, as an only child, enjoyed spending the long hot summer days at the seaside cabin with his cousins. To be honest, Dan also enjoyed spending time with his brothers, *braaiing*, fishing and generally catching up on family news over the evening campfires. Perhaps if he felt comfortable that all the pumps were working and all the maintenance work was up to date, he could leave the farm for a week in January just before the schools opened again. His family usually spent four weeks over Christmas at the cabins, going back home after the New Year. He wouldn't tell Alex yet, just in case it didn't work out.

Sara had to admit that Buhle was an excellent cook; her *pap* was just the right consistency and cooked to perfection. It was a real skill. Preparing it for the proper length of time was something Sara could never do. She knew she was too impatient, and the *pap* ended up lumpy and undercooked, or she put salt in, which Buhle didn't. The *pap* was sweetened by adding sugar when you ate it for breakfast.

Alex and Themba sat on the *stoep,* each with a bowl of steaming *pap*. Dan came into the kitchen and had his breakfast while Sara packed sandwiches, some cake and biscuits and a flask of coffee for him as it was going to be a long, hot day out on the farm. Dan rarely came back at lunchtime; he preferred taking a break with the lunch Sara had packed for him.

So, the family routine started with Buhle cooking breakfast, the boys eating together, and Dan eating and heading out on the farm for the day. Sara used the spare time to catch up on the farm's accounting and bookkeeping. Buhle wasn't very talkative, but Sara thought she'd let her settle in, and hopefully, she would with time feel safe on their farm. Ever the teacher, Sara thought she'd share her recipe books with her and prepare Buhle for housekeeping when she was back to teaching after the school holidays, and also preparing lessons and marking papers at home.

∼

Buhle and Themba soon settled in with Gogo. Themba slept on a mattress on the floor in the living area and kitchen. She shared a double bed with Gogo who was kind and treated Buhle like a daughter. She told Buhle that her daughter lived in Johannesburg, and she had not seen her for years and missed her. Her husband had died, so she was now all alone, but she was glad she had them for company.

Buhle felt relief that she and Themba were finally away from Kasteel. She always had to be on her guard, never sure when her *baas* would be in the house, shout at her or slap her if she did something he didn't like. Making the coffee too strong or weak, not making sure his food was piping hot when she served it. Also, she hated the nights when he would come to her room at the back of the house.

She tried not to think about those nights. She loved her son Themba, even though his father had raped her. She wanted to protect him, keep him away from the *baas*, but this had become more difficult as Themba would often roam the farm without any fear. Themba usually stayed in the workers' compound with the other children, while she had to remain in the back room at the main house. She would sneak off during the day or evening to see Themba, so she was unable to keep him under control.

# CHAPTER 4

AFTER BREAKFAST EACH DAY, ALEX and Themba would begin working side-by-side on the wire car. The workshop was quiet, with the two boys' heads together. Alex's hair was brown and short like his fathers and Themba's was dark and curly. They started by using the pliers and tools to bend the wire and to attach the parts of the car they were building.

By late morning, the shed was becoming too hot and uncomfortable. Alex asked Themba if he could swim. Themba shook his head no. Alex told him it was time to learn, and they would go down to the river. Alex was a strong swimmer, but he always had to tell his mother when he went down to the river. Alex called out to his mother, who was pouring over the farm's accounts.

"Mum, I'm taking Themba down to the river to learn to swim," he said.

"You'd best check with Buhle first," she replied.

Alex and Themba ran into the kitchen where Buhle was preparing vegetables. "Buhle, is it okay if Themba and I go down to the river? I want to teach him to swim."

Buhle thought Alex seemed strong and confident. She knew he was a good swimmer; more importantly, she trusted him. "Yes, okay, but come back for lunch," she said. Themba and Alex looked at each other, smiled and nodded.

The day was like any other Karoo summer day: hot and dry, no wind, with clear blue skies. The boys walked down to the river, which was a well-trodden path from the farmyard. After about half an hour, they made their way through the thicket leading to the river bank.

"You see that Themba?" Alex said, pointing at the dangling rope hanging from a thick branch of the acacia tree, with a make-shift seat at the bottom end. "That's what we swing from to jump in the river." Themba looked at it, horrified. "Don't worry, I'll first teach you to swim."

The boys stripped off their clothes. Alex's face, arms, neck and legs were tanned brown, while the rest of his body was white. Themba's body was a consistent brown and not as dark as the other farm children's, Alex thought. He went into the water first, coaxing Themba to join him. Once he was waist high, he told Themba to lie on his front, and Alex put his hands under his stomach to stop Themba from going under. Alex would then give instructions to Themba to kick and move his arms. He alternated this with showing Themba how to swim breaststroke while kicking his legs.

Themba, despite trying very hard, did not always get his coordination right and would start to go under. Alex would grab him and lift his head up, with Themba spluttering and laughing.

"I'll always catch you, man."

Themba slowly began to trust that Alex would hold him and not let him drown. A bond of blind trust between the two was born. Alex always looked out for Themba, wanted to protect him, and Themba, in turn, always trusted Alex to keep him safe from harm. The two boys instinctively knew that as a black child, Themba was more vulnerable.

Alex caught the rope from the tree while standing on the river bank, sat on the wooden seat, lifted off and swung over the water, letting go with a loud *whoop*. Themba laughed and splashed Alex who had a fit of the giggles.

After a while, the boys started to get hungry. They lay on the rocks on the river bank to dry, eating the peaches they had picked up from under the tree in the farmyard. Eventually, they put on their clothes and made the trip back to the house for lunch.


After lunch, the boys went back to the shed to carry on working on the wire car for Themba. They busied themselves, each with pliers and wire in their hands. Alex frowned and looked at Themba.

"Do you believe in God, Themba?"

"I don't know, I don't think so. Why?"

"We go to church every Sunday, and I say my prayers before I go to bed. I love God; he looks over us and protects us."

Themba shrugged his shoulders, not particularly interested. He was more focused on getting his car finished.

Alex was confused by this. The church in Cradock was only attended by white people, and black folk usually held their own services outdoors on the farm. Sometimes they had a black pastor, but more often, one of the workers led the service. Alex thought he might join them one day, just to see if their message was the same. He knew the Bible was in English and Afrikaans, but he had never seen an isiXhosa one. Not all of it quite made sense to Alex, but he supposed because the workers spoke mostly isiXhosa they would want to worship in their own language.

They were nearly finished for the day when they heard the first loud clap of thunder. They both jumped with fright.

"Come," said Alex, "let's go to the *stoep* and watch the storm." They ran around the side of the house and sat together on the top step of the *stoep*, where they had a bird's eye view of the approaching storm.

Alex and Themba sat transfixed by the spectacle in the sky. Flashes of lightning, like flaming branches across the backdrop of dark, brooding clouds, illuminated the hills and trees across the *veld* in flashes of brilliance. There were deep rumbles of thunder with unexpected bolts of lightning, which made them jump and then laugh. This aerial display of raw power seemed to last forever - until the start of the slow puffs of dust on the ground where the large raindrops fell. You could smell the rain coming – dampness caught in the air and blown in the wind. Their senses recognised the dampness after days of dry dust and sun-scorched veld. Then came the dramatic increase in large raindrops and the loud noise showering the corrugated iron roof of the farmhouse and *stoep*. The swelling cacophony of the balls of ice hitting the tin roof above them meant the boys couldn't talk to each other, so they just sat hypnotised by the mighty Karoo concert before them.

~

Alex's father and the farm's foreman, Bongani, took the workers once a month on a Saturday morning to do their shopping in Cradock. Alex usually went along, sitting up front between the two men. On this next trip into town, Alex persuaded his father to take Themba with him.

Themba was excited. He did not go into town very often. Sara gave Alex some money to buy them ice cream but reminded Alex that he could not go to the main café with Themba, as it was "whites-only."

"Ag," said Alex. "I'll just go to the other café at the bottom of the street with Themba." Sara asked Alex to post some letters for her, but he would also have to first buy stamps at the post office.

The boys jumped excitedly into the front cab with Dan and Bongani. A group of the farmworkers sat in the back of the *bakkie*.

Cradock was bustling with the usual Saturday market and with shops busy doing trade. Farmworkers had to go to the shops at the bottom end of Church Street, which was the main street in the small town. Dan told Alex to go to the post office, get their ice cream and he would meet them back at the *bakkie* in an hour.

With his money rattling in his pocket, Alex motioned to Themba to follow him. He made his way down the busy sidewalk towards the post office, jostling with people of all colours, speaking different languages: isiXhosa, Afrikaans, English and some languages he did not know. For a moment, he stood outside the post office and did not know what to do. Themba was standing next to him. He pointed at the large sign, but Themba just lifted his shoulders in a question, not understanding what Alex meant.

"You see that sign, Themba?," asked Alex.

"Yes," said Themba with a questioning look.

Alex took a deep breath in, reading to Themba who could not understand. "It says, white's only," said Alex. "That means you can't come in with me."

"Why?" asked Themba.

"Because you're not white yet," said Alex not knowing what else to say. "I tell you what, you wait here for me." With that, he walked into the post office, leaving Themba to wait patiently outside in the hot sun.

After about twenty minutes, Alex came back out again.

"Come, Themba, let's go get ice cream," said Alex in a bad mood, his forehead all scrunched up in a frown. He knew that he could not go up the road to the "white" end of the main street, so he turned left and went down to the café where black people went.

The boys could smell the freshly baked bread before they got to the café. Their tummies rumbled, their mouths moist with saliva. They walked inside the shop, which was so busy, nobody noticed them. Once at the counter, they chose chocolate ice cream in a cone and went outside and sat on a wall to enjoy themselves. Themba stuck his tongue out, licking the ice cream, copying Alex in the process. He couldn't remember ever having had one, and the coolness on his tongue and mouth was delicious. He closed his eyes to the harsh sunlight and carried on licking. The ice cream started to melt and ran down his hand. He opened his eyes and saw Alex biting into the bottom of the cone to catch the melted ice cream. He did the same. Not a word was said, as each sat and relished the sweet chocolate flavour on their tongues and pleasant coolness in their mouths. They were completely oblivious of the hustle and bustle around them.

When they eventually got home, Themba went to his mother and Gogo, babbling away, telling them about his trip into town. Alex was still confused and went to his father in the shed.

"Pa," Alex asked. "Why am I not black?"

Dan stood still, thinking, and after a bit, he said, "Son, your mother and I are white, that's why. If we had been black people, you would have been black."

Alex thought about this for a while, and said, "Pa, then who is Themba's father? He isn't a lot black like his mum."

Dan did not know what to say. After some hesitation, he answered, "Son, I don't know who Themba's father is, but his mother is black and Xhosa, so he must be as well."

"Oh, that's okay then," thought Alex out loud.

Nobody ever spoke about the signs outside public buildings, so Alex was growing up with them as the norm, although he didn't understand them, or the concept of apartheid, as nobody had ever explained this to him. Themba had not yet learned to read, so he was only aware of the physical division of people, by the fact that black people went to the bottom of the street in Cradock, while the white people went to the top end near the big church built of lime-stone. White people were the farm owners, and black people were the farm workers. Neither child thought to question it.

If Themba had been a white child, Alex instinctively knew he would not have been confronted with the dilemma of the post office segregation. As a young child, he was now forced to confront it in confusion. In his child's mind, it didn't make sense. Being confronted with these rules led him to consider what this meant for Themba.

Alex sat curled up next to his mother on the sofa and spoke to her about his confusion.

"Mum," he caught her attention from reading a book, "why can't Themba go into the post office with me? Why is there a sign that says 'white's only'? There's another sign on the other side that says 'non-whites only.' Is a non-white a black person?"

Sara sighed. She knew this question was going to surface at some point, but she didn't expect it so soon. "Well, you know how you and Themba are different?" she said.

"I know, he's smaller than me and doesn't like vegetables, but he does like chocolate ice cream like I do, so sometimes we are different, and sometimes we are the same. Oh, and he can't read yet, and I can." Alex babbled on about the things the boys liked that were the same and what things weren't the same.

Sara knew this was going to be challenging to explain. "You know that the people who make the rules in the country are the government?"

"Yes," Alex answered slowly, not sure where this was going or what it had to do with his question.

"Well, they made the rules and decided that black and white people can't be together, live together or even marry each other."

"That's silly," replied Alex with childlike wisdom. "What if a black person is my friend? Can't we be mates and do things together? Why does he have to go into the post office by another door? I suppose that means he can't go to school with me?" He stamped his foot angrily, and threw himself on to a chair, folding his arms in disgust.

"Well, you can play together on the farm; it's much easier as we are on our own. Themba can't go to school or church with you. If you think of your class at school, are there any black children?"

"No," said Alex, never really having thought about it before.

"This is called *apartheid,* my son, and whether we like it or not, it is the law of the land."

"Well, I think it's stupid. Why should Themba be treated differently than me? The only thing different is the colour of his skin. His brain works the same as mine, right, Mum?" he asked.

Sara nodded, saying, "Yes, you're right." For now, that was enough for Alex, but she knew this was going to be something that she would have to explain repeatedly over the coming years. The closer he and Themba became, the more heartbreak she could foresee for them both in the future. They would most likely not be able to continue their friendship if either of them left the farm as adults. Themba was destined to work on the farm, and perhaps Alex would go to college or university, or take over the farm from his father. They would inevitably be separated by apartheid.

Themba and Alex were oblivious to the grown-ups' concerns, and enjoyed their long summer days together, building Themba's wire car, and eventually racing it across the yard. When they felt too hot, they went down to the river to swim, with Themba slowly learning to remain afloat. He hadn't quite got the confidence to use the swing.

They passed each day in the same way: sitting on the top step of the *stoep*, with a bowl of *pap* for breakfast. Then they would go their separate ways, water the garden they were each responsible for and gather eggs from the chicken coup. Then they went to the shed to make more wire cars, continuously improving their designs. Going down to the river to cool off soon became a habit.

Sometimes the farm worker's children would play a game of soccer. Alex and Themba would join in, although they were older. Mostly, they would race their wire cars. Your car had to be aligned and run smoothly, and you, the "driver," had to be fast on your feet to win. The boys made a track to race, with a finish line. They were competitive and would try and cut corners to beat the other one to the finish. Sometimes they'd argue, accusing the other of cheating, but then they'd grunt, make up and carry on playing.

After his evening meal with his parents, it wasn't long before it was bedtime. Before getting into bed, Alex would say his prayers on his knees. Once in bed, he enjoyed reading. Invariably he was so tired, he would fall asleep with his book on his lap.

~

Dan decided to tell Alex and Sara that they could go to Port Alfred for a week, as he was now up to date with all his maintenance work. The family was sitting at the kitchen table, having their evening meal together.

"Well, I've finished servicing and fixing all the boreholes, so I've decided to take this last week of the school holidays off. We can go down to Port Alfred before you start back at school, Alex."

"Woohoo!" shouted Alex in delight. He loved going to the beachside cabin for the summer. All his aunties, uncles and cousins would already be there. "Can Themba come with?" he asked.

Dan thought carefully and said, "it's not usual for us to take people from the farm to the cabin." He then got stuck and couldn't think of what else to say or to come up with any reasonable excuse. This was something they'd not confronted before, and he wasn't sure what his family would say. They usually just packed the *bakkie* and off they went. Bongani was left in charge of the farm, although he often had a sort of holiday as well, by spending more time with his family and only doing basic tasks. Bongani had lived his whole life on the farm, as had his father before him, and he could keep the farm running in Dan's absence.

"I'm not going without Themba," Alex said firmly, crossing his arms and leaning back on his chair. "I'll stay at home and look after myself."

Dan and Sara looked at each other and knew that when Alex was stubborn, there was little hope for convincing him otherwise. As an only child, they usually gave in to him, as they wanted him to be happy. They had seen how content he was on the farm, building his friendship with Themba, going to bed tired and satisfied every night.

"I suppose I could do with Buhle helping me give the cabin a good clean and help with cooking," Sara proposed tentatively.

Dan always trusted his wife, and added, "Okay, if you speak to Buhle and see if she'll agree, I can't see it being an issue for the family."

~

A few days later, the family left the farm in the early morning before the sun got too hot. The journey was long and slow, as the cabins were near the town of Port Alfred. Alex always enjoyed the approach to their cabins; it was a steep decline on a dirt track. Dan manoeuvred the *bakkie* along the narrow opening between the thick bushes on either side. The screeching sound against metal making them laugh and put their hands over their ears.

The cabins were on a farm that bordered the Indian Ocean. The family knew the farmer, and for years, they had been renting the cabins on a sort of verbal agreement. They kept the cabins in good condition, usually painting and undertaking repairs when they visited each year, but they were basic structures with no electricity and outside toilets. They collected freshwater from a central tap for use in the cabins.

When they reached their cabin, all was quiet. Alex knew his cousins were down on the beach below. That was where they were every day, only coming back to their cabins when they were hungry or when it became dark. The family unpacked the *bakkie*, and Sara showed Buhle and Themba the back room where they would sleep. It was attached to the cabin but had its own entrance door.

Alex put his bags in the front room, where they had breakfast each day. Next to his bed was a chest of drawers. His parents had their own bedroom, and the kitchen was open to the front room with a large table and chairs. They had a good view of the beach below, which was curved and had rocky outcrops to one side. This prevented the tide from coming in too strongly and created a natural tidal pool. Playing cricket on the beach, swimming in the protected area, or looking for crabs and fish in the pools between the rocks filled the children's days. Alex and his cousins knew they could not swim outside this protected area, as the current was so strong with the waves crashing with brutal force against the sandbank that fell away suddenly. It was too dangerous.

This part of the beach was usually where Dan and his brothers fished during the day. They would catch the "spotted grunter," which could get to a size of 90cm and a weight of around 10kg. It was an excellent white fish that could be cooked on the *braai* for a large group. If they were lucky, the men would catch a "white" or "black mussel cracker", which could reach a maximum length of 120cm and weigh up to 30kg. Dan and his brothers preferred the "mussel cracker" that weighed under 10kg as they found it to be tastier, usually releasing the more substantial fish back into the ocean.

Alex rushed outside, down the opening between the bushes, and on to the beach. He greeted his cousins, who were playing cricket; some were swimming.

After chatting to his cousins for a while, he heard his mother calling him for lunch. He reluctantly broke off to go up to the cabin, remembering that Themba would be waiting for him.

∽

Buhle opened the door to the outside room of the cabin. It creaked, and she turned her head around the door. It smelt a bit musty but seemed clean. There was a single bed, and although small, she was content with it. She and Themba could sleep top and tail at night. She unpacked their few belongings into a chest of drawers while Themba bounced on the bed and decided he quite liked it.

"Come, Themba," she said to her son in isiXhosa, "let's go and see if Missus Sara needs us to help her."

They entered the cabin through the back door and found the kitchen and living area, which also smelled musty. There was a bed in the corner that Buhle presumed would be for Alex. She called out, and Sara came through, opening the windows to get rid of the odour. When they had opened all the windows, the fresh sea breeze, the sound of the crashing waves and the smell of salty sea air rapidly filled the cabin. Sara asked Buhle to unpack the groceries and make the beds

Buhle turned and looked through the windows and could see the sea above the line of the bushes. She had never seen the ocean before and was utterly transfixed by its beauty. The rolling waves smashed against the rocks creating a sea haze while leaving rockpools as each wave receded. While marvelling at its beauty and strength, she also felt frightened, sure the waves could sweep her away. They roared each time as they broke, with a regular rhythm. The sound felt deafening to her, but she thought she may get used to it.

She turned to the kitchen and began unpacking while Themba watched through the window. She knew he was waiting for Alex to come back to the cabin.

Before long, Themba saw Alex running up towards the cabin through the opening in the bushes. Themba started to frantically wave, but Alex did not notice him. Soon, the back door swung open. Alex came in and put his arm around Themba.

"See, I told you it was the best place ever!" Alex babbled. His cousins were playing a game of cricket on the beach. "We need you to play wicket keeper for us," he said to Themba.

"But I don't know how to play," said Themba, hanging his head down to his chest, his bottom lip sticking out.

"Don't worry, all you have to do is stand behind the person who is batting and catch the ball when he misses, or fetch the ball when it goes behind you. You need to just run as fast as you can and fetch it back!" Alex reassured him.

After the boys had their sandwiches and something to drink, they headed down to the beach.

Alex had eight cousins. His father had two older brothers, and the cousins were of varying ages. He had two girl cousins who were teenagers. They liked to boss him about and tease him by ruffling his hair. Yuck. He ignored them. He had six boy cousins; the oldest was fourteen and the youngest was a year younger than him. Alex hero-worshipped his eldest cousin, Frik. He was smart and was the leader of the gang of cousins; all the children looked up to him. He decided which games they played and who batted first, and he was the arbitrator in their disputes. The cousins deferred to him in all matters. He was also much taller than any of them.

Today was a day for playing cricket. Nobody wanted to be wicketkeeper, as they all said it was boring. His cousin, Frik, also had a black boy, called Liwa, with him from their farm. They had repaired the cabins with the adults at the beginning of their holiday. They painted the exteriors and cleared away any rubble or foliage. The cabins were surrounded by sand and wildly grown brush, and they all faced the ocean. Behind the main buildings was the communal area, where the toilet cabins were and parking for the *bakkies*. There was also an open area where they would *braai* every evening. There was a storeroom where they kept their fishing rods, general tools and decorating kit. Part of the informal lease agreement was that they would maintain the cabins and the surrounding area every year, without fail, or the farmer would withdraw his consent to them staying there.

The farm was close to Port Alfred, where they could go to do essential shopping, but it was far enough away to be remote and secluded—the perfect spot for tired farmers to unwind and to enjoy each other's company in peace.

They had finished their chores during the first week, and all three cabins had a fresh coat of paint, and the window frames were fixed and repainted as well. The more people there were to do the work, the quicker the job got done. Liwa and Frik had grown up together on the family farm and were firm friends. They came down every year, repairing the cabins together like they worked on the farm.

Each cricket team had a captain, and this was usually one of the eldest boys. Alex was on the side with his cousin Koos, who was thirteen and nearly as tall as his cousin Frik. Standing behind the batsman for long periods wasn't a favourite position, so Themba, as the youngest and the new-comer, was given that unpopular job.

They explained the rudiments to him, with Frik doing the explaining in isiXhosa.

The game began. Each batsman faced the bowler, with varying levels of skill. There was lots of shouting, swearing in Afrikaans, English and isiXhosa. There were a few fracases, which took the heat out of the moment and were over quickly. These were usually settled by Frik, who was the de facto leader. Playing the game was the most crucial objective.

They could never remember beyond a day who had won the match. There were usually stories, teasing and bragging around the campfire each night, but each day brought a new game, a new challenge.

Themba tried to be an efficient wicket-keeper, but he wasn't very good at catching the tennis ball if the batsman missed it. His body usually took the hit. The ball stung him and sometimes left a perfectly round red mark on his body. He was, however, very fast in fetching the ball and bringing it back to the stumps. He even managed to stump a few batsmen out who were away from the crease! He was satisfied that he had passed the test of being part of the "gang" of cousins.

What Themba didn't know was that in a proper game of cricket, each team would typically have their own specialist wicketkeeper, but for the children, this was done by Themba, who seemed to be entirely happy with his job. He would only find out when he was older that being the permanent wicket-keeper was a set up by the other children and was usually delegated to the youngest or smallest child, desperate to play and to be accepted by the older boys. They did the job no one else wanted.

The children started playing just after breakfast and continued until they had enough, and then they would swim in the rock pools. Themba could float now, so he hesitantly joined the other children, staying in the shallower water. They usually ended throwing the tennis ball at each other in the water. This lasted until there was a yell from one of the mothers that lunch or supper was ready.

The children ate outside, wolfing down sandwiches and inevitably some cake, which was washed down with homemade lemonade or ginger beer. Once supped up, they went back down to their cricket match on the beach. Supper was the inevitable *braai*, with the fathers stoking up a fire in an old oil drum that had been sawn in half lengthways, and a grill placed on top. This was made of a sheet of metal mesh welded on to an iron frame for stability. Once the coals were "just right," the meat or freshly caught fish was placed on the grill and cooked to perfection. Buhle, who became the undisputed queen of *pap*, made the other version, which was *stywe pap*. This was the same as breakfast *pap* but a much thicker consistency, and you could roll it into balls in your hand. It served as a way of mopping up gravy or any other leftovers on the plate.

Everyone ate together. Afterwards, the adults sat around the fire, drinking brandy or illegally home-distilled moonshine, often made from peaches. The children would head back to the beach until it was dark when they returned to sit by the fire. The younger children usually went to bed first, tired from running around on the sand all day and swimming. The older boys would sit with the adults and occasionally were allowed a tot of alcohol, although they were to be "seen" and "not heard" during the adult conversations.

Themba lay curled up in bed with his mother, telling her all about the game of cricket and what he did and how the bigger boys would fight each other if they tried to cheat. He talked on about who won, who lost, and who was the strongest.

Buhle held her son in her arms, stroking his hair and listening to his happy babbling in isiXhosa. She had never seen him so happy. She was relieved he was not the only black child there, that there was an older Xhosa boy, Liwa. She had spoken to the boy and asked him to look out for Themba. She knew that Alex would always protect his friend as well, so she was content that her son could enjoy himself without anything untoward happening.

Children, if you left them to their own devices, were not racist. She knew they would just play with each other, fight and bicker, and make up again. She instinctively knew that as a black person, you always had to be on your guard. Her experiences so far in life had taught her that you could not depend on everybody. You had to be very selective. She trusted Mister Dan and Missus Sara to some degree. She knew they would not deliberately harm her. She would never confide in them like she did with Gogo. Gogo understood her without Buhle having to say anything. Gogo had also suffered hardship and racism throughout her life.

There was an underlying, unspoken understanding of what Buhle had gone through and how it had affected her. They never spoke about the abuse Buhle suffered from her previous *baas* and how the missus had turned a blind eye. Her separation from Themba, who was looked after by the women in the compound, was never acknowledged as harmful. These were unspoken things that Gogo knew without Buhle having to tell. There would very rarely be any form of justice for a victim. Well, maybe only if there was a murder. These were matters commonly experienced by black farm workers and their families. The workers' wellbeing was always tied to the generosity and kindness of the farm owner. She knew that being a white Christian would not stop some people from being abusive to their workers.

Being with the white families on their holiday was something Buhle had not experienced before. She had lived on a farm throughout her life. Firstly with her parents, and later on her own, as a domestic worker or farm labourer. She knew the art of remaining invisible amongst white people. And here she instinctively did the same—staying in the kitchen, keeping it clean and tidy, preparing meals for the day, sweeping and mopping the cabin. Cleaning the windows.

Missus Sara would be with the other women, also cooking or preparing food or just generally chatting with each other over a cup of coffee, or reading a book. The front windows gave a view of the beach. This made it easy for Buhle to keep an eye on Themba throughout the day.

Buhle could feel Themba's soft breath against her shoulder and snuggled down with the blanket over them. She couldn't fall asleep. Just as her eyes were closing, her mind wandered back in time. The nightmares never left her; they always snuck up on her when she was trying to sleep. The smell of stale man-sweat, his breath smelling of brandy. His slurring and heavy clumsiness.

Those long days and nights at Kasteel, how she had to steal time with Themba. In the evenings, she had to wait for the family to finish their meal she had cooked, and go in and clear the dining table, wash the dishes and clean up the kitchen. After she was finished for the day, she would quietly go to her room behind the homestead. She'd take a bucket outside her door and wash herself.

Sometimes, the *baas* would sneak up behind her. She'd jump with fright but did not dare to scream out. His hand covered her mouth from behind, putting his hand into the front of her blouse and grabbing her breasts and squeezing them until the tears ran with the pain. She would freeze, knowing what was coming. He would lift her off her feet and drag her into her room, slamming the door shut with his boot. He pushed Buhle on to the bed. Hitching up her skirts before undoing his trousers and getting on top of her. He pinned her down. His weight suffocating her, crushing her. She would panic, unable to breathe, taking in short, shallow breaths. But she had to do as he wished, or he would take his belt and beat her. He would strike with the buckle end, breaking her skin, the leather bruising her. She would do the housework, dragging her aching body around the house, wincing in pain.

She always closed her eyes and tried to take her mind away from what was happening. She would think of the veld, walking through the long grass, the sun on her face. She remained utterly passive while he groaned as he penetrated her. Once he had finished, he would slap her head and tell her to clean up. If he had been drinking a lot, he would sometimes fall asleep on the bed on top of her. On those nights, she dared not move. When he woke up, he would sometimes get up and go back into the main house, or he would rape her again.

Even though her son was mixed race, he was no different from many of the children on the farms. While being Xhosa meant you were black, some farm children were mixed-race or coloured. This was dependent on the farmer and whether he wanted a black "mistress." Buhle's experiences were limited to the farms she worked on, so she wasn't sure how widespread this practice was. She knew from talking to other farm workers at Kasteel that this kind of relationship was rarely consensual, but rather the powerful abusing those who were without a voice.

Buhle had fallen pregnant soon after starting work at Kasteel. She was only sixteen at the time the *baas* had taken a liking to her. He would make excuses to come into the kitchen, rubbing himself against her or putting his hands through her housecoat, undoing or tearing it open and aggressively feel her breasts with his large rough hands with their broken and long nails. His hands would sometimes go down between her legs, scratching her, tearing her. She would freeze, terrified of what may happen. He was such a big man compared to her. She would never have the strength to fight back or even know how. Buhle had been a virgin when she first worked in the house. Women in the compound told her what they had to endure from the *baas* or from other men on the farm, or she would lose her job or suffer worse beatings. She lived in fear of what might come her way.

Buhle's pregnancy was difficult, and the visits to her room by the *baas* did not decrease during this time. When she went into labour, one of the farmworkers took her into Cradock to the government hospital. She endured two days of labour before the doctors decided to do a caesarean section. Buhle had been talking to the other women in the workers' compound and felt confident to ask the doctor to sterilise her at the same time as delivering her baby.

Themba was a beautiful baby; his dark eyes, long eyelashes and abundance of hair tugged at her heartstrings. She breastfed him for as long as she could, even though he had to stay with the women in the compound, and she had to steal time to go and be with him. If she missed a feed, one of the other lactating mothers would feed him.

~

The week went by in a flash. Very soon, the families were packing up and leaving the cabins behind. Everything had to be cleaned and tidied, packed away and locked up, ready for the next summer holiday in eleven months' time.

The families and children said goodbye to each other, ready to go home and start the new school year.

Alex and Themba packed into the front of the *bakkie* ready to go. Alex felt happy, and content having spent time with his cousins, but he felt for the first time that going home was not such a bad thing. He had Themba to play with every day. Now that Themba could play cricket, he was going to try and get a team going on the farm. It would be such fun.

They started the journey home just before sunrise before the heat became unbearable in the *bakkie*. Themba, Alex and the grownups reached the farm by early afternoon. They unpacked the *bakkie*, and the boys went straight down to the river.

# CHAPTER 5

*January 1978,*
*first day of a new school year*

ALEX TOOK OUT HIS NEW khaki-coloured shorts and short-sleeved shirt from his cupboard for the first school day in his second year at school. It was Sara's first teaching day for the year as well, and they were travelling into Cradock, together.

Alex was looking forward to seeing the friends he had made last year and catching up on all the news on what they had been up to over the holidays.

He felt sad that Themba couldn't go with him. Even if he could, it would be tough to be the only black boy in the school. Sara had arranged for Themba to attend Soetewater's farm school. A new government teacher was coming to teach all the farm children over the age of seven. Buhle wasn't sure if Themba was six or seven, but they said seven on the forms Sara had to fill in and submit to the education department. A disused farm worker's hut was a makeshift classroom. There was a bench for the children to sit on and some tables. Sara had managed to get these items a few years ago, which were discarded furniture from the local white schools in Cradock. There would be about fifteen children, of varying ages, attending on the first day, but the dropout rate was high.

Sara had not met the new teacher yet, but she would go and sit in on one of her lessons on a day she was not working. The previous teacher had been popular with the children, even though his teaching methods were well below the level of the school she taught at. The farm teachers were not highly qualified and were rarely subjected to any sort of regular inspection. The quality of the farm school was very much dependent on the generosity of the farmer. The previous teacher was elderly and had decided he no longer wanted to teach and had given his notice at the end of the last term.

Sara asked Gogo to settle the new teacher in, while she and Alex went into Cradock to start their day.

~

Themba had also woken up excited to start his first day at school. He was completely unaware that his little class was different from that of Alex's. He knew most of the farm children already, and he sat on the bench with them, waiting for the teacher to arrive. Gogo brought her in, flustered and hot from her bicycle ride from Lingelihle, the Cradock township where she lived.

The front wall in the classroom was painted black. This served as a blackboard for the teacher to use for her lessons.

The day's learning began, with each pupil quiet and expectant.

Sara and Dan paid Alex's school fees at the government-run school, where class sizes were small and according to age. Teachers were fully trained, with Sara being one of the teachers and some of the others were her friends. Alex's school also provided sporting facilities and various inter-school competitions for each sport. Alex played cricket for his school in the summer and could play rugby in the winter if he wished, although he didn't seem interested at the moment.

~

The evening before the start of the new school year was always an opportunity for Sara to prepare for the year ahead. She sat at her desk in the lounge, checking all her lesson plans for the children. Sara managed the farm school jointly with the government. She wasn't yet sure how the new teacher would perform, but given she was young, it was perhaps an opportunity for Sara to mentor her. Sara was looking forward to that. Teaching was in her blood; she could not stop herself.

Sara had no choice as to who the teacher would be; this was the government's decision. Fortunately, she had managed to encourage fifteen pupils to start the year, with some coming from neighbouring farms. She was so pleased, as this meant that she had met the annual quota, but she knew there would be a drop-out rate and that every year, she had to work hard to keep the school open.

She finished her paperwork and accounts for the farm, making sure her wage envelopes were completed for the week, including the new teacher's. The government subsidy was in their bank account, so she was all prepared for the first Friday's payday.

Sara was worried about how she would manage with the limited funds paid to her. She looked across at Dan, who was relaxing on the sofa with the newspaper. He was deep in thought, but she felt they needed to discuss this.

"Dan, I know we both want to keep the farm school running, but how am I going to buy materials and pay the teacher with this meagre subsidy the government gives us?"

Dan looked up at his wife. "Well, I suppose you could ask the other teachers in your school to help gather any unused or surplus material to pass on to the farm schools in the area? The government will never increase the subsidy; it's not a priority for them."

"I know; that's a good idea. I usually do the clearing out of the stock room at the end of each year. I'll get permission to do that at the end of each term instead. I can then distribute to our farm school and any other farm school that needs materials. The principal is not really bothered, as long as I do the job nobody else wants to, so I can't see him disagreeing."

"Why don't you ask our minister if we can have a collection in church for funds to buy pencils and books for the farm schools in the area?"

Sara thought about Dan's suggestions. It was going to be a lot of extra work and commitment from her, but she had a few good teacher-friends whom she could call on to help her.

"You're such a good man, Dan." She laughed and went to join him on the sofa. She curled up next to him, putting her head on his shoulder. "Can I ask you to try not to use some of the older kids in school at harvest time or when you are shearing the sheep? I worry that they will miss out on too much of their work."

"I'll try, but sometimes Alex likes to come along as well. I could try and do it during the school holidays. We'll see."

Sara snuggled up to Dan; she knew he would try his best. She peered across to the newspaper, and they read together. Then they took turns reading articles to each other. Sara enjoyed being close to her husband; he smelled of soap and shaving lotion. Dan always shaved in the evening, as he was in such a rush in the morning.

He kissed her head and slowly moved to gently kiss her on the mouth.

"Come, it's time for bed," he murmured softly. He took her hand, switched off the lights and led the way to their bedroom.

∾

When Alex and his mother returned from their first school day, Themba was waiting on the *stoep* steps for them. Alex changed out of his school uniform and reverted to his shorts and t-shirt. He and Themba went to the shed to work on some wire cars, and Sara spent time with Buhle, catching up on domestic chores.

The family were developing their new routine of education, housework, homework and play. Dan was out early each morning on the farm with Bongani. In the hot summer months, he was often out at 4am, returning for breakfast and only returning home late in the afternoon.

As the days went by, Alex flung himself into his new curriculum. He was a diligent learner and always did his homework without his mother having to prompt him. He usually achieved good marks in tests, and he always wanted to come first in his class.

Themba was like a sponge. He absorbed information as soon as it was presented to him. He was learning to read very quickly, and when it was not a school day, he practised his alphabet and read additional books that Sara or his teacher gave him. Schooling for him was in a mixture of Afrikaans and English. Themba tended to use mostly English as his mother was adamant that he should become fluent in speaking, reading and writing the language. She instinctively felt that Afrikaans was the language of the oppressor, and he would do better in life if he could speak fluent English.

Themba enjoyed the breaks in the school day, and their young teacher allowed them to play soccer in the yard. They let off steam before going back to their afternoon studies.

Sara managed to supply the farm school with second-hand books from Alex's school, and any other materials she could get her hands on. Themba was, therefore, using the same tools as Alex had the previous year. She was able to buy some basic stationery from the money they had collected at church.

Themba's thirst for learning, and his natural abilities, led him to achieve the level of his first grade within six months of starting school. Once Alex saw that Themba was working hard, he would do his homework on the *stoep* with Themba by his side. Soon he was telling Themba what he was doing, and would almost be teaching him. Themba was eager and hung on to Alex's every word. This "teaching," questions and answers, and sharing knowledge, resulted in their bond becoming even more durable.

Once the boys had finished their homework, they would either play cricket in the yard with the other farm children or build or fix their wire cars and race each other around the tracks they had made. When the weather got too hot, as it always did in the Karoo summer, reaching temperatures of over 40 degrees centigrade most days, they headed off down to the river.

Themba got more confident in his swimming and tentatively started to swing on the rope, jumping off when Alex could catch him as he fell into the water.

On this blistering afternoon, Themba was swinging confidently, and on his third attempt, he seemed to lose confidence and fell awkwardly, elbow first, into the river. Alex watched. Why did Themba not surface? Where was he? Was he trapped underwater? Alex watched the water slowly turn red.

"No, no!" he yelled. "Themba where are you?" Alex had at first thought Themba may be playing a trick on him, but the red water was a hint that this was serious.

Alex repeatedly dived, trying with his hands to find Themba's body. He had to come up for breath a couple of times before he felt a body and pulled him out of the water holding under Themba's armpits so that he could hit the surface to breathe.

Themba was motionless in Alex's arms. Alex patted his face, calling his name, but no response. Alex dragged Themba over to the sandbank and lay him down.

Themba started to splutter, water gushed out of his mouth. He started coughing, more fluid spouting. Alex held Themba upright so he could breathe easier, with Themba now throwing up bile and breakfast.

Alex sat tucked behind Themba, with him seated in front with Alex's arms around his body, keeping him upright.

"Themba, Themba, are you okay?" Alex kept repeating, trying to get an idea if Themba was conscious or not. Alex twisted around and noticed the blood pouring down Themba's face, on to his chest. He grabbed his T-shirt and wound it around Themba's head, trying to stem the flow.

Themba seemed to be able to sit upright now, but kept crying, "Ow, ow! My arm! it hurts."

Themba held his left arm close to his body, cradled by his right arm.

Alex heard Themba's raw cry of pain, which pierced through his body. He needed to get Themba home to their mothers.

Alex managed to get Themba's shorts on him and used his shirt to tie Themba's arm to his body. Alex quickly got dressed and got Themba to use his good arm to lean on him, dragging him along the track to the house. Each step was painful, and Themba was crying louder and howling now.

When they got to the farmyard, Alex shouted out for his mother and Buhle. They both came running towards them.

"What's happened!" the two mothers shouted in unison.

"I don't know. Themba was on the swing and fell over in the river. His head is bleeding, and his arm hurts!" Buhle scooped her son into her arms and sat him down on the *stoep* stairs.

"Let me have a look, Themba?" asked Sara. He nodded. She lifted the T-shirt and saw the large gash to his head, just below his hairline. It was deep and still bleeding. She dashed inside the house and got a large towel and wrapped it around his head. She then removed his shirt and saw his arm swelling up and very tender to the touch. She made a makeshift sling from a sheet, for his arm and told him to hold it close to his body.

"Buhle," she said, "I think he may have broken his arm. That injury on his head needs to be looked at and maybe needs stitches. I'm worried he may be concussed. I'll get the car ready. We must take him to the hospital to see the doctor."

Buhle nodded, she had seen farm workers with injuries and broken limbs before, and she knew Themba was in a lot of pain.

They all climbed into Sara's car and headed towards Cradock. Buhle sat in the back, cradling Themba, who seemed to have calmed down now he was with his mother.

Alex sat in the front next to Sara, crying, not sure what was going on, only that it was severe and Themba needed a doctor straight away. *It must be my fault. I wasn't watching him. Themba will hate me now. I made him go on the swing when he didn't want to.* These thoughts kept going round and round in his head, spinning like a merry-go-round, unable to jump off. He worried what Buhle may be thinking, that he'd not looked after Themba properly.

They got to Cradock Hospital where they went towards the non-whites entrance and Sara told Buhle and the boys to sit in the waiting area while she parked the car. Themba seemed to flit between conscious and unconscious, and she was worried. The place was thronging with people, mostly adults with various ailments and injuries. There were a few nurses behind the reception desk, taking information from each person who patiently waited their turn. Sara held her breath; she knew that it was sometimes a whole day's waiting as the Accident and Emergency was usually overcrowded and under-staffed.

When she had waited her turn in the queue and got to the front desk, Sara explained to the nurse what had happened to Themba and she thought he may be suffering concussions, had a big gash on his head and may have broken his arm. He was in a tremendous amount of pain and repeatedly losing consciousness.

"You know you're not supposed to be in this side of the hospital. It's for non-whites only," the brusque old white nurse responded without acknowledging or showing concern for the injured young child.

Sara could feel her hackles rising, the bile in her mouth tasted bitter. "Listen, I have a young child here who is injured. He is my responsibility as he lives on our farm. I will not be chased out of here. I don't care what you say," Sara said in a firm school-teacher tone, her eyes unflinching as she stared at the nurse, daring her to challenge her. She was ready for a fight!

Out of the corner of her eye, Sara saw the matron, a familiar face. She was the mother of one of her pupils. Sara had helped her daughter, who was struggling at school, and whom she suspected had special needs. Sara had invested extra time with the child, believing that she could do better with targeted additional teaching. Sara had worked together with the child's mother towards a better outcome for her daughter. Sara thought she'd use this to her advantage.

Sara called out to the matron, "Glynis, hi! Could you help us, please?" She had caught Glynis' attention, who walked over to Sara and asked how she could help. Sara explained what had happened to Themba and that she was worried he had concussion due to the injury to his head, and he may have broken his arm. Glynis told her to wait with Themba and Buhle; she would deal with it.

Sara walked back to where Themba was sitting huddled next to his mother, his face drawn and streaked with tears. Alex looked shocked and pale, wondering what was the matter with Themba. Sara reassured them that her friend Glynis would look after Themba, they must just wait a little while.

Glynis was true to her word and shortly came across to them, bending down and made eye contact with Themba.

"Do you speak English, Themba?" she asked him.

"Yes, a little," he muttered.

Glynis took his good hand and spoke to him in a mixture of English and isiXhosa. "Themba, we're going to do something called an x-ray with a machine. It won't hurt you. It's a special machine that looks at your bones in your arm and tells us if it is broken. If it is, then the doctor will tell us to put a plaster cast on your arm to stop it moving so that your arm can heal. We also have to take a look at your head injury, and you may need stitches if the wound is deep. Is that okay? You need to be brave for a little bit longer. Mum, you can come through as well."

Both Themba and Buhle nodded and walked gingerly through the swing doors with Glynis, to the treatment area.

Sara and Alex waited amongst the farm labourers and other patients who were most likely from the surrounding Cradock area. They got a few interesting looks but were largely ignored. The nurse, whom Sara had initially spoken to, gave her intermittent hostile stares but said nothing. Sara thought to herself that it was often about "whom you knew" when you wanted to get things done. How long would Themba have had to wait to be seen? Hours maybe? She shook her head and flinched thinking of the pain the poor child was in.

Eventually, after about two hours of waiting, Glynis came through the swing doors towards Sara and Alex.

"Hi, we've x-rayed Themba's arm, and it is broken in two places. We're giving him a plaster cast to stop him moving it and to allow it to heal. We are worried about his head injury. The doctor has stitched up the wound and wants to keep Themba overnight for observation. His loss of consciousness is a concern."

"Thank you so much for your help," Sara said, "I don't know what would have happened if you hadn't been here."

Glynis smiled, knowing what Sara meant. "We try and see the children first as they are the most vulnerable, but sometimes they can get lost in the milieu of patients waiting. If you come back tomorrow afternoon, we will know whether Themba can be discharged or not. His mother will stay overnight with him."

Alex was quiet on the journey home. Sara knew he was worried about Themba. After supper, they talked through the day's events. Dan wanted to know everything that had happened and why Themba had been injured so severely.

"Pa, I know it's my fault. I shouldn't have let him on the swing. He didn't want to go on it, but I forced him. He's much littler than me, I should have known." Alex hung his head.

Dan looked at his son, who was torn up by guilt, fear and remorse. "Son, you aren't to blame. It was an accident that could have happened to you or to Themba. It was unfortunate but something we can't change. We'll all look after Themba when he gets home so that he can get healthy again.

"I tell you what—tomorrow, Bongani and I will go down to the river and check whether there is any large logs or boulders that have been swept downriver and clear them from where you swim. I think, for now, we'll take down the rope swing as well."

He felt a bit better with his father absorbing his anxiety and worry. His pa was in control and would make sure that the river was safe again. Alex was sitting next to his pa. He put his head on his chest with Dan wrapping his arm around Alex, holding him close.

The next morning seemed to drag for Alex; he was desperate to go and see how Themba was doing. His mum said they would go to the hospital after lunchtime.

Dan and Bongani went down to the river. Both took long sticks and felt under the water for any hazards. They had managed to fish out a large log with a prominent branch sticking out of the one side. This may have been what had caused Themba's injury. They combed the whole area, ensuring there was nothing submerged that could harm the boys. They agreed to take down the rope swing as a precaution in case other debris was brought downriver after the summer storms.

Alex walked through the hospital ward and saw Themba lying on the bed, with Buhle on a chair beside him. His head was covered in a wrap-around bandage. He managed a beaming smile as he saw Alex coming towards him.

Buhle looked tired but relieved. Alex went towards her, putting his arms around her neck. "Buhle, I'm so sorry. I didn't mean for Themba to get hurt. It's my fault; I should have looked after him," Alex cried.

Buhle hugged Alex back, saying, "Shh, it's okay; it was an accident. Themba's fine. Look at him." She placed her hands on his shoulders and turned Alex around so that he could see his friend smiling at him.

The boys hugged, with Themba wincing. His face was swollen, his eyes puffy and the bridge of his nose was twice it's normal size. His face had a dark blue tinge to it.

"You look like you've been in a boxing match, Themba," Alex joked, hoping Themba and his mother would see the funny side.

Buhle smiled. "Alex, thank you so much for saving Themba. He would have drowned if you hadn't been there to pull him out of the water," she said in a whisper. "The doctors say that Themba had a mild concussion and the head injury always looks worse than it actually is. They've put stitches in and say the swelling will eventually go down. He has to have the plaster cast on for another six weeks so his arm can heal."

Alex let out a big sigh. Relief. He didn't feel that he deserved the thanks from Buhle but accepted it graciously.

Themba smiled, his dimples on either side of his cheeks showing. "You did save me. All I could see was the water over my face, and I kept sinking deeper down, down. Then it went blank, and next, I knew I was getting sick, and you were holding me up. Guess there won't be any swimming for a while now?"

"Definitely not," said Sara and Buhle in unison.

Themba felt gratitude towards his friend who had saved him from inevitable drowning. An unfortunate accident. Alex was always so big and strong, and Themba could depend on him. Themba wanted to go home now; he felt tired and didn't like the restriction of being in the hospital.

The nurses discharged Themba with a list of concussion symptoms for Buhle to be aware of. Sara didn't tell Buhle, but she and Dan had agreed to pay the bill for Themba's treatment. Even the government hospital wasn't free! They were their family now.

Alex put his arm around his friend as they walked out the hospital and to their car.

# CHAPTER 6

SARA AND BUHLE WERE DEVELOPING a comfortable relationship, although rather superficial. They each had a specific role in the house. Preparing meals and doing household chores fell to Buhle. Sara did the farm accounts and managed the wages every week. She also taught three days a week at Alex's school. She and another mother took turns driving the children to school and bringing them home.

Relationships and bonds were forming between the children and adults. Sara observed the change and deepening friendship between Themba and Alex, which was strengthened by Themba's accident in the river. It was as if another layer had been added to their bond. They each looked out for the other, always wanting to know where the other was. The affection between them was observed by all the adults around them. They were inseparable now. It was not only their circumstances that allowed the bond to develop, but also the match in their temperaments. Sara had observed this with her pupils at school. Some became natural firm friends and others natural adversaries.

Buhle watched Themba slowly recover from his injuries; his face returned to its regular colouring and shape, and he got used to playing and sleeping with an arm in a cast. She also felt the boys had a natural close fit in their personalities and their relationship. The traumatic river incident seemed to cement their bond.

Sara was teaching Buhle to read and write. Buhle would sometimes sit with Themba and practise writing the alphabet with him, and they would do his reading homework together when they were in the hut with Gogo in the evenings.

Sara kept an eye on the young farm teacher, giving her some of the lesson plans she had developed to use with her own pupils. Sara knew the training of farm school teachers was not equal to the requirements for teaching that she had to attain at college. This disadvantage was unfair and not the fault of the young woman. Sara shook her head at her thoughts, knowing she could not leave this teacher to flounder.

Sara realised the teacher had a challenge as the ages of the children in her class did not match their capabilities. Sara guided the teacher to be more adaptable in her teaching. Some of the older children could not read and write very well, so she had to engage them at a level with the younger children. Sometimes there were squabbles and resentment by the older children having to learn with the more inexperienced teacher. Sara would then have to coach the teacher on how to manage their unruly behaviour.

The summer heat slowly started to wane. The nights turned colder, and the day took longer to warm up. The winter cold was harshest overnight, sometimes going below zero but warming by midday. The lower and limited daytime temperatures meant that it was less appealing to go swimming, which was just as well as Themba had to endure the plaster cast for six long weeks. Fortunately, it was his left arm, so he could continue writing with his right hand.

Themba's broken arm healed, and he developed a scar on his forehead just below his hairline—a reminder of his near-drowning. The boys tended to spend time in the shed or playing cricket or soccer in the yard with the other children after they had finished their homework.

In the early evening Themba would go down to Gogo's hut and have his supper. Afterwards, he would join Alex on the *stoep*, and the two would sit at the table doing their homework, or Alex would show Themba his homework, which they would do together. They often tested each other on the work they had done, trying to catch each other out. Sometimes they would squabble, but it always ended in laughter.

～

Buhle saw her son completely absorbed by learning, and to some degree, she was learning with him. They practised the alphabet, writing and eventually reading together. Buhle was amazed that by the time winter came, Themba had mastered the basic reading books, which she was still struggling with. The tables had turned, and he now helped her with reading.

Buhle was worried that there may come a time when Themba would surpass the other pupils in the farm school. Where would he go then? Would he end up having to work as a labourer on the farm for the rest of his life? She knew from her own family history that once a boy started work as a farm labourer, usually by the age of fourteen, it was almost impossible to escape farm life. Themba would have to have the farmer's permission to move into any other industry or work. Farmers used this as a way of ensuring an ongoing supply of farm labourers. The pay was poor, with no conditions for old age or sickness. The apartheid supremacy of the white government sustained the enduring flow of cheap labour. The "homelands" policy prevented black workers from owning any land in the white designated areas.

If Themba was viewed as surplus workforce, he could forcibly be removed and relocated to the "homelands." These were self-governing areas, usually allocated by cultural groups scattered across the country.

Buhle was worried about the future if Themba was to move to secondary education, she knew she would need to move to a township and enrol him in one of their high schools. She would consequently lose her job and income.

She wanted more for him. She wanted him to be able to work somewhere where he could prosper beyond the hopes and dreams of a farm labourer. A farm labourer's fortune was very much entwined with the success, or not, of the farm they worked on, or indeed what kind of employer the farmer was.

The future was unknown, but Buhle knew there was time yet, perhaps a few years before she would need to decide what to do. She did not have many choices, but they would have to work hard. The only other option was to join one of her family members who lived in the big city, where the schools may offer Themba more than what a farm school could and a better opportunity for employment for her.

Sara enjoyed teaching, helping students to reach their potential. She was confident that Alex enjoyed his schooling and was satisfied that his school allowed him to use English as his first language and Afrikaans as his second. He would be tested in English. She knew he was academically able but also a hard worker.

She watched closely as he did his homework. She wanted him to develop his own thirst for learning, which would drive him to want to succeed. She was not a pushy parent, nor was she a parent who believed in harsh punishment if a child did not conform or achieve. She believed in instilling a strong love of learning, and a drive to succeed, which came from within Alex himself. An inner motivation to succeed, was in her view, more effective in getting a child to learn and reach their own potential, than enforcement.

Sara was worried about where Alex would go for further education once he got to high school. There was only an Afrikaans high school in Cradock, and she wanted him to be educated in English. Sara dreaded him having to go away to boarding school. Secretly, she was hoping he would go on to university, and she knew the more progressive universities taught in English, either in Johannesburg, Grahamstown or Cape Town.

That was a dilemma for the future; for now, Alex had another three or four years in primary school, and she would keep a close eye on him, making sure he stayed motivated to do his best. She did not share her concerns about her son's education with Dan, as he was focussed entirely on the "here and now" of the farm. Decisions were made on a day-by-day basis so the revenue would continue to come in. She kept a close eye on the bank accounts and knew that the farm operated on a narrow margin and they rarely made any sort of profit. In fact, if it was not for her income from teaching, they would really be struggling. She was able to fund Alex's schooling and also the household budget. Buhle and the farm labourers' wages came out of the revenue they got from the farm.

The livestock and wool prices were currently stable, but this could change very quickly. If there were a drought or a disease that spread through the livestock, they could lose everything in a season. Farming was stressful and full of risk. Dan was all too aware of this, and this motivated him to keep his farm functioning efficiently at all times.

~

Alex felt his muscles aching with every slight movement of the car. He kept quiet, hoping his classmate's mother, who was giving him a lift home, wouldn't notice and ask him what had happened.

They arrived at the farm entrance, where Alex got out, said thanks, and started the long walk down the dusty road to the farmhouse. He was still angry at Klaas Junior. They didn't call him that; they just called him Klaas. He had wound Alex up, telling him he heard Alex now had a black brother on the farm, and why didn't he have any white brothers? "Is something wrong with your mum or dad? Does your dad have a black girlfriend?" Alex stayed silent. Incessant taunting by Klaas, with his Afrikaner buddies in the audience, kept on and on and on. Eventually, Alex lost his patience, turned to face Klaas and threw the first punch at his fat belly.

That knocked the wind out of Klaas, but not for long. He was soon up and ready to fight. Alex was just as tall as Klaas but leaner and more muscular. The boys pulled each other's hair or ears and punched whichever body part they could access with their fists. It was mayhem, with the audience shouting and rooting for either boy.

Eventually, the principal pushed his way through the crowd of children, blew his whistle, and told both boys to come to his office. A chill ran through everyone; they knew what that could mean: a caning.

Each boy sat on a chair on either side of the principal's office door. Alex sat frozen. Klaas's teeth were chattering. He made them sweat it out and wait. After about half an hour, the principal called them in. He gave them a stern lecture that he did not care what the argument was about, he would not have this kind of behaviour at his school. Each of them would get the maximum of six canes.

He sent Alex out of his office first, with Klaas staying behind. Alex could hear the whip of the cane, and Klaas's yelp after each strike. Alex was determined he wouldn't make a sound. Klaas came out of the office, blubbering and crying. Snot running from his nose, as he ran out the building into the playground.

Alex went in, bent over and waited for the first whip. His buttocks stung. The pain etched further and further down his legs and up his back with each strike.

He didn't make a sound. Afterwards, he went to his classroom, where everyone was packing up for the end of the day.

When he got closer to the house, Alex went to the back door where he dropped his satchel and went straight to the shed. He usually went through to the *stoep*, where Themba would be waiting for him, but not today.

Themba must have realised Alex was back, so he went around the back of the house, saw the satchel, and popped his head in the kitchen where his mother nodded towards the shed.

Something must have happened. Themba tiptoed into the shed, where Alex was at the workbench, frantically sanding a piece of wood. The sanding motion was repetitive, purposeful and seemed to be calming Alex down. Themba saw the bruises and scratches on Alex's arms, legs and cheeks. He stood next to Alex and picked up a piece of wire and pliers and started to bend a wheel for the car they were part-way through constructing. He didn't say anything or even look at Alex.

After a while of silence, Alex turned to Themba and said, "I've got a game we haven't played yet."

"What is it?" asked Themba.

"Mm, let's get those cardboard boxes over there and flatten them, and then I'll show you."

They walked over and folded the boxes to flatten them. Alex said, "Right, let's head up the boulders." This was a smooth, solid stone hillock set behind the shed. They were red and too hot to the touch to play on in the summer. The weather was colder now, so the game would be more inviting.

Each boy took his flattened box. "Come, follow me, Themba," Alex called as he was crawling up the rock dragging his box behind him. As always, Themba trusted his brother and followed him to the top.

They were breathless by the time they got there. "You see that long marking all the way to the bottom," Alex pointed out to Themba. "Well, that's where we're going to slide down this big rock, sitting on the boxes!"

Themba shook his head. "No, I can't do that. I'm scared!"

Alex turned and looked at Themba, put his arm about his shoulder. "Watch me go down first a couple of times, then we'll go down together. Then you can go on your own when you're ready. We don't want another accident!"

Themba thought about it and reluctantly said, "Okay!"

Alex set his flattened cardboard box in front of him. He reached out to the forward part of the box and bent it slightly back, holding on with his body doubled over. "Right, you need to push me now!" he said to Themba. Themba put his hands on Alex's back and gave him a forceful shove.

Alex shot down the hill, sliding smoothly, yelling and screeching at the top of his voice despite the pain resurging through his body. When he got to the bottom, a dip and a sandbank stopped his forward motion. He jumped up, yelled, and flung both arms in the air. "Yes, yes, yes," he said. "That's ace!"

Alex did a couple more slides, with the same reaction at the end. Eventually, he managed to persuade Themba to sit behind him, legs on either side of Alex's body, and they pushed themselves forward, finally shooting down the rock. Themba clung on to Alex, petrified. Once they were at the bottom, Themba felt a satisfaction that he had done it. "Let's go again," said Themba.

After that were several more joint sledges until the cardboard broke, and they had to use the second one. Themba didn't want to go on his own; he preferred the security of Alex in front of him, clinging to his back, speeding up, wind in their faces and then the abrupt stop at the bottom when they would both fall over, laughing, adrenalin racing through them. Pain is forgotten when you're laughing.

~

Most Sundays, Alex and his parents went to church in Cradock. The imposing building on Church Street dominated the town. Alex left his parents at the front doors and went around the back to the smaller building. He spent the next hour learning about Christian values and stories from the Bible. He loved the exciting stories, especially the one about Moses leading his people and parting the sea.

After the children's Sunday school and the congregation's service, the parents gathered together having coffee and cakes. The children usually ran around playing in the gardens.

Sara avoided having direct contact with Karen and her family at church services. Klaas Senior had done some scripture readings as part of the service today. Sara felt a churning in her stomach. *Bloody hypocrite!* she thought. *Acting pious, and spouting omnipotent wisdom to the congregation.* Sara thought she wanted to throw up but managed to conceal her feelings by holding her hand in front of her mouth and keeping her eyes downcast. Everyone fawned over Klaas Senior after the service, and he lorded over everyone, literally.

As they were having coffee afterwards, Karen came up to her and asked, "How are things on the farm?"

Sara replied, understanding the hidden question. "We're all good, thank you. Alex has started his new class and is very busy with his schoolwork and homework and has barely any time for his sports after school."

Karen seemed relieved, saying in a whisper, "You won't believe it, but Klaas Junior came home the other day from school, having been in a fight with another boy. He was black and blue and even had to go to the principal and got a caning. So unfair, it wasn't even his fault. Poor boy, I had to keep him out of school for a few days to calm him down."

Sara smiled, saying, "Oh dear." She had seen Alex's cuts and bruises and had waited until he was ready to tell her what had happened. He had told her briefly what Klaas had said and how he had retaliated. She felt that Alex had been standing up for his friend Themba and that Klaas was a bully only challenging him with an audience. She, in a way, felt relieved that her son would always stand up for what was right and would not be bullied by others. Themba was now more than a friend; they were like brothers— inseparable. Quite ironic, thought Sara, as Klaas Junior was actually Themba's half-brother. Of course, that fact would have been kept a secret from the child!

Karen seemed to lose interest and soon walked off to talk to her other friends and to join her husband. Sara stayed out of Klaas Senior's way. He did not acknowledge her, and she was sure he did not even remember that she had been on his farm those months ago. Relieved, she found Alex and Dan and said she wanted to go home to get lunch ready. Sundays were Buhle's day off from cooking, and she wanted to share the rest of the day with her family.

Through the winter months, the boys would go to school, and afterwards, they did homework together, with Alex teaching Themba from his textbooks as well. They seemed to enjoy sharing knowledge, and there were plenty of discussions and questions about geography and history. Themba challenged Alex, saying that history seemed only to be about white people. Alex didn't know what to say and asked his friend to explain.

Themba said, "Well, there is Xhosa history, the chiefs and their battles, say with the Zulus. Then there are the Zulu kings. Lots of African history that I don't know but must be there."

The boys spoke to Sara about this, and she acknowledged there was no black history in the textbooks unless it was when the white man battled with, say, the Zulus. Sara was not sure if there were any books on African history, and she thought it might be a good idea if she went to have a look in the library when she was next in town. She doubted she'd find anything to enlighten the children, as the library was limited. She knew Cape Town library would have more information, but she was unlikely to get there for some years yet.

The boys moved on to doing maths homework, and here Alex excelled. He was patient and explained things to Themba. Themba, on the other hand, was good with his languages. He spoke isiXhosa, but could not read nor write it, but he could talk reasonably fluent English, and his grasp of reading and writing was improving exponentially. He was also learning some Afrikaans; as the government actually wanted all Black children to be taught only in Afrikaans, he had no choice but to learn it.

Sara had somewhat rebelled against this and insisted the farm school taught mostly in English but used Afrikaans in a tokenistic way. IsiXhosa was more a common language the children used in play and when explaining something to each other. In fact, farm children were learning three languages. In contrast, at Alex's school, they were learning primarily in Afrikaans, or with a few children learning in English. IsiXhosa was not spoken at the white school.

Everyone was in a routine, and so the winter passed.

# CHAPTER 7

*Spring.*

EVENTUALLY, THE DAYS GOT WARMER, and the nights less frosty. By the end of October, the heat was reaching 30 degrees Centigrade most days.

Alex and Themba started going down to the river again, with Themba now being far more confident and with a physique that was more muscular from all the games he and Alex played. Themba seemed to have gotten his confidence back since his accident. Dan and Bongani had rechecked their swimming area before they were allowed down to the river to play. The boys often wrestled and threw each other in the water, testing their new-found strength. Hours of fun!

Buhle had also settled into her routine. She was experimenting with some cooking, using Missus Sara's cookery books, which she could more or less read. Sometimes she would ask Sara or one of the boys to help her.

The house was quiet, the boys were at each of their schools and Missus Sara was teaching. Mister Dan was out with Bongani for the day. Buhle had the house to herself. She thought, *I'll experiment today and impress everyone with something new!*

Buhle lifted the heavy *Mrs Villiers' South African Cooking* book off the kitchen shelf. She went to the *Contents* page as Missus Sara had shown her, and scrolled down the list with her finger. She found what she was looking for: a mutton stew with dumplings. Buhle had made various kinds of stew many times before, but the dumplings were something novel.

She browned the meat and afterwards added the vegetables, and she let it simmer for about two hours. By mid-afternoon, the meat was tender, and she decided to start on the dumplings. She measured out the flour, baking powder, salt and milk, rubbing the butter into the dry mixture with her fingertips. Buhle double-checked the recipe as some measurements were with a small *t* and some were with a *T*. One was teaspoon and the other tablespoon. She thought she got it the right way round.

She rolled the dough out, used the biscuit cutter to press out circles and placed them on top of the stew mixture. Now she just had to wait.

Buhle always left the cooked food in the pots, ready for the family to eat when they came in. She dished out food for her and Themba and made her way home to Gogo.

Sara and Alex came home from a long day at school. Alex met Themba on the *stoep*; both boys were tired but did their homework. Once they finished, Themba went back to his mum and Gogo to have his supper.

Alex walked into the kitchen; the smells made his mouth water.

"Hi, Pa," he called out to his father as he came through the back door.

"I'm hungry after such a long day. Bongani and I went all the way out to the far side of the farm to check on some sheep. They were caught in the fences. It was a struggle to get them loose." Dan sat down at the table after washing his hands.

Sara dished up, and Dan said grace before they dug in.

"Buhle's been creative today with dumplings," Sara quipped. She and Dan put their forks in their mouths at the same time. The dumpling stuck to the top of their mouths, the saltiness taking their breath away. They both spat it out into their napkins.

"Oh my goodness, what has she done?" shrieked Sara, looking at Dan's face all scrunched up in disgust. They couldn't contain it; they burst out laughing at the same time. Alex looked at both his parents, not quite knowing what was going on. He put his fork in his mouth.

"Yuck! What happened?" Alex said while spitting the dumpling mixture out of his mouth into his hand.

They all had a fit of the giggles, turning into belly laughs. It must be Buhle's reading, getting the quantities of the ingredients wrong, they exclaimed in unison.

"You haven't done a good job of teaching Buhle to read, Sara," said Dan between fits of giggles.

After they'd managed to calm down, they pulled the dumplings off the stew and carried on eating the rest of the meal, which was delicious.

74

At the same time, Gogo, Buhle and Themba were digging into their stew and dumplings. Gogo tried to be polite after the first mouthful. Buhle screeched in isiXhosa, "What's happened here?"

Gogo said she must have misread how much salt to add. Buhle was mortified.

"Oh, no!" she said, holding her head in her hands. "What will I do? I've got the mixture wrong! Am I going to get a beating now?"

Gogo knew she was frightened after her experiences at Kasteel at the hands of her old *baas*. She tried to reassure Buhle. "Don't worry, Mister Dan never lays a hand on any of the workers!" She hoped that would pacify her, not sure it was working as Buhle still looked stunned.

Buhle went up to the farmhouse the next morning, like she did every morning, and started making the *pap* for breakfast. Missus Sara came into the kitchen while she was busy stirring the *pap* so that it didn't turn lumpy.

"Buhle, what happened to you?" Sara giggled, putting her hand in front of her mouth. "Were you trying to poison us yesterday?"

Buhle looked at Sara, her mouth hanging open. *No*, she thought, *I'd never do that.* Then she saw Missus Sara's smile and giggle. *It's okay*, she thought, *they think it's funny.* Buhle saw the funny side of it and started to laugh as well.

She showed Missus Sara the recipe that she had used, and they worked out she had got her small and capital *T's* muddled. It was a teaspoon of salt, not a tablespoon.

Mister Dan and Alex also walked into the kitchen, and they all laughed at Buhle's mistake and told her not to worry, the stew was delicious. They had second helpings, so there were no leftovers for lunch today.

Buhle felt relieved; it had not been the response she was expecting. If she had been at Kasteel, her *baas* would have slapped and punched her for making a mistake. He would also take it out on her in her room later that night.

She felt reassured nothing 'bad' would happen to her and was happy to laugh at her own mistake.

By December, the school year over, the boys were ready to close their books and play the days away. The family, now with Buhle and Themba joining, would soon be going to the cabin in Port Alfred to meet up with the rest of the family.

They packed up the *bakkie*, with Buhle and Sara sitting next to Dan, and the boys ensconced behind the front cab, between the bags and boxes of groceries.

Bongani waved them off, quite happy to be left on his own. He and mister Dan had chatted about the few things he needed to keep an eye on, but mostly he had his days to himself. He'd spend them with his children and his wife, fixing things around his little house, maybe even giving it a coat of paint. Bongani had free access to the shed and the equipment, so he could help himself to whatever he needed.

This year, they were one of the first families at the cabins, and soon the rest of the Smit brothers and their family joined them.

Themba and Alex got together with the boy cousins from last year; all had grown a bit taller and had finished another year of school.

They all quickly got back into a routine of cricket, with Frik as leader. Themba also wanted to bat this year, so in between the games, Alex or Frik would teach him by throwing the ball for him to strike. There was much laughter when Themba missed, but he soon got into the rhythm of watching the tennis ball, keeping his eye on it, and swinging his bat at the ball at the right time. He got his timing, and although he was slightly smaller than the other boys, his swing technique was excellent, and he could hit it quite far.

Themba became part of a team. It was now the turn of one of the younger boys to be included in the game and to be given the job of wicketkeeper.

Buhle felt a sort of home-coming to the cabins. It was far enough from Cradock to make her feel less anxious and fearful. She rarely went into Cradock to shop, and usually she gave Themba a list of what she needed. Themba would go with Bongani and Alex once a month to get supplies. Buhle saved money every month and put it in a tin under her bed.

Having "run away" from Kasteel still played on Buhle's mind, and she only felt comfortable when she was at Soetewater, with Missus Sara nearby. She slept behind Gogo's back every night, and this helped with the nightmares. If she woke, shaking, thrashing her arms and legs, Gogo would take her hand and hook it under her arm. Buhle would curl up behind Gogo's back and eventually fall into a fitful sleep. It was like having a mother, someone who would calm her down when she was anxious, who understood why she had nightmares.

Being at the cabins was a relief for Buhle; nobody could find them here, least of all her old *baas* Klaas. It was a safe place to revisit what had happened to her and to reframe the trauma she had suffered. She had to learn to tolerate the memories so they wouldn't frighten her so much. They slowly but surely became less threatening to her.

*Baas* Klaas was a brute of a man; he used his fists with his farm labourers or anybody who got in his way or didn't do what he wanted fast enough. When he snapped his fingers, everyone had to jump. You were on tenterhooks all the time, never sure where his mood would take him or who would be his victim that day. Would you be on the receiving end of his whip, or would he remove his belt and hit you, the buckle tearing at your skin and clothes?

A young fourteen-year-old girl had just started working in the house before Buhle left to come to Soetewater. Buhle understood that Missus Karen wanted her to teach the girl the household and cooking routines before she was to leave the farm. While Buhle was doing the washing or cleaning, she would often think about the girl; what was her fate at Kasteel? The *baas* liked younger girls, and his preferences seemed to be getting younger and younger each time. When Buhle got to be about twenty, she had been at the farm for about four years, with Themba being about three years old; the *baas* came less often to her room. He was still as brutal with her. He remained generous with his hands and would come into the kitchen and slap or punch her if the food was not to his liking. He'd shout and swear at her; it was almost as if he were angry because she was now a woman. She might have served mutton stew, but he would come in and shout that he had wanted a *bobotie*. How should she know what he wanted? She cooked whatever the mis-sus told her to. Well, she knew the missus also suffered from his power-hungry anger and his brutal fists. She often saw bruises on her arms, and sometimes her one eye was black, even though she tried to cover it with makeup.

Each time Buhle thought about Kasteel, she would shiver, remembering how trapped she used to feel. She had to endure the pain and the smell of the man, allow her mind to wander, trying to leave her body and fly away while he raped or groped her, hoping and praying that one day she would be free.

The safety of the cabins, and the general babble of the children, the adults laughing and joking in a carefree way around the fire every night, made her feel safe. She liked being invisible to them. She quietly went on with her work. Sometimes she would go down to the beach, sit in the sand and watch the children play. She would put her hand into the warm white powder, lift it up and let it run through her fingers. She would do this over and over again, enjoying the dry warmth on her palm.

It gave her joy to see all the children together, intent on their game, competitive, squabbling. Frik or Liwa broke them up if it got too heated. They collapsed with laughter when the batsman missed the ball or a fielder dropped it when trying to catch it. Themba was always the joker – adding an extra roll or flip when he failed to catch the ball. There was lots of teasing as each team tried desperately to win only to head off in unison to swim when the game got too heated or when it was over.

Sara could sense that Buhle needed quiet space, and she did not put pressure on her to talk. She just let her get on with the chores with each day being more or less the same as the last day. It was about putting the world to one side, sitting back and putting your feet up. She loved to see her husband joking with his two brothers, both older than him. They were a close-knit sibling group, and the annual get-together was essential to them. They shared advice about farming, checking on how each was doing, what new plans they had for their farm, or what the latest farming methods were. They stood around the *braai* every night, cooking together like they always did, no instructions needed.

She enjoyed the company of her two sisters-in-law; they were kind and thoughtful. Although their relationship was superficial, they were comfortable in each other's company. They were home-makers, typical farmers' wives, while she was working, albeit part-time. She felt they respected her, often asking her advice about their children's schooling.

Frik's mother, Johanna, was very proud of him. She told them that he was going to university next year in Grahamstown. Frik would be the first in the family to study further.

"I'm worried," said Johanna. "Frik will be away from his family, living at the university, not knowing anyone. I'm going to miss him." She sighed, wiping a tear from her cheek. They all sympathised, wondering how they would feel when their children would first leave home. They all reassured her he would be fine; he was very independent and a born leader.

"Liwa is staying on the farm, and they'll miss each other. They've been together since they were babies." Liwa's mother worked in the farmhouse, and when he was a baby, he was always with her, usually tied with a blanket or towel to her back. When he was older, he would toddle about after his mother or play with Frik. They were inseparable.

# CHAPTER 8

*Cradock*

ANOTHER TWO YEARS WENT BY, uneventfully. The farm was becoming more successful, although they were not rich by any means. Dan managed to buy the family a more comfortable car, albeit a second-hand Zodiac with a long front seat and a long back seat. This larger car was a big step up. They kept the *bakkie* for farm work and mostly for Bongani to use.

Buhle felt at home with Gogo. Sara settled back into teaching in town, and she supported the teacher on the farm school, bringing books, etc. that were no longer needed in the town school. Routines and relationships were well established. The farm school was also doing well, with the young teacher growing in confidence under Sara's guidance. The farm children enjoyed learning, and there was still a steady number of students at the start of each year.

Alex and Themba's relationship grew and changed. At first, Alex was the leader and Themba the follower. Still, slowly as Themba's confidence grew, particularly physically in the games they played, his learning leapt ahead and was at least on par with Alex now; the relationship was equal.

Alex was more of the hot-head, doing things spontaneously, but always fiercely loyal to his brother Themba. They called each other "brother" now, squabbling, teasing and building a bond to last. Themba was the peace-maker, the sunny-natured optimist, who always saw the positives first. He would play tricks on Alex, who was more serious, and laughed when he caught him out. Alex would get cross but quickly burst into raucous laughter. They would rough and tumble with each other, each trying to outsmart or over-power the other.

# CHAPTER 9

*Cradock,*
*June 1981*

THEMBA FINISHED HIS MID-YEAR TESTS at the farm school, and Alex had already finished his. They were packing their school-books away, ready for the winter and a two-week holiday ahead.

It was late morning, and the sun was beginning to warm the *stoep* of the house. Sara was inside finishing off the farm accounts and the banking for the month. Buhle was in the kitchen preparing lunch for the boys and peeling the vegetables for supper.

They all stopped what they were doing, hearing the *bakkie* coming to a screeching halt in front of the house, driven by Bongani. Dust kicked up like a tornado. The vehicle was covered in fine brown powder. Bongani had obviously been driving fast for a while.

"Missus, missus," he shouted, climbing out the cab, waving his arms trying to attract attention. "Come quickly. Mister Dan is sick." Sara heard the panic in his voice and rushed out.

"What's the matter?"

"He fell over in the field, missus. I don't know what's the matter. He said his arms ached, and he threw up. Then he passed out." He stuttered, panicked, tried to get his words out, but failed. He mumbled in isiXhosa and English, before finally running out of words.

Sara looked at her husband, propped up on the front seat of the cab. His face was ashen white and blue around his lips. Sweat covered his face. "Bongani, we need to get him to the hospital quickly. I'll get in and hold on to him, and you drive as fast as you can."

Buhle had come out to the *stoep* to see what all the commotion was.

"Buhle," Sara shouted, "look after Alex while I take Mister Dan to the hospital in Cradock."

"Yes, ma'am."

Alex and Themba sat open-mouthed on the steps, looked at each other and waved Sara off, oblivious to the emergency.

When they got to the hospital, Dan was wheeled in on a stretcher, leaving Sara and Bongani standing in unified shock in the reception area. One of the staff came over and told Bongani he had to wait outside.

"Missus, I'll wait in the *bakkie* for you." Sara nodded and went over to sit and wait.

Sara sat on the hard backed-chair for what seemed an eternity. Eventually, a stern-faced doctor in a white coat approached her and asked to talk to her in private. They went into a side room.

"Mrs Smit," the doctor said, "your husband has suffered a massive heart attack. We've tried to resuscitate him, but he is not responding. I'm afraid I don't think we can save him. I think you should go in and see him."

Sara was shaking, not fully understanding, but blindly followed the doctor into the room where Dan lay. He was hooked up to all sorts of machines that bleeped and buzzed, but she did not notice these; all she saw was him lying on the bed, pale. His eyes were closed. She stood next to him, held his hand and stroked his cheek. She felt her throat choke, and her chest contract, squeezing her breath out of her body.

"Dan, I love you," she said, stroking his face, tears streaming, her whole body shaking with emotion. "I'm sorry if I didn't tell you often enough. You're my rock, please don't leave me on my own!" He did not respond, but she saw his lips move into a slight smile.

She sat with him, holding his hand until it eventually became dark outside. A nurse came in occasionally and spoke to her, but Sara didn't hear or respond.

Bongani sat in the *bakkie*, his head on the steering wheel, tears streaming down his dark cheeks. He was so worried Mister Dan would die. "Please don't die, please don't. It's not your time to go," Bongani said to himself in isiXhosa. He carried on muttering prayers, talking as if directly to Dan.

⌁

The day turned into night, and all went dark and cold. Bongani continued to sit in the *bakkie*, shivering with cold and shock. He could not go inside the hospital, and he didn't want to make a scene as Missus Sara would already be upset.

With the dawn slowly breaking, Bongani lifted his head and saw Missus Sara walking out of the front door of the hospital, looking around as if trying to find him. He climbed out of the pickup so Missus Sara could see him. She caught his eye and ran towards him. She flung her arms around his neck, sobbing, her whole body shaking. They clung to each other.

"He's gone, he's gone, Bongani," she mumbled into his neck. Bongani kept his arms around her and guided her to the passenger side of the *bakkie*, realising he could get into trouble hugging her, a white woman. Sara sat in the seat, looking up at him. "I don't know what to do; he's gone," she sobbed, her shoulders shaking. She sat frozen, her left hand holding up her head, her elbow leaning against the window.

Bongani went around and sat in the driver's seat. He held Sara's hand, squeezed it, saying, "Missus, he's gone, but Mister Dan is in heaven. He was a good man, and we all loved him. You will need to be strong now. You have to tell Alex."

Sara just nodded, squeezing his hand back. Bongani started the engine and slowly drove the *bakkie* out of the parking lot and along the road back to the farm. He drove as slowly as he could, giving Sara time to think.

Eventually, they turned on to the dusty road to Soetewater. Sara let out a deep sigh, covering her eyes with her hands.

When they pulled up in front of the house, Bongani said, "Missus, it's nearly sunrise. You go to bed, and I'll go to my house. You'll have to tell Alex when he wakes up. I'll come up to the house later, make sure you're okay. Don't worry about the farm; I'll carry on with the jobs." Bongani didn't want her to worry about the farm; he'd lived all his life on it and had worked so closely with Mister Dan that he knew what tasks needed doing.

Sara nodded at him, climbed out of the cab and up the steps of the *stoep*. Bongani let out a sigh, knowing that she had a terrible day ahead of her. He pulled away and went to park outside his home. He quietly climbed into bed next to his wife so as not to wake her.

Sara felt drained and numb. Life had seeped out of her body and mind. She went and lay on her bed, their bed, putting her hand out to where Dan would have been. She closed her eyes tightly, tears rolling down her cheeks. Sara took his pillow and put her arms around it, smelling his body. She fell into an exhausted, fitful sleep.

Alex woke up. The house was quiet, and the sun had risen. He could hear Buhle in the kitchen. Where was his mum? She was usually up and coming to wake him. He then remembered his father being ill and going to the hospital.

He tiptoed over to his parents' bedroom, opened the door, and saw his mother, fully clothed, lying on the bed by herself and holding on to a pillow next to her. Alex climbed on to the bed, on his father's side, lying next to his mother. She turned as she sensed Alex next to her. She opened her eyes to face him. Her face was swollen and pale.

"Where's Pa?" Alex asked.

Sara sighed, took her son in her arms, and explained that he had a massive heart attack and the doctors couldn't save him. He had died in the night. She held his hand and was with him until the end. His Pa wasn't alone when he left this world.

Alex's body went stiff. Shock. He had seen sheep die on the farm, their lifeless form lying there in the veld where it had fallen. His Pa and Bongani would bury it. His Pa was dead now, lifeless and would also need to be buried. He sat up in bed, pulled his knees up to his chin, and wrapped his arms around them. He started to shake uncontrollably. Sara didn't know what to do. She let him absorb what she had said. Eventually, he turned to her and flung himself in her arms. They both lay on the bed, bodies entwined, their joint grief overwhelming them to silence.

Bongani came up to the house and spoke quietly to Buhle, who was in the kitchen. Themba came in, and Bongani told them that Mister Dan had died. Buhle hugged Themba, tears running down both their cheeks. She knew that he was worried about his brother.

# CHAPTER 10

*June 1981,*
*Soetewater farm, the funeral*

THE HILLS WERE A GREY silhouette against an azure blue sky. A deep shadow against the intense African rising sun. Sara looked at the familiar scene from her perch on the *stoep*. The world around her looked the same as it always had, but her life had dramatically changed. She was like a precious vase, broken into a million pieces. Reluctantly, she got up and prepared for the day.

Dan's brothers arrived at the farm to accompany Sara and Alex to the funeral. Sara was grateful they had come to escort them to the church. She didn't feel up to driving into town, and she couldn't ask Bongani to take them. He was making preparations for the burial in the farm graveyard in the afternoon.

She felt some relief that Dan's parents did not have to go through this agony as they had both passed away. His brothers looked drawn and in shock. Dan was their little brother. It was never going to be the same when they met up at the cabins at Christmas. It did not hold the same allure anymore.

Frik and some of Alex's older cousins came to sit with him. Sara was relieved as she was finding it difficult to deal with her own grief and with Alex's. Themba was a comfort to Alex, but he could not be here today. The church was exclusively for white congregation members.

She just wanted it over so she could be back home to the farm, with the familiar around her.

The formal Christian service proceeded. All members of the family sat together and people from Cradock who knew Dan, Sara and Alex were there as well. Sara and Alex sat together, their heads bowed, tears rolling down their pale cheeks.

The service went past in a blur for Sara and Alex. The minister's words washed over them like a wave over which they had no control. They shook hands outside with members of the congregation but could not remember who had spoken to them or what they had said.

Time went past in a haze of sorrow and tears.

Later that day, Dan was buried on the farm in a private family ceremony. Only a few family members and the farmworkers were present. There was a small graveyard alongside the dusty road leading to the farmhouse. The family gathered around, and Dan's brothers committed him to the ground, each saying prayers and reading texts from the Bible.

Bongani performed the *Thetha*, speaking to Dan in isiXhosa, as he was worried that Mister Dan's spirit was still held within his body. Bongani wanted to talk him into being released from his earthly form, through to the afterlife.

Eventually, Bongani and Dan's brothers lowered the coffin into the ground. The workers sang an isiXhosa hymn, swaying gently to the rhythm of the music. Sara was moved by their sadness, the slow rhythm and gentle voices calming her mind. She felt for the first time that she could grieve without constraint amongst people she and Alex knew. The families on the farm, Dan's brothers and Bongani all stood around Sara and Alex, tears rolling down the white and black faces, joined in their grief for the loss of a good man.

Earlier that morning, Bongani had slaughtered a sheep by slitting its throat, the *umkhapho* to help Mister Dan move quickly into the afterlife. The meat would not be spiced and was to be eaten on the day of the burial. Bongani put the spit roast over the coals. It would take all day to roast before they could feed the family and the farm workers.

Buhle and some of the women cooked *pap* to go with the meat. A table was set outside to serve the large group. Alex and Themba helped put plates and cups out for the meal.

Dan's brothers carved the meat once it was ready and served everyone.

It was dark by this stage, and Bongani stoked up a massive fire that reflected light and shadows over dark and white faces, all grieving. Everyone sat on large logs or chairs formed in a circle. The fire cast a glow across all the workers and the family. Voices were quiet and peaceful, the African darkness absorbing their pain. The stars came out and seemed to shine in a pure African sky spectacle. Themba and Alex lay back on the logs, looking up at the sky, deep inky blackness speckled with shining stars.

There was dancing and singing around the fire until the early hours. Dan's brothers had a bottle of brandy to toast Dan as they shared anecdotes and memories about him. There were laughter and tears with each of the stories told with poignancy and love.

Sara did not want to stop Alex experiencing this night; it would be one he needed to remember. She felt this was part of his grieving process, so she quietly went off to bed, telling Alex she'd leave the *stoep* light on for him.

Themba and Alex sat around the fire, talking to Alex's cousins. The family had all congregated at the farm but stayed overnight at the hotel in Cradock.

Frik, now nearly twenty years old, sat with Themba and Alex. They eventually lay on the ground, looking up at the stars, like they used to do at the beach cabins. Frik pointed out the constellations to them. Allowing their eyes to adjust to the dark sky he pointed to the Milky Way, with its cluster of sparkling lights spread across the pitch-black, clear sky.

"You guys know I'm at university now," Frik reminded them, after stoking the fire and sitting back on the logs.

"Yes, we know," said Alex. Themba nodded as well. "That's why you don't go to the cabins at Christmas."

"Yes," said Frik. "I'm studying law at Grahamstown." The boys nodded that they understood. "Well, I belong to a political group at university, and we're discussing all sorts of things."

92

"Like what?" asked Themba, lifting his head, eager to hear some grownup snippets.

"Well, apartheid for one, whether it is right that only white people can vote and sit in parliament and make the laws. The other is, if it's wrong, then how can we move to a system of one vote for all? Why do we allow people to suffer through apartheid? Why should one group, whites, have the power over others, black, Indian and coloured people, just because of the colour of their skin? These are big questions that we need to think about. We, the next generation, need to think about whether we want to carry on living like this, or how we can change things."

Alex and Themba were due to start high school next year. They had heard some of the grown-ups talking around the fire when they were at the cabins on holiday, but they didn't quite understand it all.

Frik continued, trying to explain to them what apartheid was, and if they could do anything to change it. Alex and Themba listened quietly, soaking it all up and trying to understand. Some of what Frik was telling them was something they were vaguely aware of in their day-to-day lives, but they did not understand that things could change or be improved upon or that they could be a part of that change.

"You see, boys, here's an example. Four years ago, the government wanted to make a ruling that all black children had to be taught in Afrikaans in schools. This led to students being angry and resulted in an uprising in Soweto, which is just outside Johannesburg. Lots of students were injured and killed by the police, even though the protest was peaceful. None of this information was reported in the South African newspapers, but it was well publicised in the rest of the world, like in America and in Europe."

Frik carried on educating them. "You see, we, the next generation, are the future, and if we're not happy with the way things are, then it's up to us to make changes. Now that I'm over eighteen, I can vote, but only for a white person. What if I don't want a white person in government? Say I thought Bongani should be in government; why can't I, or any other person, vote for him? We can't. So, we are stuck."

Frik put more logs on the fire. The boys stared into the flames, the sparks flying from the wood being placed on the fire, absorbed by what he was saying.

"Well," said Frik, "I for one won't be voting until we have a free and fair government that represents everyone. Liwa can't vote either."

Themba and Alex looked at each other, mouths open. Alex was aware that his parents sometimes went to vote, but he had never understood why or how it worked.

"I'm going to be a lawyer," said Frik, "and I want to be part of the future and force things to change. The government does not tell people what is going on. They're hiding things; people who disagree with the government disappear without a trace. I want to study constitutional law and criminal law. This apartheid doesn't help anyone."

Alex thought about this and said, "How are you going to do that?"

Frik spoke in hushed tones. "Now don't tell anyone, but I'm going to start working in my uni holidays at a law firm in Jo'burg, which advises the ANC. That's short for the African National Congress. There is a chance they may offer me a permanent position once I'm finished studying."

"What's ANC?" both boys asked at the same time.

"It's a banned political organisation that wants to bring about a free and fair country, giving the same rights to every person. I want to be a part of that. Once I've finished my studies, I'm going to move to Johannesburg permanently. I'm going to take Liwa with me. He's not cut out for working the rest of his life on the farm. The ANC is banned, so you can't talk about them. The leaders live outside the country so they don't get arrested. The main leader is Nelson Mandela, and he is in jail for his beliefs. If the secret police find out I'm sympathising with the ANC, they will arrest me and also put me in prison. My friends and I must be very careful when we meet up and talk about them. The police gather information, build a file on you and then pounce when they are ready to put you in jail."

Alex and Themba sat with their mouths open, thinking that it was very harsh to be imprisoned for something you believed in!

This was their first momentous "awakening" into the reality of South African politics. Themba and Alex listened to Frik. He had always been their role model, and they both looked up to him with trust. This was a night they would never forget.

Alex swallowed nervously, taking in the enormity of what Frik had said. "Please, Frik, be careful. We don't want you to go to prison and never see you again." Alex looked at Themba, nodded and said on behalf of both of them, "We'll never tell anyone, not even our mothers, we promise."

"You know that Nelson Mandela is a lawyer and also Xhosa. He went to prison for his principles and political activism in 1963. Nobody is allowed to talk about him or even mention his name. You must pretend you have never heard of him if anyone asks you. The secret police are everywhere and very happy to arrest anyone they think is a threat, or a 'communist,' even if they're not.

"Listen, nobody knows this, but last year three ANC prisoners escaped from prison in Pretoria, and they went to live in countries bordering us. One white prisoner, who went to prison for life at the same time as Nelson Mandela, is still in prison. His name is Denis Goldberg, and he helped them to escape. One of his accomplices, a guy called Tim Jenkin, made keys from wood so they could unlock several gates to get out of the prison that night."

Themba and Alex had now left the last of an innocent childhood behind them and started the move into adolescence. There ideas were being formed; the big questions in life were starting to be raised and they'd attempt to answer them. Their emotions and thoughts would be passionate and at times, extreme. Their views on fairness and justice were being cemented into their personalities. The cloak and dagger of the freedom struggle would permeate their lives. The days of innocent childhood were slowly falling away, revealing a core of strength and commitment to a cause each of them would take up, despite the dangers involved.

This turning point in their development was significant, as was the events outside their control. All these would be added to the mix that would shape the men they were to become. Politics in South Africa invaded everyone's life, whether they wanted it to or not.

Themba and Alex stayed up all night. Once the fire died down and they had run out of wood, the boys took blankets, curled up together and slept next to the dying embers. The workers had gone back to their homes, and the rest of the family went back to Cradock and their hotel, ready to return to their farms the following day.

This is where Sara found them the next morning, curled up, tucked under the blankets. She let them sleep and went back to the kitchen to start breakfast: bacon and eggs and some pumpkin fritters.

# CHAPTER 11

SARA KNEW SHE COULD NOT make the farming decisions like Dan had. He was the farmer, not her. She was feeling anxious and insecure about what path to take in the future. Although Bongani was a good manager, it was always Dan who had made the day-to-day decisions or plotted and planned the way ahead, leading them all in his quiet, unassuming way. She could not fill Dan's shoes and continue his legacy. Being realistic is what she needed to do.

Once the boys were taken up with school, she made an appointment to see the family lawyer and a land agent who handled the sale of farms. She already knew that Dan's will had set out that she inherited everything. She had many a sleepless night over this, tossing and turning, dreaming of every which outcome, but she realised she had no choice. She had to put the farm on the market to sell while it was still a going concern. She couldn't wait for it to flounder and then try and sell it.

This was her one opportunity to create a future for her and Alex. With the proceeds from the sale, she could buy a small house near her mother in Cape Town and save the rest of the money to fund Alex going to university. This was her plan.

Now that she had made up her mind, Sara went through to the kitchen and spoke to Buhle.

"Buhle, I've had to make some difficult decisions. Bongani and I can't manage the farm without Mister Dan. I am going to have to sell the farm, but I don't want to tell Alex and Themba yet. It might take months to sell, and I don't know when or if we will get a buyer. It's not fair to have this hanging over them and worrying. I will tell you as soon as I have accepted an offer, and we can plan together how we'll tell the boys."

Buhle agreed; this was something she had thought would happen, but she asked, "Can I telephone my sister, as I don't want to stay behind if you and Alex go back to Cape Town?" There was no way Buhle wanted to remain behind in Cradock with the ever-presence of her old *baas* on Kasteel nearby. She always felt she was in a protected "bubble" here at Soetewater.

Sara agreed, as they both needed to start making plans based on what they would do if the farm sold.

Buhle considered her options. Once the farm was sold, Buhle could go to Alexandra, to her sister Lulama, and her husband, Sipho. Her sister had invited her and Themba to come and live with her family in Alexandra some time ago. She had been waiting for the right opportunity. Buhle knew any break from the farm and Alex would upset Themba. She would only make this break when she absolutely had to and not before. Themba could go to a local school in Alexandra, while she would take up her sister's offer to help her find work.

Sara confided in Bongani as well, promising him that any buyer would need to keep him on as manager. She stipulated this as part of the conditions of the sale. She would ideally like to keep all the workers on as they had been loyal to the family, but this would ultimately not be her decision but that of the new owners.

～

Life returned to a new kind of routine. Sara knew she had to be patient. A bit of routine would help to settle Alex, as he slowly had to get used to life without his father.

Each Sunday, they would go to the farm graveyard, tidy the headstone, and sit for a while.

"Mom," Alex asked, "do you think Pa has gone to the afterlife or heaven already?"

"Yes, I think so. Your Pa is with your grandparents now. He won't be on his own."

"Do you think he knows what I'm doing? What my grades are in school?"

"Maybe, I don't know. I tell you what, when you say your prayers every night, say a prayer for him, and tell your father what you have been doing and how you are feeling. A bit like talking to him over a telephone."

Alex thought about this and put his head on his mother's shoulder. He held her hand. They sat on the hard-brown earth, each with their own silent thoughts.

Sara hoped she was making the right decisions. What would Dan have wanted her to do? She knew he would want her to make sure Alex was happy and doing well at school. Sara shouldn't be lonely. Without Dan beside her, she felt the need to see her own mother and sister. Both were in Cape Town. Although she spoke to them on the telephone, it wasn't the same as seeing them or hugging them. She had told her mother about her plans, and it was agreed she and Alex would stay with her until she bought a small house of her own.

Alex missed his father. His had been a quiet presence. Pa was always there when he ran into difficulties, like how to fix the wire cars. He and Themba would sit in the back of the *bakkie*, the wind racing through their hair, dust everywhere. Pa and Bongani up front taking them to check the sheep and cattle furthest away from the farmhouse. They needed to make sure the livestock had enough feed and water, particularly in the dry winter months. Now it was just Bongani upfront in the *bakkie*.

Afterwards, if it was hot, he and Themba would go down to the river to swim and get rid of the dust. Alex remembered when he was little, it was his father who taught him to swim. His father always had said, "If you fall into the river, you need to know how to float and get out." Alex thought about how he had taught Themba to swim, just like his dad had taught him, holding him up under his tummy, kicking his legs and moving his arms until he could float on his own.

Alex knew his father's influence was no longer there, but he felt him in spirit, talking to him in his prayers. He would now have to float on his own without his father to guide and keep him safe.

Sara heard the phone ringing from the kitchen. She dried her hands and picked it up.

"Mrs. Smit." It was her agent. "I have an offer for the farm."

Sara listened carefully. The offer was from Klaas Senior from Kasteel. He wanted to buy her farm as it was adjacent to his. His proposal was two-thirds her asking price.

Sara didn't need time to think it through. Firstly, she would never sell to him, and secondly, he had just insulted her by offering a ridiculous price for a well-run farm.

"No, I don't accept the offer," she said firmly and confidently. "Tell Klaas that I decline." With that, the conversation ended.

Sara carried on with her chores. Alex would soon be back from school, and she wanted to spend some time with him. She needed to make sure he was still motivated to do his school work. Themba would join him, and they would sit on the *stoep*, at the little table, heads together, pouring over their books.

About an hour later, the phone rang again. Sara picked up the receiver. It was Klaas Senior.

"Hello," he said cheerily. "So, you have declined my offer to buy your farm. You know it is a good offer for such a little farm. You can't keep the farm going on your own, and you know it. It's better that you sell to me; it's a cash sale that can go through quickly. I can come over and discuss it with you. I have the offer already drawn up and ready to sign. Are you available today?"

Sara thought carefully about how to respond. "Well, as you know, my agent has told you I have declined your offer. I don't want to see you; there is no point. Please don't phone me directly. I've asked my agent and lawyer to deal with all the offers and business relating to the farm. My answer is still no." With her hands shaking, she put the telephone back on the receiver and phoned her agent back, telling him that under no circumstances would she sell at a ridiculous and insulting price, and please to handle all offers.

Feeling relieved at her assertiveness, she returned to her chores. She told herself if Klaas phoned her again, she would just put the phone down on him. You cannot allow a bully to bully you; you need to stand up to them, or they would trample all over you. Her and Alex's futures were on the line here. She had to fight for a good deal to secure their future without Dan.

She was still nervous that Klaas might come over to her house, and for a few days, she watched the road anticipating him coming to strong-arm her into changing her mind. After a week, she realised her agent must have made a good case for her. He didn't come near the farm or phone her again.

~

The days slowly began to get warmer. The nights were not so cold anymore. Themba and Alex started to down to the river again like they did every spring. Time was slowly creeping towards December when Sara would have to decide whether to go to the cabins in Port Alfred, with the rest of the family.

Sara was busy finishing off marking exam papers when the phone rang. Her agent told her that someone from Port Elizabeth had made an offer for the asking price. They had come and visited the farm about a month previously. They also agreed to keep Bongani on as farm manager and the rest of the workers for now.

Sara felt a sense of relief but was also nervous as now their lives were about to take a turn in a completely different direction. One they had not anticipated nor prepared for. She agreed to the offer and went to see the agent and lawyers. They completed the paperwork, and set a date for Sara to move out. It would be before Christmas. She was relieved as she could use the time to settle Alex before the new school year in January.

Sara told Buhle. They decided to explain to the boys separately that the farm was sold and that they were going their separate ways.

Buhle and Themba went down to Gogo's hut, where she told him the farm was being sold, and they were moving to Alexandra to her sister's. Themba would go to school there, and she would find work. Themba wanted to know about Alex. She told him he was moving to Fish Hoek near Cape Town. His *gogo* lived there and he'd go to school there.

Themba listened to his mother, not fully understanding the enormity of what was about to happen. He knew he had to do what his mother wanted; he was dependent on her. He'd never met his cousins, or his aunt and uncle. Alex was his brother; how would he manage without him by his side? They were like two sides of a coin.

He knew things hadn't been the same since Mister Dan died; the situation felt unsettled and precarious. They tried to carry on as usual, but it wasn't the same.

Sara told Alex they had no choice. Sara and Bongani could not manage on their own, without Dan to guide them. She had sold the farm, and they were moving to stay with his granny in Fish Hoek until the funds came through; then she'd buy them a little house, and he could go to the local school.

Alex thought about this; he remembered visiting his Granny and going to the beach. He didn't believe this was such a bad idea. Soetewater seemed quiet and lonely without Pa. His Pa was always behind the wheel of the *bakkie*. Now it was just Bongani on his own. Alex struggled with all this. Pa was like a ghost all around him on the farm. He dreamed of reaching out to him, but the image of his Pa always disappeared before he could touch him. Alex felt confused; there was a big gap in his life where his father used to be. The farm had changed, and he was not able to tell his mother how he felt; he couldn't describe it even to himself. Alex loved being with Themba, but they would now be separated. Leaving this place that felt hollow and empty, he would be leaving Themba and his father behind. It was so confusing for him; he shook his head, bit his lip and thought to himself that he had to just endure what was happening around him and follow his mother's lead.

"What about Themba?"

Sara told him that he and Buhle were moving to Alexandra to be with his auntie and cousins, and Themba would go to a big high school there. Alex had no idea where Alexandra or even Johannesburg was, other than on a map which shows it was northeast of where they lived on the farm.

Alex couldn't comprehend a world without Themba. How would it feel? He knew how it felt to lose his father, and now he was losing Themba as well. On the other hand, Alex would see the other members of his family. He didn't know how to feel. He knew his mum was missing Pa as well. She cried when Alex wasn't looking, and she still kept all his clothes in the cupboard like he'd just gone away for a while and would come back. Alex felt the need to be strong for his mother. Being separated from Themba was the price he was going to have to pay. Life was cruel.

Alex had to be brave, but his brother was such a part of him, of his everyday life, and now this was all going to change.

Sara felt powerless and guilty, but nonetheless responsible for Buhle and Themba as well. Although the pass system had historically required Black men to hold and present this "internal passport," such a system never included Black women. Farm workers had no rights nor freedom of movement. Nonetheless, Sara needed to make sure this move for mother and son went as smoothly as possible. She wrote a letter "to whom it may concern" saying that Buhle and Themba had lived on the farm in her employ, and were now moving to Alexandra to join their family as the farm was being sold. Sara wrote a separate document giving a reference regarding Buhle's skills and loyalty. She also, as the manager of the farm school, gave a report on Themba's schooling and got the teacher to co-sign this. Sara gave Buhle three months wages, to give her time to find work and to settle in. She listed her mother's address and telephone number in Cape Town, if anyone wanted to speak to her or if Themba wanted to talk to Alex.

Buhle and Sara promised to help the boys write to each other, and perhaps when they were a bit older, they could visit each other. Given the restrictions of apartheid, neither of them knew how they would manage this, but they felt they needed to reassure the boys that this was not the end of their relationship, but it would change.

# CHAPTER 12

SARA AND BUHLE DECIDE ALEX and Themba should say their goodbyes on the farm. They didn't want to distress them by doing this at the station. It was private on the farm; they could hug each other and cry if they need to.

Themba and Alex were on the *stoep*, alone.

"Bro, don't forget about me," said Alex, choking on his words, not knowing what to say. He'd never had to say such a big good-bye before.

"No, I won't. You don't forget me either—we're brothers, you know. I will write letters to you; please write back and tell me what you're doing. I've got to go to a big school, and I'm scared." Themba glanced down at his feet, tears rolling down his cheeks, no smiles or friendly dimples to be seen.

Alex looked at him, tears in harmony with Themba, started to flow. He tried to wipe them away, but they kept on coming. He grabbed Themba by the shoulders; they looked at each other's wet faces and clung to each other. No more words. What could they say?

Eventually, Bongani came up the stairs and hugged the boys together. He said to them, "You have to be men now. Remember, this is going to be hard for your mothers, and you need to be strong for them." The boys noticed Bongani's eyes well up, but he kept his emotions in control. "Come, Themba, your mother is waiting for you in the *bakkie*."

Themba's shoulders rounded, but he followed Bongani, wiping away the tears on his sleeves. He daren't look back at Alex, or he knew he would not be able to be brave.

Alex watched Themba climb in next to his mother, and the *bakkie* slowly pulled away. Themba lifted his arm through the window and waved. Sara watched as Alex ran down the track behind the *bakkie*, dust in his face mixed with the tears forming caked mud on his cheeks.

Slowly, the *bakkie* turned left on the tarred main road, and he saw Themba's face and waving arm through the passenger window. Alex waved back, standing still. He watched while it disappeared into the distance. He turned around and went to sit in the little graveyard, next to his Pa.

"Pa, we have to move to Cape Town," Alex whispered a conversation with his father. "I miss you, and now I'm going to be far away from you." Alex felt his world had suddenly shrunk in size, with him a little toy figure about to be packed in a box and taken away.

A long shadow fell over Alex, and he turned to look up at Bongani. The two of them sat silently by the graveside, each with their own thoughts. Bongani reached out and held Alex's hand.

"*Umntwana* - I will visit your Pa's grave and out of respect for him I will make sure it is kept tidy. Remember, Mister Dan is not

108

here, he has left his earthly body and is in heaven with his ances-
tors. Wherever you are, he will be with you – in your heart and your
mind."

Alex put his head on Bongani's shoulder, trusting the wise
words spoken.

~

Alex and Sara packed up their belongings, and a large truck
came to collect the furniture. Alex took a last walk down to the river.
It was cool, not inviting at all. Not like in the summer when he and
Themba would spend hours down there. He threw a stone in the
water, making ripples that disappeared. It was like a faded drawing
or painting, losing its lustre and vitality. He wished he hadn't come
down to the river. He turned around and walked back on the well-
worn track.

Alex knew he had to be brave. He missed his Pa, and now
Themba, his brother, was gone. He and Themba had pored over
an atlas of South Africa and pinpointed their new homes - on either
side of the country. They had no idea how big South Africa was or
how far apart they would be. Even if you had told them it was 1400
kilometres apart, they would not have been able to grasp it.

They packed the car after the removal truck had left with their
belongings. He went to Bongani, who hugged him, tears rolling
down his dark face. Bongani rubbed Alex's hair, talked to him softly
in isiXhosa, almost like a blessing for the future.

"I'll miss you, Bongani," Alex said.

Bongani clicked his tongue in agreement. "Remember, be
brave for your mother."

Sara spoke to Bongani, shook his hand with her other hand on his shoulder and tears in her eyes. They had shared such a traumatic event together. Bongani was the only person with her when Dan died. He had been there for her when no one else was.

The new owner had come over from Port Elizabeth to meet Bongani, and they had spent time together. Bongani took him around the farm, explaining what he was currently doing. Bongani had seemed satisfied with the new owner and felt they could work well together. He told Sara all of this so she would not worry about him.

Alex climbed into the front of the car next to his mother, the car pulling away, kicking up dust. They drove gradually to the front gate of Soetewater. Alex looked through the side mirror of the car, watched the house and Bongani waving to him in the distance, getting smaller and smaller. He turned, stuck his head out the window and waved back to Bongani. Alex felt a burning need to open the door and jump out and go back in time to when everything was right in his life. When they turned on to the tarred road, he slipped back in to his seat. He was frozen where he sat, his mother driving carefully forward to their future.

# CHAPTER 13

*February 1982*

FISH HOEK WAS IN A bay with mountains on either side, hugging the brilliant white beach in the basin. A road ran through the town, connecting each hillside. The continuing coastal road eventually meandered to Cape Point, the southernmost point of the Cape Peninsula.

Alex started high school. He'd had a lonely summer; everyone on his street was away on holiday or visiting family. It was like a ghost town. He and his mother spent time with his granny or on the beach. His mother bought him a belly-board. He'd spend the whole day down on the beach trying to catch the waves.

He was a strong swimmer, and eventually, his mother allowed him to go down on his own. Being on the beach reminded him of the cabins at Port Alfred, his cousins and Themba. Playing cricket with Frik bossing them about. Lazy days. Fun and laughter. Sometimes these thoughts made him happy; other times, he felt angry and sad.

They had just moved into their own two-bedroom home after living with his grandmother for two months until the farm's money had come through. Life was so different now. He had never been lonely on the farm; he'd always had things to do with Themba— building cars, playing cricket or soccer with the other kids, swimming and also doing their homework together sitting on the *stoep.* Sounds of his mother and Buhle chatting and laughing, Buhle cooking with the smells wafting through to where he and Themba were doing their homework.

Sara got a teaching post at the local primary school in Fish Hoek. Alex often came home to an empty and quiet house. No sounds of Buhle clattering about in the kitchen, isiXhosa everywhere, farm workers shouting at each other, chattering, singing while they worked. Themba waiting for him on the steps every day after school. Now he had to do his homework on his own.

Alex was finding it difficult to make friends at school. Everybody already had their "gangs" before he arrived. He had come from a small rural school, and this high school was big with hundreds of pupils. Alex felt overwhelmed. He struggled to find his way from classroom to classroom, often getting lost, which led him to be late for his next lesson. He would get into trouble with the teacher for being late. It made him angry; nobody bothered to help him or even offer to help him. Nobody was interested in who he was or where he came from. They never asked about his story.

Sara noticed that Alex was subdued and angry, lashing out at anything and anyone. He often had to do detention after school for being late or for being confrontational with others. Even teachers bore the brunt of his verbal aggression. She suggested to Alex that he start writing letters to Themba, as Buhle had given her the address of her sister in Alexandra.

For his Christmas present, his mother bought him a Polaroid Instamatic camera that printed the photograph as soon as you took it. He took pictures and included them in his letters to Themba—a view of the beach, of his home and his bedroom.

Sara worried about this anger that was boiling over into school life. She felt helpless in trying to get him to open up; nothing she did seemed to alleviate his rage. Alex was grieving for the loss of his father and also Themba. She knew that, and although she identified the reasons for his behaviour, she did not know what to do to help him. She couldn't go back in time, and she couldn't bring Themba or his father back. Sara was finding life strange, like a bad dream, although it was familiar, as she had grown up in Fish Hoek. She had her mother to talk to about her feelings; her own father had died when she was young. Her mother understood how she was feeling—at a loss and adrift in the world.

Kids at school teased Alex because of his accent, and they called him "farm boy." Eventually, he retaliated and got into a fight with a boy. Alex's physical strength and height from years on the farm dominated all his interactions with people. They felt intimidated by him. Now they had a new name for him: "tough boy." Kids started to stay away from him; they were scared of his anger and teased him at a distance.

One particular afternoon, as he stepped from the corridor, outside the building he noticed a boy, about the same age, sitting on the ground outside. Alex greeted him, the boy responded, and they started up a conversation. Alex saw him later in the day before it was time to go home.

"You fancy coming for a smoke behind the bike shed?" he asked. Alex had never smoked before, but thought *"what the heck."*

They went behind the shed. The boy introduced himself as Phil. They sat on the ground and Phil took a packet out of his bag. Alex sat next to him and watched. Phil took some tobacco and rolled it into a paper, licking the sides to seal it. He had matches and lit it, drawing on it to make smoke. He handed it to Alex, who took a draw and started coughing.

"No, man, don't pull so hard, just gently," instructed Phil. They finished the cigarette and Phil invited Alex to come to his house after school. Alex didn't hesitate to say yes. His empty home did not appeal to him.

They're late for class, but Alex talked his way out of another detention, saying he was in the toilets.

They met up behind the bike sheds after school. Alex and Phil walked out the grounds together, and towards Phil's home, which was only a few blocks away. Alex had never been to this part of Fish Hoek, which seemed to be on the outskirts of the town.

Nobody was home. Phil explained his mum was at work and his step-father was out. Alex had never seen a house in such a mess. Coffee cups were everywhere with mould growing out of them; there were cigarette butts in ashtrays that were overflowing, and beer bottles lined up next to a sofa that was full of stains and an old blanket.

The windows were closed, and the smell settled in Alex's stomach and made him want to throw up. He daren't. They went through to the kitchen, which was covered in dirty pots and pans. Oil spills on the stove were black with grime. Dirty dishes piled up everywhere and congealed food stuck to plates. Phil took a tin from the top of the cupboards, and motioned for Alex to follow him outside.

Phil rolled up a cigarette, like he did behind the bike shed at school, but he added some "tobacco" from another packet to it. He rolled it up as before, licking the paper to seal the cigarette. Phil lit up and drew on it. He passed it to Alex.

Alex tried and spluttered again; he realised this cigarette was different from the previous one. "What's this then?" he asked, turning to Phil.

"Ag, just a bit of weed. Nice, hey? My step-dad sells it to all the locals."

Alex took another drag and started to feel his body relax, and his surroundings didn't seem to bother him anymore. He felt dizzy and lay down on the ground. After smoking another two "cigarettes," Alex began to feel very drowsy. He didn't have any more worries and settled into a semi-state of paralysis.

Alex woke up when it was starting to get dark. Phil was laid out next to him. He looked at his watch; shit, his mum would be home already. Alex's mouth was dry. His body was not really doing what he wanted it to, which was to stand up. After a couple of attempts, he managed to stand by steadying himself against the wall. Alex noticed people were inside, but he made his way along the alleyway at the side of the house and slowly walked home.

Sara was in the kitchen when he got back. "Where have you been? I've been worried sick."

"I was just helping granny at the café and got a bit carried away."

"Oh, okay. Go and change and let's eat our supper."

Alex and Phil regularly skipped the last few lessons of the day, and went and smoked cigarettes mixed with weed, behind the bike shed. This didn't go unnoticed. His teachers reported him to the principal.

~

Sara waited outside Principal Malherbe's office. His secretary had phoned and asked her to come in and see him. She felt nervous and anxious. Alex had been behaving strangely. She knew he lied to her about going to her mother's café every day after school. Her mother had said she'd not seen him for weeks. Then there was the smell of smoke on his clothes. He showed no interest in his schoolwork. He just sat outside in the garden in the dark, brooding silently.

She tried to talk to him, to ask him what was wrong, but he had put up a brick wall between them.

She startled when she heard her name; the secretary asked her to come into the principal's office. She had met Mr. Malherbe before when she explained Alex's background and her worry that he had been getting into fights.

"Mrs. Smit, I'm worried about Alex." She nodded; the feeling was mutual.

"He's missed the last four weeks of afternoon lessons. One of the teachers spotted him behind the bike shed with another pupil whom we know has a troubled family life. You explained to me about Alex's background, how he lost his father, his brother Themba, and life on the farm. Coming to Cape Town will have been a big shock for him too, having come from a small-town school. He's also had to adjust to the move to high school."

Sara explained Alex's absences from home, his lies, the smell of smoke on his clothes. She was also worried but felt powerless. He wouldn't talk to her or tell her what was bothering him.

"With all due respect, Mrs. Smit, he knows you have also been grieving for the loss of your husband, and he is unlikely to want to burden you with his feelings. He may also be struggling to articulate these feelings. These losses are like nothing he's ever experienced before, and he doesn't have a reference point or the skills to deal with them.

"I hope you don't mind, but I'd like to advise you to support him seeing a grief counsellor. Children often find it easier to talk to a 'stranger' who has no emotional investment in their family life. If he talks to you, he will feel he will only upset you. He is unlikely to burden you with his own feelings.

"I must add, that it's not just cigarettes these boys have been smoking; they are laced with weed. That is not good; it is already affecting Alex's school work and performance. We need to try and deal with this now before it's too late. The effects of the weed will be numbing his current upset, and he will continue to use it as a crutch unless we give him an alternative: talk therapy."

Sara felt guilty. She'd uprooted Alex, changed his life completely, and was not able to be there for him. She'd been so wrapped up in her own grief and trying to make a life for them. She now worked full-time and ran the household without help. She felt exhausted and powerless.

"Mrs. Smit, with your consent, I can send a referral letter to a grief counsellor I know who is very skilled in helping young people. She's based here in Fish Hoek. Some years ago, my wife passed away, and my daughter and I were struggling with this loss. My daughter went to see her regularly, and with time, she was able to deal with her overwhelming feelings. I also attended some sessions with my daughter, and we were able to grieve together. It also brought us closer again."

Sara agreed; she didn't know what else to do. Mr. Malherbe planned to speak to Alex today, and Sara would follow-up with a chat with him tonight.

# CHAPTER 14

THEMBA AND BUHLE SETTLE IN at his aunt and uncle's house in Alexandra township. He started high school, which was much larger than the farm school, with hundreds of students and a jumble of multi-storey buildings all packed together, which he was not used to. Buhle noticed he went into his shell, did not talk to anyone and tried to remain invisible. He'd lost his smile, cheekiness and playfulness. There weren't many children who spoke isiXhosa, so he mostly spoke English. He was finding it challenging to navigate the school and the children. Buhle was worried that his education would lag behind.

Buhle's sister found her work as a cleaner and kitchen worker at a large computer company in Sandton. Sandton was a very upmarket area of Johannesburg, and Alexandra township was east of Sandton and north of central Johannesburg. Alexandra was a vast area made up of shacks, houses, dirty streets and gutters overflowing, with large spotlights to illuminate the city at night. It was a sprawling mass of humanity that could be seen from the highway that ran alongside it. They lived in the older section, on

Fourth Street, where Themba's uncle managed to buy a house before apartheid took away black people's land rights.

His uncle had a fleet of taxis that worked the route from Alexandra to Johannesburg. A mechanic lived in a room in the yard behind the garage. He serviced and repaired any faults on the fleet of minibuses. Running a flourishing business from home meant there was a constant stream of drivers and minibuses in and out the yard. Many different languages were spoken, lots of people milled about inside and out on the street. Themba tried to keep out of their way. He was struggling with the noise and the sheer number of people around him.

Themba liked his cousins, Auntie Lulama and Uncle Sipho. This was the first opportunity he had to spend time with family other than his mother. They were kind and generous people and made him feel welcome. That didn't stop him from missing his brother Alex.

When Buhle enrolled Themba into the local high school, she put his age down as twelve turning thirteen this year so he could start immediately. She didn't have a birth certificate for Themba, and she didn't know how to get one. The school didn't query Themba's age, and so he started high school in January.

Themba went to school with two of his cousins, boys who were much older than him. He also shared a bedroom with them. They always talked about cars, girls and things Themba didn't know anything about. He felt like an outsider. He missed Alex, their antics and doing their homework together, building wire cars and swimming in the river. He had never been alone before.

Buhle talked to her older sister and her husband one evening when Themba was asleep. She told them about her worries that he had withdrawn into his shell and wouldn't talk about how he was feeling. Her brother-in-law looked pensive and finally spoke.

"He's a boy who's never had a dad, he's lost his home and his brother, Alex, and a life that was very different to here in Alexandra. Perhaps he just needs to adjust, but I'll spend a bit of time with him and see if that helps."

Buhle's family knew Themba's background that his birth father was her *baas* on the farm. This was not uncommon and nothing they had not heard of before.

Sipho had raised his two sons: two teenagers who were well behaved and respectful of their elders. They went to school every day, and he hoped they would one day take over his business.

He enjoyed being a father and felt nostalgic for the time he used to spend with his sons. Getting to know Themba would be a joy for him.

The next morning, he saw Themba sitting outside the back door, looking at the comings and goings in the yard. His mechanic was busy working on an engine, and his sons were visiting their friends—typical Saturday activity. The taxi business carried on seven days a week, although it was a bit quieter on Sundays.

Sipho sat on the bench next to Themba. He took a flick knife and started shaving a piece of wood. Themba looked at what he was doing.

"What are you making, Uncle?"

"I'm making a Zulu king, to go with my queen."

Themba was intrigued. "Why, Uncle?"

"Have you ever heard of the game called chess?"

"No, what's that?"

"It's a board game, but I make my own pieces. Do you want to see them?"

Themba nodded.

Sipho took a block of wood out of the box next to him. He placed the block of wood between them. The piece of wood had 64 squares on it. Sipho reached into the box again and put figures onto the squares in a set pattern.

"See, you have two players, Themba. Here's a castle on each corner. There are two of each piece—a bishop, knight, or at least a horse. On the front row are pawns. In the middle at the back sits the king and queen," explained Sipho. He'd made the English pieces into African pieces carved by hand. The rooks, or castles were round traditional African huts; the other figures were also African symbols, two in each set. One set was polished black, and the other was brown.

Sipho explained the movements each piece was allowed to make and started playing a game of chess with Themba. The two quietly played, each waiting patiently for the other to make a move. Sipho was a skilled player and enjoyed giving Themba advice along the way, teaching him to think ahead, to develop a strategy that led to check-mate. Sipho gently teased Themba when he got too worried he might make a mistake. This was Themba's first older adult male relationship, and he enjoyed the camaraderie with his uncle. It felt very different from being with Frik or Liwa.

～

Themba got his first letter from Alex. Themba read it, frowning thinking about how Alex was struggling in school; he was struggling as well. He liked the photographs and put them on the wall next to his bed. He wrote back straight away, telling Alex what life was like now.

Hi, Alex,

Well, we've made it to Alexandra. The train journey was long and boring. My auntie and uncle fetched us from the station. Their house is big, and I share a room with my cousins. They're teenagers, and I don't see much of them.

My auntie is my mum's older sister. They are a lot alike. I like her; her name is Auntie Lulama.

I miss life on the farm and what we used to do. The school here is huge and noisy. I don't like it. It's tough to make friends when you're the new kid that nobody knows.

My uncle Sipho makes amazing wooden figures, and he builds chess sets. He's teaching me to play chess. It's a complicated game, but I enjoy it.

His taxi business is hectic, and the yard outside the house is always full of people speaking all sorts of languages. Sometimes I talk to the drivers, and they tell me about all the places they go. They tell me funny stories about some of the people who are regular passengers. There's one old man they always have to wake up when he's at his stop. He snores so loudly; everyone laughs at him. One lady is so fat, she takes up two seats but will only pay for one.

Good luck with school, bro.

T

Buhle was worried Themba was not progressing with his school work as he should. Her instinct told her he was underperforming. It was all too easy for him. He finished his homework usually at school. Learning was no longer a challenge. She was working as an office cleaner and a kitchen worker in the staff canteen with her sister. By asking around at the office, she managed to find the name of a retired teacher who lived in Alexandra. She arranged for Themba to go to her every Saturday for extra classes.

Even with these extra classes, Buhle was still not satisfied that Themba was getting the best chance. She knew he was very bright, but not how much exactly.

Buhle started cleaning the offices early, at about 7.30am. She always chatted to the lady, called Irma, who worked in the human resources department. Buhle was not sure if she was the manager. She told Irma about coming from Cradock to live in the big city. Irma had also moved to Johannesburg from a small town. They had a comfortable and pleasant relationship, enjoying the quiet office in the early morning before the throng of people came. Buhle found out there were over three hundred people who worked in this vast building.

Buhle always checked the notice board next to the water cooler, practising her reading and seeing if there was anything of interest. One early morning, she saw a sign on the noticeboard, saying the company would be starting the process of recruiting several candidates to be awarded scholarships to a Johannesburg private school. Each grade would have one successful candidate for the following year's intake.

Buhle plucked up the courage to ask Irma if she could put forward her son for the scholarship programme. She gave Irma a flavour of Themba's capabilities. Irma gave her the forms and said, "Of course, he can apply. He will have to undergo stringent tests and an interview as part of the selection process."

When she got home, Buhle talked to her sister and brother-in-law, asking for advice. Was this an excellent opportunity for Themba? They both agreed it was rare for a young black boy to have the chance to get an exceptional education. It was an opportunity they must grab with both hands. They talked to Themba, and he was not sure what it entailed other than a different school. He wanted to do well, and he knew in his heart that the schoolwork he was currently doing was far too easy for him. After months of hard work with his tutor every Saturday, Themba was prepared for the tests and the interview at the company.

Themba's uncle took him and his mother to the big building in Sandton. Themba felt nervous in this strange place. It was quiet as it was a Saturday. A friendly lady came to greet them, and took Themba off to do the tests.

Themba remembered his mother telling him to take his time and to concentrate. This he did, just like he and Alex used to focus and work quietly together. He opened the first sheet of paper. It was an English language test—Themba's top subject. He felt confident and slowly started working his way through the documents. He was so transfixed by the challenge of the paper, that his nerves were forgotten.

After two hours of tests, Themba was asked to wait with his mother. There were two other black boys as well, and they also seemed nervous. Themba knew his English was excellent and felt confident going into the interview.

There were four grownups behind a desk and one empty chair in front of them. Themba sat down, and they tried to make him feel comfortable, asking him about his interests. He told them about his love of cricket, how he and Alex used to do their homework together. He loved swimming and making things. After about an hour, they thanked him, and he returned to his mother.

There was a month-long nail-biting wait. Eventually, Irma called Buhle to her office and passed her a letter regarding Themba's application. Buhle opened the white envelope and read. Themba had been accepted to the high school sponsorship programme. Buhle broke down, shaking, tearful thanking Irma. She felt it was an unattainable goal, but nevertheless, she and Themba had to try.

"Don't thank me; your son is classified as 'gifted.' Well done. He will start his scholarship this year, halfway through the year. His performance was clearly over and above any of the other candidates, and the South African company directors and the American director do not want him to lag behind this year. He will start at St Paul's Academy as a weekly border at the start of the next term."

Irma handed her a prospectus of the school and some consent forms she had to sign. If he continued achieving well, he would qualify to apply for a university bursary in about four years. The company would pay for his school uniforms; she gave Buhle the forms to complete for this. Themba would, at some point, be interviewed by visiting American managers of the company's social responsibility programme. Themba must make himself available for these as part of the programme.

Buhle told Themba. The whole family celebrated, and his uncle made them a *shishinyama*, with entire legs of meat cooked on the fire they made in the yard. It was a joyful day.

Themba wrote a letter to Alex to share his news.

*Hi, Alex,*

*Well, I've made it. I've been accepted onto the scholarship programme. I can go to St Paul's! I start in two months. I can't believe it.*

*Hey, they think I'm 12 going on 13 when I'm only 11. Ha, my mother is cunning!*

*They've got a cricket team, which I might join. Also, there's a debating club, which seems cool. My uncle says there may be a chess club, so I'll check it out. I'm going to be a weekly border, so I will go home every Friday, and then back on Sunday. My uncle owns loads of taxis, so he'll give me a lift.*

*Thanks for the photos. You live near the sea, you lucky thing. I can imagine you belly boarding all day. Have you got any friends?*

*I've got my cousins here; they're nice but older than me and are interested mostly in girls. They don't spend time with me like Frik and Liwa did. I hope I make friends at my new school.*

*Write to me again.*

*Your bro,*

*T*

Fish Hoek was set in a small bay with a long white beach hugging the town. The opposite end of the beach had dark black rocks with monstrous waves crashing against them. The bathers didn't go there; only the surfers dared to venture on the giant waves.

Every day after school, Alex went to the café, called *The Green Parrot* on the corner of the main street. His granny ran it and allowed him to sit at one of the tables and do his homework. He hated going home to the empty house. On Wednesdays, he went to his counsellor's house, which was on the street close to his granny's café. He found Jane easy to talk to. He talked about the farm, Themba, his Pa, Bongani, and all his cousins. Alex liked talking about his family and the farm. He's started looking forward to the sessions as he felt "lighter" after each visit, like this heavy load was bit-by-bit lifting off his shoulders.

The principal and his mother banned him from being friends with Phil or from going to his house. He found out from some other kids that Phil had been expelled from school. Smoking was out of the question as well. Mr. Malherbe gave him a long lecture on the damage weed caused to brains and to mental health. It wasn't the answer to dealing with his pain. It could only mask it temporarily.

When he got to his granny's café, she gave him a sandwich and a drink, and the day's newspapers to read. Ever since Frik had introduced him and Themba to the idea of politics, he had been fascinated. He read the political sections of the paper most days. He followed Bishop Tutu, Helen Suzman and Allan Boesak's attempts at challenging the government, particularly about their harsh crackdown on black unrest in the townships.

Alex chuckled to himself. Helen Suzman, MP, could not be kept quiet. She was the thorn in the flesh of the Nationalist government. Because Helen Suzman was a Member of Parliament, the press could report on what she said and did. She used this to its full extent.

One minister said in parliament, *"The Hon member for Houghton, it is well known, does not like me."*

Helen Suzman replied, *"Like you? I can't stand you!"*

Alex enjoyed the humour; he read it aloud to his granny when no one else was in the café. They laughed together and added their own comments, making it even funnier.

Alex and his granny loved that despite the white male parliamentarians continually insulting or demeaning her, she never cowered or held back her voice of dissent. Alex respected that. In one of her speeches in parliament, she reflected, *"I do not know why we equate – and with such examples before us – a white skin with civilisation!"* No wonder they hated her. That got granny laughing.

Alex was fascinated by the antics of Helen Suzman. He read how she would visit prisons and campaigned to improve warder brutality and their living conditions. She visited Nelson Mandela on Robben Island and made representations to the authorities to improve his and the other prisoners' living conditions.

She often put insults and arguments to good use. When it was shouted at her in parliament that her *"number one man in South Africa was Nelson Mandela!"* she retorted, *"Let him go!"* She was mocked in parliament for her admiration of Nelson Mandela and her view that he (Nelson Mandela) was the only man who, according to her, could counteract the present unrest situation in South Africa and negotiate peace.

She interjected, *"That's right!"*

Alex would read these bits of the newspapers out loud to his granny when they came out every week. Eileen would shake her grey curls, make a cup of coffee for them, and go and sit with her grandson and go through the newspapers alongside him. They both developed a routine of Alex reading to her and sharing the comments. They shared the thought that Helen Suzman was one of the most remarkable of all the current white politicians.

Everyone who was fighting apartheid was doing it in their own way. The students in the townships fought for a better education and demanded equality. The religious leaders, who were not banned, called on the government to change, supporting those who were disadvantaged and did not have a voice. Helen Suzman fought the system from inside its apartheid belly. Surely this was pushing the government into a corner. These were Eileen's thoughts, and she and Alex talked through the different political challenges.

# CHAPTER 15

EILEEN LOOKED AT HER GRANDSON, reassured that he seemed less angry now. He was getting used to living in Fish Hoek rather than on the farm. Jane, his counsellor, had slowly but surely given him a safe space to express his pain and a toolkit to manage his strong feelings.

She still worried that he didn't have many friends, and she wondered how she could help him. She knew Jane has been a God-send but felt she needed to try and encourage Alex to build interests and friendships. She had a plan.

"Alex, I'm shutting early today. Do you fancy coming with me to a new shop around the corner facing the beach? You might like it."

Alex nodded, thinking he had nothing else to do. Eileen locked up, and they walked the short distance over the road and around the corner.

There was a shop sign in big, bold letters that read *Newly Open,* and *New Owner was* sprawled across the front windows, sandwiched between two surfboards. Eileen walked in with her grandson. She knew the young owner and had been longstanding friends with his parents.

"Hi, Ed," she greeted him with a handshake. "This is my grandson, Alex." Alex shook his hand. Ed was well over six feet tall, with below-the-shoulder curly brown hair that was bleached blond by the sun. He had a light brown bushy beard with no moustache and a wide smile.

"Can you show him around the shop?" Eileen asked. "I've just forgotten something at the café. Alex, when you're finished, you may want to go home; I'll catch up with you later."

Alex was a bit confused by his granny's behaviour. What was she doing? He nodded at her, and in turn, was polite and chatted to Ed, who showed him around the shop. There were rows of surf-boards and wet suits of varying sizes and colours.

"I make the boards myself, mostly."

"Wow, they're cool." Alex was really impressed, thinking of his little belly board.

Alex saw a sign in the shop about surfing lessons. Ed noticed this.

"I'm doing a taster surfing lesson this Saturday; you can come and try it out if you'd like?"

"Yeah, that would be great!"

They settled on a time. Alex would meet him at the shop and help him carry the boards to the beach, which was just across the road.

Alex was delighted. He loves the sea and felt he had out-grown his belly board. He was thirteen now; he needed something a bit more grown-up and a new challenge.

Eileen popped in to see Alex later. She noticed he was beam-ing from ear to ear. Her little plan had worked.

"So, how was it?" she asked.

"Ah Granny, it's great. Ed has asked me to come for a taster lesson on the boards on Saturday. If I like it, I'll have to ask Mum if I can go for regular lessons."

"If it goes well, I'll give your mum some money towards the lessons."

"Cool. If you like, Granny, I'll help you out at the café when I've finished my homework to pay you back."

"Deal!"

∾

The wind was blowing a gale, but Alex got up early, dressed and made his way down to the surf shop. Ed was waiting for him, and they carried the boards across the railway track to the beach. There was a group of about five other teenagers of varying ages waiting for them.

After greeting each other, Ed took them to waist-deep in the water and showed them how to set off.

"You put your belly down on the board, then paddle out to the wave, turn to catch the wave, then push up with your feet, back foot forward, front foot forward between the hands, hands always on the board. Try and stabilise your position, then stand up, feet well-positioned, knees bent. Keep your hands flat; don't balance on your knees. Sue," he called out patiently, "break with your back foot first; this keeps speed and stability. Keep your body upright." Ed called out this string of instructions which they tried multiple times until the sequence was etched into their minds.

Once they had mastered these basics, they paddled out to the first small waves. Alex tried to catch a wave but struggled to get his sequence right. He wobbled and fell over. Most of the others were also struggling.

Ed was patient and ran through it again, and again, getting them all to repeat the moves in the shallower water. Once they felt a bit more confident, they paddled back out to try and catch a more significant wave.

After much falling off, laughter, and Ed patiently going over the sequence of moves, they each started to be more successful in catching a wave.

Breathless and exhilarated, they gathered on the beach after-wards. The young surfers chatted amongst themselves, and Alex talked to Ed and another brother and sister, twins. They found out they all attended the same school, but the twins were a year ahead. They all decided to continue lessons with Ed next Saturday.

Alex said goodbye to his new friends and headed home. He excitedly told his mother all about it.

"Mom, it was great. It's challenging to stay on the board, but Ed showed us all the moves you have to do. You really have to concentrate hard, so you don't fall off. I'm going to write to Themba to tell him all about it." With that, he went off to his bedroom to start writing.

Sara sighed; she was relieved Alex had taken to surfing. It had been her mother's idea to introduce him to Ed, and it had worked. Well done, Granny!

*Hi Themba,*

*Thanks for your letter, I'm so excited you've got in at St Paul's School. It sounds very posh. Hope you fit in. They still call me "farm boy" here in Fish Hoek.*

*I was too late at school to start playing for the school cricket side this season, but I have managed a few training sessions. I hope to play for a team next summer.*

*We have a surf shop here in Fish Hoek, and my granny took me there. The owner is a guy called Ed, and he is really cool. He makes most of his surfboards himself. He has all sorts of colours and sizes of boards, and a workshop at the back.*

*Anyway, I went to a taster lesson today, and it was brilliant. I eventually managed to stay on the board after lots of falling off. It was hilarious. You would've laughed at me!*

*I'm slowly getting used to school, but it is so big, and I keep getting lost. I bet your school in Alexandra is big. Maybe St Paul's won't be so big. Little farm boys like us, ha.*

*Good luck with your new school. Write and tell me how it goes.*

*Your bro,*

*A*

Alex drew a surfboard with a stick figure on it so that Themba would know what a surfboard was, and enclosed it with his letter before posting it.

Having enjoyed the surf lesson, and written a letter to Themba to share his news, he tucked into his homework on Sunday. He did enjoy the school work, especially maths and science, which he was good at. Alex started to feel the flutter of his competitive spirit, kicking in again. He was determined to show everyone at school he wasn't just some "farm boy" but that he had a brain as well. He would go and visit Ed in the shop this week when he'd finished helping his granny and doing his homework. Lots to look forward to.

Alex went to the surfing lessons every Saturday and slowly became more confident and skilled. The twins were called Peter and Sue, and they were already fifteen.

After their surfing lessons, the three of them piled into Granny's café for milkshakes and to analyse their performances.

Sue was probably the best in the group. She was a girl-version of Peter, very close to identical. Alex was fascinated and liked their casual, easy-going company. They would visit each other's houses after school and spend most of their spare time down on the beach, surfing. Peter and Sue had their own surfboards. It seemed like their parents weren't short of a penny.

After school, Alex often helped his granny in the café, unpacking stock, cleaning tables and sweeping the floor. He also did his homework but usually had more to finish off when he got home later. His granny didn't mind that he left before she shut, so he could go and visit Ed at the surf shop.

Ed was usually sanding down boards in the workshop at the back of the shop. Alex asked him about the process of building a surfboard and how long it took. Ed told him about the different shapes and how they affected the way they would perform on a wave. Building a board took time and patience, as you had to build up the layers, wait for one to dry, and then repeat the process on the flip side of the board.

Alex had mastered the surfing basics, so Ed went on to show him more advanced moves at their Saturday afternoon group lessons. Ed was convinced that Alex was hooked into surfing. Alex and his friends Peter and Sue enjoyed talking about surfing, and they learnt from each other and developed a routine of surfing most weekends and school holidays.

Alex knew he could never afford his own board, but he was desperate to have his own so that he could have the freedom to surf whenever he wanted.

"Ed, if I get the materials, would you help me build my own board? If you like, I'll help you in the shop on a Saturday as payment for your time." Alex had often watched Ed while he worked on a surfboard. Heavy rock music played loudly as the sander bellowed out dust. The workshop was messy, but everything had its place.

Ed was enjoying Alex's company and agreed.

$\sim$

Alex and his mother went to the hardware store in town armed with a shopping list that Ed had drawn up for him. His mum and granny agreed to buy the materials.

The weather was slowly turning to winter, with persistent rain and blowing winds howling across the beach. Alex missed the dry Karoo weather, with summer thunderstorms and dry, dusty winters. This was utterly different: wet winters, windy and dry summers. Ah well, the summer weather was best for surfing, with a blustering south-easterly wind blowing across the bay. The winds gave the surfers the gift of powerful, churning waves.

Alex worked in Ed's workshop every Saturday afternoon after the chores in the shop were finished. There weren't many customers over the winter, but Ed wanted to keep the opening times consistent throughout the year. He usually closed on Mondays and Tuesdays, then opened from Wednesday to Saturday. Ed said extending opening hours on a Saturday to all day in the summer months would be something that may be worth considering. He wanted to ensure his profile remained visible throughout the seasons. Ed was building up a steady customer base and was hoping he could eventually get a bigger shop, like those in Muizenberg. The beach there was by far more prominent than Fish Hoek's and was where the majority of surfers went.

The winter months proved to be a productive time for Alex. He slowly built up the surfboard by spending time and concentration on getting the shape of the board right. He used the building board, cut it into two pieces, glued them together and then started to shape the board with a hot wire cutter. He had made a template from one of Ed's finished boards, and this gave him the shape he wanted.

He started sanding the shape and blending the curves. Then he started the lamination process by placing sheets of fibreglass on the board, using hypoxia liquid to seal the layer, and then he put another layer on top once the first was dry. This fibreglass would protect the shape of the board. He repeated this process on the underside of the board.

It was a lengthy and time-consuming process, but Alex didn't mind. He was used to working in his father's workshop, building wire cars and remodelling them until they were perfect. It was almost like going back in time, concentrating on making something he would use that would bring him pleasure.

Once he had sanded the edges until they were smooth, he pasted on the three fins, or "skegs" as Ed called them, and put fibre-glass over it as protection. Alex painted more resin on and started the final sanding process with an orbital sander. He then dusted the surfaces and applied pigment final resin coats to decorate his board. Then came a final transparent layer of resin on both sides, including a wet sanding of the board. He finished off with car polish to build a shine on the board.

Alex admired his handiwork. He couldn't believe he'd finished it. He thanked Ed for his help before going to test it on the waves.

∾

Alex wanted to tell Themba all about his surfboard. He started writing the letter during the week, adding to it each day and then fin-ishing off at the weekend when he had completed the next stage of the board. He took a picture to include it in the letter before posting it on Monday.

Themba responded quickly, updating Alex on how his life was changing.

*Hi Alex,*

*Well, I've started at St Paul's School. I had to get this smart uniform with a blazer and hat. I look ridiculous. Feel like I'm dressed in cardboard and can't move.*

*There are mostly white boys here, and I stand out. I have made a friend, who is Indian and not white or half-black like me. Two brown boys. Luckily, we're in the same class. There are some black kids, but they're in the grades above me. I don't speak to them much.*

*My friend's name is Kaashi Naidoo, and his family lives in Durban. He goes home at the school holidays, but I go back to Alexandra most weekends. This might change when the cricket season starts as there are matches on Saturdays.*

*All the teachers are white men. They are strict. Some classes are taught in Afrikaans, but mine are all in English. Of course, there's no isiXhosa in the curriculum here. It's not seen as necessary. I only speak it now when I go home to Alexandra. It is quite weird going from the private school, back to Alexandra where life is more chaotic, less regimented, with people hustling on the streets and corner "spaza" stands with fresh fruit and vegetables. There's always someone to talk to, and I know most of the people who live on our street. I love my weekends with the family when I can just be myself. I don't have anything in common with the middle-class kids at school who always talk about their skiing holidays in Europe or going down to Plet—that's Plettenburg Bay—for their summer holidays. The only holidays I know about were when we used to go down to the cabins in Port Alfred. I just walk away when they keep going on about "holidays."*

Remember we used to talk about history only being white? Well, it still is. I don't even know of any black people in our history. My friend Kaashi says there are ones. He's invited me to go and visit his family in Durban in the next school holidays. That will be cool; it will be great to see the sea again! He loves cricket, as well. We're hoping to play in the same team next summer.

Some of the kids call me Tom. They can't be bothered to call me Themba. I usually ignore them. They think because I'm shorter than they are that I'm not strong. Well, they found out...

Sometimes, if one of the kids in our age group "misbehaves" in the dormitory, something like crying after dark, then we all have to do a punishment called "afkak."

A couple of nights ago, one of the boys was having bad dreams and crying. An older teenager came in and told him to "shut up," or we'd all do afkak. The boy then wet his bed. Well, we did afkak. We had to run around the rugby field until this stupid, pimply teenager told us to stop. The poor kid who had been crying couldn't manage it and passed out. They had to carry him off. We still had to carry on running as if nothing had happened.

I bet you're thinking, "How did Themba do?" Well, I showed them, bro. You know how I can run. To start off with, I kept my pace reasonably slow, and then I just ran and ran and ran until the spotty teenager got bored and told us to stop.

Even though this school is expensive, and only rich kids or those like me on a scholarship can go, they are just as racist as the white kids in Cradock were. I have to stick it out, as I'm getting a good education and may even be able to go to university. My grades are good, but I know I have to work much harder than the *white kids to get anywhere. That's what my mum keeps telling me. "Work hard, work hard, be cleverer than them." Mum may be right.*

*So, I'm determined to do as well as I can at school. Kaashi's parents pay for his schooling, and they are also strict with him. He's not allowed to fail anything; he has to work very hard. He's top in the science subjects. Even when he goes home for holidays, they make him do homework every day. Same as my mum.*

*Hope you're doing well at school. How's your maths and science going? What about geography? You're not so good at that. Soon you'll be able to choose your subjects for the last 2 years at school. Hang in there, bro.*

*Your surfboard is so cool. I can't believe you build it yourself! Try and send me a picture of you riding the waves with it. Wish I was there to watch you fall off!*

*T*


Themba put the letter in an envelope, ready to give to his uncle Sipho to post on their journey back to school after his weekend back at home in Alexandra. Themba packed his bag and dressed back into his school uniform for the return to St Paul's.

He hated the uniform; it itched and constrained him. He couldn't fidget in it or stretch out. Uncle Sipho watched Themba in the passenger seat. He always looked so glum when he took him back on Sundays. It was awful to see the youngster so sad. He knew he wanted to stay at home, but they had no choice.

"Themba, you know that black kids like you, and my boys, don't get an opportunity like you have very easily. Black people have to put up with whatever they are given, which is often not a lot. We always have to make do."

"I know, Uncle Sipho, but I can't help how I feel. I know I don't fit in at school. All the other kids are wealthy, they live in big houses with servants and go on fancy holidays to places I've never heard of. They talk about it like everyone has the same experience. I don't. I love my family, and I like being in Alexandra with you all. I feel like a fish out of water, and I don't know what to do."

"My boy, you have to stick with it. I don't know of any other kid from Alexandra, or even Soweto for that matter, who has the opportunity to go to a school like St Paul's. You never know, you could even go to university if you do well enough. That would be a first in our family! Remember when you did those tests?"

"Yes, Uncle."

"Well, the lady said you are 'gifted.' Do you know what that means?"

"No, Uncle."

"It means that before you even start with your studies and schooling, you are ahead of everyone else. You know how you find studying easy?" Themba nodded. "Not everyone finds it easy; for most people, it is a hard slog and grind to pass any exams. Not for you; you are a smart young man. You must make the most of the talent you have. It will be your ticket out of poverty and towards success. Don't mess it up. Your mum was cunning to get you into the programme, so keep your head down and ignore the imbeciles who don't know any better."

Themba thought about what his uncle had just said. He wished Alex was with him, so they could talk through what they were worried about. Uncle Sipho was right; he'd have to rise above it and focus on schoolwork, cricket and anything else he was interested in. For his mum's sake, he had to come out of this with flying colours!

~

Eileen watched her grandson slowly creep out of the dark place of despair and pain. She knew her daughter was a kind and thoughtful mother. She knew that Sara carried her own losses and guilt about her decision-making and whether she had done the right thing to sell the farm and upend all their lives and move to Cape Town.

As a grandmother, Eileen was that step removed from Sara and Alex's relationship and would try and influence and help where she could. Part of the process of overcoming such losses and trauma was to do something for others. Eileen knew how altruism made her feel. On the one hand, it could be seen as selfish, wanting to make yourself feel useful by undertaking community work. On the other hand, it could be argued that it's in helping others that the Bible tells us equates to being a good Christian—standing alongside another human being in need, not turning away, but doing whatever is in your power to alleviate hardship without being judgemental of them.

She enjoyed Alex's visits to the café every afternoon. The doorbell clanged as he pushed the café door open with a bit too much strength. She always knew it was Alex coming through the door; he didn't know his own power sometimes.

Eileen put the newspapers on the table where Alex usually sat, by the window. He'd read the papers while having a snack she prepared for him, then he would start on his homework. Just before closing time, he would go to Ed's surf shop, unless she had a few chores for him like lifting heavy boxes or taking out the rubbish.

Today was no different, except it was a Friday. Phyllis, who helped in the shop, would go and do her shopping in the supermarket soon, and then Eileen would take her back home to Ocean View after the café closed. Ocean View was a township outside of Fish Hoek, on the way to Kommetjie, another small seaside resort on the Atlantic Ocean. Fish Hoek was in False Bay, a slightly warmer ocean where bathing and surfing was more popular.

"Hi, Granny," Alex shouted, throwing his bag on the floor next to the table. Eileen returned his greeting while getting his sandwich and coffee ready.

"Alex, would you mind helping me today? You know I take Phyllis back to Ocean View every Friday after the café closes. What I also do is visit a family who lives in the dunes in a shack near Kommetjie every week. I take the leftovers from the café, and I need to give them some Germylene, as their little toddler has injured herself. They light a fire in the living area, and the little one got burnt. Can you help me to carry these bags over the dunes to them? I find it's getting more difficult; you know my arthritis!"

"Sure, Granny. I'll go to Ed's tomorrow anyway; we don't do much on a Friday, just chill usually." Alex started reading the papers and munched absent-mindedly through his snack.

Alex started chuckling. "Granny, listen to this." Alex began to read the paper out loud to Eileen.

"When Helen Suzman gets racist and obscene phone calls because she is Jewish, she responds by blowing a shrill whistle into the mouthpiece. Nice one!"

Granny said she'd use that tactic if anyone called her to try and sell her something she didn't want or need.

Alex continued reading, "One Afrikaner woman tried to remind her in a letter to the press that her people, the Voortrekkers, had brought the Bible over the mountains to the interior to the blacks. What were Helen Suzman's people doing?

"Suzman replied, '*You say your people brought the Bible over the mountains and ask what mine did. They wrote it, my dear ...*'"

Alex fist-pumped the air, and Eileen laughed. They both enjoyed Helen Suzman's antics, as a way of getting back at the apartheid government. They could not silence her, not like other anti-apartheid activists who couldn't.


After shutting the café, Alex carried the bags his granny had packed, out to her car and put them in the boot. Phyllis sat in the front with Eileen, and Alex sat in the back, wondering where his granny was taking him. He'd never been to Ocean View before and was intrigued.

During the journey, Phyllis gave Alex the history of the area.

"You see, Alex, my parents used to live in the white area in Glencairn, a cute little house overlooking the sea, the other side of Fish Hoek. Then during the 1960s, the apartheid government forced them and the coloured people to move to Ocean View, which they used to call Slangkop, which means 'snake's head.' It was a bitter time, and my parents never got over it. Ocean View, you will see, is far from anywhere, no shops or towns nearby, and we all have to catch taxis to where we work. The young people can't find jobs, so they form gangs and get into too much mischief."

Alex could see talking about this upset Phyllis; he knew she had a son, so he wondered if she had personal experience with the gangs or whether her son was involved in them.

The township bordered on the main road, Kommetjie Road, that they were travelling on. Alex could see the town was built predominantly on sandy soil. Nothing grew on it except some grass! They turned left into the township, on to Milky Way, then turned again on to Flamingo Road. They stopped outside Phyllis's house, a small brick building with a yard in the front. They said goodbye to Phyllis, and Eileen turned the car back on to the main road.

They continued toward Kommetjie, and turned right, following the straight road, which eventually took some twists and turns until they reached a cul de sac. Eileen parked and they collected the bags and made their way through the sand dunes.

Alex could see how his granny would struggle; the sand was soft and powdery, making it challenging to walk on. Eventually, he could hear the waves, and they were able to look out on to the most beautiful long stretch of beach, indeed the largest and most spectacular he'd ever seen. Alex stopped for a moment, holding his hand over his eyes to see better. In the distance, he could see a group of horses cantering along. There must be stables and a farm nearby. It was a peaceful and spectacular setting.

"Come on, Alex," his granny called, walking through a group of high sand dunes. He followed. Eventually, they came into a clearing, where there was a small huddle of shacks, mostly made of corrugated iron and bits of scrap metal.

They came to one shack, and his granny shouted out "hello". The occupants opened the door, greeted her and welcomed them inside.

It was a one-roomed shack, with a fire in the middle. The fire was dead but it had clearly been used recently. The family had put stones around the fire area, a makeshift firepit. There was a sleeping area with just a mattress towards the back. There was a single ring gas camping stove, where they must do some cooking. Alex greeted the family and put the bags down.

His granny clearly knew the family well, and she gave them the Germylene and showed them how to put it on the toddler's burnt skin. Alex couldn't believe the child did not cry out as his granny put the pink cream on the child's bottom.

His granny spoke to the family and said she'd be back next week to see how they were doing.

On the journey back in the car, Alex was quiet and thoughtful. This was the first time he had ever been in a shack. He knew people lived in informal squatter camps, but he had never seen them up close. The level of poverty made him feel sick in his stomach; why was nobody doing anything to help? Just on the other side were people riding their horses—an expensive pastime! Poverty and privilege co-existed.

"Granny, can't we do something more?"

"My boy, I know your frustration. We all have to do our little bit. If we can make one other family's life easier, make sure their child does not go hungry, then we have done a good thing."

By the time they had gotten back to Fish Hoek, Alex had an idea. Eileen dropped Alex off at his home and came in for a cup of coffee. She could see Alex wanted to explore this further.

"Granny, I'll go with you every Friday to take food to the family in the dunes." Eileen nodded in agreement.

"Can't we put up a sign in the café for people to donate any unwanted clothes? We could keep it in the storeroom at the back, and take it along with the food every Friday. I can ask my principal if I can have a clothes collection point at school. That family is living in filthy rags; that child does not have warm clothes. What about the people in the other shacks?"

Eileen thought about this. "Alex, I'm getting on a bit, and you know how my arthritis affects me. I'm happy to do this, as long as you commit to helping me. I can't do it on my own."

"Deal, Granny!" Alex chuckled with satisfaction.

On her way home, Eileen thought her germ of an idea, of getting Alex to develop his altruistic side was a success. This turned out better than even she could have predicted!

# CHAPTER 16

*1982.*
*Alex and Themba's second year in high school*

THE WARM SUNSHINE PERMEATES THE kitchen, lightening it up into a summer room. Sara enjoys the mornings here, pottering about in the kitchen, getting breakfast ready for her and Alex. She hears him in the bathroom and knows he'll soon join her in the kitchen.

"Morning mum," he greets his mother with a peck on the cheek. His mum is smiling and seems happy this morning. "What's up?" he asks her.

"I got a call from Frik, he's coming to stay for a week!" she blurts out.

Alex grins from ear to ear. "That's cool. Why's he in Cape Town?"

"He has to do some training with another lawyer. He's shadowing him on a case in the Courts for the week. So, he'll stay with us."

Alex is excited that Frik's coming to stay. They won't see each other in the day, but at least they'll have the evenings and the weekend. He can see his mum is excited and looking forward to Frik's visit. No doubt to get updates on the family as well.

He'll take him to the surf shop so he can meet Ed. Alex wonders if Frik would be up for some surfing. It's not something they've ever done before.

Alex finishes his breakfast and heads back to his bedroom to get ready to go surfing with his friends.

*"Hi Themba,*

*You won't believe it, Frik came to stay with us. He's working for this big law firm in Johannesburg. He had to come to do some training. He stayed with us and took the train into Cape Town each day. It was brilliant to have him here. He told me all about university life, how hard his studies were, but he passed with a Cum Laude, which is a bit like a distinction grade. He's super smart.*

*Anyway, he's working and living in Johannesburg, and he's a new lawyer, so has to do more training with experienced lawyers. He's busy assisting on a case in Cape Town court. He stayed all week with us, going into town each day.*

*My mum loved having him here, fussing over him, asking about all the family, his parents, what they were all doing. I couldn't get a word in. I had to wait for her to go to bed so that I could talk to Frik.*

*He says the family still go down to the cabins in Port Alfred, but he hasn't gone for ages. He is busy in Jo'burg during uni holidays, and now that he has moved up there permanently it is likely that he won't be going for some time. They shorten the Johannesburg name to Jo'burg, a bit like Alexandra township being called Alex.*

*We had a proper update about the family. You won't believe it, but Liwa is living in Jo'burg as well. Looks like he might be working for Frik's firm.*

*You must be careful about what you say to people at school. Be careful who you and Kaashi trust. Frik says the government has secret squads, based in the police and military, who make up dossiers of any people they think are pro-ANC or involved in any anti-government resistance. There is a lot of unrest, particularly in the townships, but you may already know this.*

*I read the newspapers at my gran's café, but they don't always report everything. Frik says they're not allowed to. A lady, called Phylis, who works with my gran, lives in Ocean View, which is a 'coloured' area, and sometimes she can't get into work by taxi because of boycotts and strikes. Although Ocean View is not that far away, it's stuck in the middle of nowhere, so everyone relies on the taxi services. I sometimes go with granny to take Phylis home to Ocean View. It's built amongst sand dunes and gum trees. Not much will grow in the sand you see on the beaches, it's near a place called Kommetjie. Can't believe how the government put the poorest people in the most remote area. Deliberately putting them 'out of the way', looks like to me. It's okay for these folk to clean their houses and look after their children, but they have to live in a remote township. Sickens me.*

*I hope your family are all safe.*

*I'll put an extra sheet in this letter with Frik's contact details in Jo'burg if you ever need him.*

*I know you're still a kid and at school, but just be careful what you say. I know you want to make things right, but you have to finish school, go to university, and then you'll be able to start doing something. Just look, listen and learn for now. That's what I'm doing.*

*Have you started practising for the cricket season yet?*

*Here's a photograph of me on my surfboard that Ed and I build. I know it's taken from a distance, but hope you can see it's me riding that big wave. I use it all the time now, and it's excellent! Not bad for a first attempt. Couldn't have done it without Ed though. He builds most of the boards in his shop. I think he can make them blindfolded!!*

*A*


Themba receives the letter and photograph from Alex, and quickly responds …


*Hi bro,*

*Oh wow. Frik!!! How cool is that? Bet you had a good catchup. If you see or speak to him again, tell him I say hi!*

*Well, I went with Kaashi to visit his family. His dad sent a driver to collect us in a Mercedes!!!!!!!!. Was a long drive, but okay. How's that??*

*Kaashi's family live in an Indian area outside Durban, called Chatsworth. His family own a couple of Indian restaurants and cafés in the city centre. They have a huge house, and his grandparents live with him as well. They were all friendly, and I had a great time. His mum and granny fussed over me. Cooked proper Indian* curries, homemade samosas and chapatis. It was a feast! We went to the 'Indians only' beach. Swam and played some cricket with his cousins. I miss our time at the cabins in Port Alfred! There were quite a few surfers as well, reminded me of you!

His family seem to trust me after they heard my story of growing up in Soetewater with you and your family. We talked about politics, a bit like we do with Frik. His family manage an underground branch of the ANC in Durban. Don't tell anyone, remember Frik told us they are banned! Maybe we should burn each other's letters, just to be careful?

Thanks for Frik's contact numbers. I might ring him one day just to chat.

I'm back at school now. I'm due to start at the debating society. I have to start a debate, and then someone else has to counter with the opposite opinion. This is going to be challenging. I think my first topic is going to be about black, or as they say 'Bantu', education in rural areas. Should black children be better educated? Should be controversial??

Like the picture of your surfboard? Wish I could visit and come and see you on it, riding the waves and falling off.

T

# CHAPTER 17

*December 1982.*

SUMMER SCHOOL HOLIDAYS. SARA AND Buhle had arranged for Themba to come and visit Alex. It's nearly three years since they have seen each other. Buhle knew that if Themba visited Alex, he would feel more content within himself. His vision of Alex was as a younger child on a remote farm in the Karoo. Now he's in high school and experiencing a very different life. Buhle felt confident now that Themba was older, that he would cope with the long train journey to Cape Town. She has a friend who is going to visit family in the Cape, and she would travel with Themba and make sure he was safe.

Sara felt that Alex's life was incomplete without Themba. The boys' lives had undergone dramatic changes, and they had not reconnected with each other, other than by letter writing. She felt in her heart, she needed to bring these two together, or they would drift further apart, and there would always be that vacuum where Themba used to be. She felt sure it would be the same for Themba.

Nobody else could fill that gaping hole each of them were experiencing. Having Themba and Alex together would help them negotiate the future and be resilient to life's knocks and challenges. Who knew what the future held, and these two boys needed to remain brothers. The separation was heart-wrenching, and she knew that she was responsible for that separation, even if she had the best of intentions.

It was going to be a hot day. The sun was already up and heating the earth. Alex woke up early. He stretched his long body and glanced through the curtains at the bright sun. He jumped up, excited; they were off to go and fetch Themba at Cape Town station. His mother was already up making coffee and toast. Alex wolfed down some toast and gulped his coffee quickly as if that would speed up time and get them to the station quicker.

The winding, slow journey along the coastline until they get to the highway was torturous. Alex wanted his mum to drive faster, but he knew she couldn't. Once they hit the highway, they sped up.

At the station, Alex went to the far end of the platform, as Themba would be in the "blacks only" section of the train. Alex fidgeted with his clothes, repeatedly ran his hand through his hair and walked up and down the platform. He told his mother to wait in the main concourse for them.

Eventually, the long, slow train drew into the station. The conductor blew his whistle loudly, and the train doors opened. Everyone was pushing and shoving each other to get out the narrow doorways. The white passengers were located at the front of the train and made their way to the concourse first. The platform became busier and crowded. It really was a benefit being six feet

tall. He could see over everyone's heads and scan the crowd, looking for Themba.

Eventually, he saw the broad smile and dimples in the cheeks
of Themba. There was no mistaking him. He waved, and Themba
sprinted over to him. They hugged each other, not caring who saw
them. The black passengers were crowded around them, and they
were lost in the milieu on the platform.

Both boys were shaking, clinging onto each other tightly. Tears
ran down their cheeks. They eventually half broke away to look at
each other's faces and smile.

"Hey bro,'" they said in unison and started laughing and slap-
ping each other on the back of the other's head. They clung to each
other, holding tight and squeezing the wind out of each other.

It was sheer joy and relief. The other one of their pair was
there, in flesh and blood. Their voices had deepened, each had
grown taller, but Alex still was taller of the two, with Themba filling out and being stocky. They were each, at their core, still themselves. The same, but growing into men.

Eventually, they made their way back to the concourse where
Sara was waiting. She gave Themba a big welcoming smile.

"Ah, Themba, we're so happy to see you," she said, knowing
that she couldn't hug him in public.

They headed off to the car, and the boys got into the back seat
while Sara drove. They talked non-stop all the way. Sara left them
to chat, concentrating on driving at a steady pace.

Once they got off the highway, they headed along the coastal
road passing Muizenberg, St. James, Kalk Bay and eventually

arriving in Fish Hoek. Themba kept his head out the window as they wound along the coast. He felt the sea spray and saltiness on his face. He opened his mouth and felt the sensations on his tongue. There were mountains to his right, and the rugged shoreline to his left. There was a railway line tucked between the road they were travelling on and the sea. He took it all in; he wanted to remember all of this when he went back home in two weeks.

When they eventually arrived home in Fish Hoek, the boys worked out their "story." Alex and Sara had already refurbished the outside room, which all houses in white suburbs have as a "live-in" servant's quarters. It was now a comfortable room with twin beds and a shower room. Alex and Themba would use this room during his stay. Alex often slept here when family or friends stayed over, and he gave up his main bedroom in the house for guests.

"Themba, I think we need to be seen working in the garden. My mum has already told the neighbours that we have a gardener coming to work with me. We're also going to lay some slabs in the back yard for a patio."

"Okay, I understand. You know, I didn't know how much Indians are also discriminated against. When I went to Kaashi's house near Durban, they have to live in an 'Indian' area; the whites live in their suburbs. Black people either live in townships or in the Zulu 'homeland.'" Themba shook his head, pulling his mouth up at the side in exasperation.

It was prevalent in white urban areas for homeowners to have live-in gardeners or domestic workers who worked in the garden and in the home and cared for the children of the white family. Themba could, therefore, be hidden in plain sight.

Themba and Alex settled in, while Sara got a meal ready for them.

Alex looked at Themba resting on the bed and couldn't believe he was actually there in Fish Hoek with him. He shook his head and lay down as well. The boys caught up with each other, telling stories of school and how their cricket was progressing.

"You know, Alex, the coach for the school's first team told me he wants me to focus on my wicket-keeping and batting training this season. Next season, he wants me to be able to start playing part-time for the first team!"

"Wow, that's incredible. I'm bowler and batsman for my age group, but because I'm quite tall now, I want to go up a couple of teams as well. We'll see; I need a good performance this year before I'll be considered."

"Yes, our first team doesn't have any real wicket-keeping talent, so my luck might be in."

After their lunch, Alex and Themba walked around the garden, and Alex told him what they needed to do. The boys agreed they would work in the garden first thing in the morning and spend most afternoons at the surf shop and the beach. Mornings were coolest, and the wind was usually up after lunch when the waves were more exciting to surf.

Alex explained to Themba, "We usually use the far end of the beach to surf. It is far away from the main swimming area that is marked 'whites-only'. Nobody will notice us there; there's lots of sand dunes and bushes. If we need to, we can always wear wet suits."

"You mean nobody will notice that one of us is white and one black?"

Alex nodded. Smiling. They laughed and joked about the "external skin" that made them the same. Maybe if they could wear their suits all day, Alex could take Themba into whites-only places without anyone noticing. The laughter and jokes were their way of making light of a hurtful and challenging situation. They were two brothers, kept apart in their private everyday life, just because of the colour of their skin.

"We'll also go to Kalk Bay, which is the 'blacks only' local swimming area. It also has a fishing harbour where I sometimes hang out with some of the fishermen and buy my mum a *snoek*. She pickles it with onions and some curry powder. Yum, I can eat it every day with fresh bread from my granny's café."

Themba told him about *bunny chow* he had in Durban. He explained, "It's a half a loaf of bread with the insides taken out, so just the crusted rind is left. Then you fill it with curry. It's tasty but very filling. It's what the manual workers in Durban eat. You just buy it off the street sellers. Oh, then for pudding, you buy a pineapple, peeled, on a stick, which is sprinkled with curry powder." Alex pulled a funny face and tipped his head to one side questioningly. "Yes, you won't believe it, but it tastes delicious. It's like the spice makes the pineapple flavour stronger!"

Themba was exhausted from the twenty-four-hour train journey, and the boys had an early night. Next morning, they made a start on the garden, before the sun was harsh. Alex could never understand how gardeners worked throughout the heat of the day.

After lunch and drinks, they walked down to Ed's surf shop. The wind had picked up, and Alex couldn't wait to catch the waves.

Alex pointed out his granny's café and the main road with all its shops. They turned the corner closest to the beach and saw Ed's shop a few doors down.

As they opened the door, a bell rattled above their heads. Ed walked through from the workshop to greet them. They all shook hands as Alex introduced Themba. "Ed, this is my brother, Themba, from Cradock."

"Hi there, Themba from Cradock!" Ed gave him a warm welcome and handshake.

Themba was impressed by all the surfboards and Ed's friendly welcome. He was a tall, lanky man, with long, curly sun-bleached brown hair. Themba had never met anyone like this. Ed wore colourful clothes, and his skin was brown from spending much time outside. Themba reckoned he must spend a lot of time on the beach. Alex called him a "hippy," but he was not sure what that was.

Alex kept his surfboard at Ed's shop, and he borrowed another from him for Themba to use. Ed told Themba to first use the board like a belly board, and he was sure Alex would show him the moves.

"Start him on the smaller waves, Alex. Don't drown him during his first lesson!" he called after them as they left the shop. They borrowed two wetsuits as well, just to be on the safe side.

Alex and Themba walked along the sand dunes, heading to the far side of the bay. When they got there, there were a couple of people already surfing. Alex knew most of them as they surfed regularly. Alex introduced Themba. They were a mixed bag of boys, girls, white and mixed race. These young people were just getting on with life as they wished. Quite a few were wearing wet suits, so Alex and Themba climbed into theirs.

Alex first modelled the basics of surfing to Themba and helped him get the sequence right. Themba got the hang of it pretty quickly and was soon surfing the smaller waves. There was lots of falling off his board and plenty of laughter. Themba enjoyed being the clown and played along to the delight of the others.

Themba eventually got tired and decided to sit on the beach and watch. He took the top of his wetsuit off and rolled it down to his waist. It was almost hypnotic to watch the surfers catch the waves and ride them. Some of the waves were violent and destructive and seemed to dwarf the surfers trying to ride them. But they twisted, turned and rode, almost as if they were taming the wave. They came off the board before the wave died out. Themba was impressed by Alex's skills; he clearly spent a lot of time on his board and had lots of surfing friends.

After a couple of hours, the boys decided they were hungry, and one of the older surfers who had a car offered Alex and Themba a lift to Kalk Bay, which was a short drive away. Themba and Alex dropped off the boards and wet suits at Ed's shop before heading off.

Themba remembered passing the harbour when he came through the day before, but today being a Saturday, the pier was full of people, children, and picnics. There was a tidal pool where children were playing. It was a joyful chaos of shiny brown bodies.

Alex and Themba headed off to where the fishing boats were moored up in the harbour. The boats were brightly painted, and nets were neatly arranged on the wooden decks. Alex greeted a couple of fishermen, and they stopped to chat with Alex, introducing Themba to them. Once the greetings were exhausted, they headed off to buy fish and chips at a kiosk. They sat on the boulders, eating hungrily. Themba had never had such fresh fish and chips, and both boys enthusiastically and silently ate every last scrap. Alex let out a loud burp when he was finished, followed by Themba. They both laughed, repeating the joke many times enhanced by their fizzy cold drinks.

Eventually, Alex headed off to one of the boats with Themba behind him. He bartered with the fisherman, who sold him a huge *snoek*. Alex had arranged for his mother to come and collect them at the carpark outside the harbour. They sat on the wall, chatting while waiting for Sara.

Alex told Themba, "We could have gone back to Fish Hoek by train," pointing to the station platform across the road. "But that would have meant we would have had to sit in different 'white' and 'black' coaches. I'd be worried you might get off at the wrong stop and not know where you are."

Themba nodded. "That's okay, bro."

Sara eventually arrived, and the boys jumped off the wall and got in the car with the *snoek* wrapped in newspaper.

Themba and Alex enjoyed having a routine together, like on the farm. Up early, breakfast, then gardening until lunchtime. After lunch, they headed off to Ed and the beach. Sometimes they waited until closing time at granny's café, and they went in the back door. Alex's granny made them milkshakes, with extra chocolate sprinkles. She couldn't admit Themba into the restaurant during opening times, as it was 'whites-only' in the seated and serving area. Black or coloured folk would come in, but she had to sell them take-away only. She would lose her license to operate if she didn't adhere to this segregation restriction.

As the days wore on, Themba became more proficient at using the surfboard. He mixed with Alex's friends Peter and Sue while they were at the beach. It seemed to him that most of all these young people's time was spent on the beach in the summer.

Alex and Themba made a fire most evenings and attempted to *braai*. Some days, the meat ended up as charcoal, but with gentle coaxing from Sara, they managed to distinguish between a beefsteak that needed quick flash cooking and the gentler and slower cooking of sausages or chicken.

Once they'd eaten, they stoked up the fire, and sat talking through the night. They reminisced about their life on the farm, their school, and what they found difficult when first moving home. They realised their mothers didn't have a choice in moving to Alexandra and Fish Hoek. They had to make the most of the problematic situation.

Themba explained to Alex that his mother enjoyed working at the computer company; the people were friendly, and the big bosses would take time to talk to all the staff. At Christmas time, they got a bonus and also had a party for all the staff, black, white and Indian. One of the sales team was managed by an Indian. Most of the technical engineers were black folk. They both struggled with this, shaking their heads. When it came to making money, the colour of your skin didn't seem to matter.

"What about the canteen; can they eat together?" asked Alex.

"Yes. Isn't that weird? Hey, money upgrades everyone to 'white'!" Themba thought about this. "If you have a white skin, you will not be discriminated against because of your colour. If you're black or another colour, the police are more likely to suspect you of something, pull you over or question you without reason. This would never happen to a white person. I've been stopped plenty of times in Jo'burg by police, asking me where I'm going, what am I doing. Even if I've got my school uniform on."

Alex nodded in agreement; he had often thought about his white privilege and how some things for him were an automatic advantage, whereas Themba had to fight harder just to be treated fairly. Alex often felt helpless about this. He loved Themba, and Themba loved him; he wanted the same opportunities in life for his brother. Perhaps just listening to Themba was a start? He'd listen to his story of life and what he suffered daily. He'd understand and accept his narrative. Maybe he could walk a mile in Themba's shoes.

"You know, Alex, I'm grateful to be sponsored and getting a good education, but I can't help but feel guilty that other black kids aren't getting a good enough education. I think of all those kids on the farm, and I know your mum did her best, but the chance of them ever leaving farm labour is unlikely. They are stuck in that job for life. How many of them are talented and able to do more? We'll never know. I want to make a difference for them, but I can't. Maybe I can in the future, but will this government ever let me?"

Alex thought about this. He knew there was ingrained inequality in this country, but he didn't know what the answer was. "Perhaps we have to start off with making everyone equal, everyone having a chance to vote. We may then be able to rid ourselves of this apartheid government. Helen Suzman is the one voice in parliament who is calling for this. Everyone else is silenced." Alex went on to explain what he had been reading about in the newspapers.

"Yes, we need a new government!" Themba told Alex he wanted to join the ANC, but he'd wait until he was at university. He wanted to go to Wits university, as they had an ethos of equality for all and a student voice that challenged the apartheid government.

"Don't jeopardise your school education," Alex said, fearful it could all fall apart for Themba before it had begun. He was worried that Themba was a risk-taker, that he thought he was indestructible.

"Finish your schooling, get into uni, then things will fall into place. Things are changing, and Frik predicts if there is continual pressure from all sides, including from overseas, then eventually the government will be forced to make changes. It's going to carry on being difficult for some time, and there will be even more bloodshed before we get a vote for all."

The time they spent together in Fish Hoek flew by, working in the garden, surfing, and spending evenings by the fireside. Alex even arranged for them to go on a fishing boat one day. He knew the coloured fishermen, and they were keen to show these teenagers how tough they were. The boys both got seasick, and left the boat after a day at sea in awe at the tenacity and skill of the fishermen. They managed to get a *snoek* as a present and some crayfish. A feast was coming!

# CHAPTER 18

*1984*

ALEX OPENED THE FRONT DOOR. The house was quiet; his mother was not home yet from school. She must be working late. Alex heard a crunch under his foot. He looked down and saw an official envelope on the floor.

It was addressed to him. He opened it. It was his compulsory conscription for his military service to commence when he finished school. He was due to start in July 1986 and would be notified of the defence unit he would be placed with closer to the time. It was a two-year conscription. Alex's heart sank; the dreaded nightmare had begun.

The letter that every white South African boy received had arrived. Alex and his friends at school often spoke about the military conscription they all had to undertake when they were eighteen and finished with school. His surfing buddy Peter had already received his, and he was due to start next year.

Alex had been dreading this. He needed to go and see Peter and talk to him about it. The day had finally dawned; as a white South African male, he had no choice about this. Why did they have to warn you so far in advance? The agony everyone had to go through was unbearable.

Alex put his bags in his bedroom, changed out of his school uniform, and left a note for his mother to say that he had gone to Peter's house.

Peter invited him in; he was hanging out with some of his friends in the back garden. Alex joined them and told them he had received his "call up" letter.

"It was bound to happen, man; we've all got them. We're a year ahead of you and will soon be finding out which unit we'll be placed in. Some of us will go into the Army and some in the Airforce. The lucky ones go into the Navy. Those buggers get to stay in Cape Town or Durban. The rest of us have to do border patrols near Mozambique, Angola or up in the Northern Transvaal."

"I don't want to do it," said Alex. How could he be part of the struggle against apartheid and then go and put his life on the line for it? He knew the dissonance between what his heart feels and his mind tells him is compulsory, would drive him nuts. Alex knew from reading the newspapers that the government was launching cross-border raids into neighbouring countries like Mozambique, Angola, and others that were either socialist governments or harboured ANC activists and Umkhonto we Sizwe military bases in their countries. The government was using the military to destabilise their neighbours, but also troops to occupy the townships, where they used violence and terror to generate fear amongst the township residents who dared to protest or undertake strike action. He felt as if his head was stuck in a vice, and his heart was being gripped tightly.

Alex knew his options were limited, and even joining the newly formed End Conscription Campaign would not help him avoid the draft.

"You've not got a choice, man," said Peter. His friends all nodded in agreement. That feeling of falling into a deep, dark abyss overwhelmed Alex. He dropped his chin to his chest and focussed on listening to what everyone had to say.

"Look, if you have a British passport, then you have the option of going into exile in another country, but you lose your family and everything you have in South Africa," suggested one of Peter's friends who Alex had not met before. "My parents got me one as my mum is British, born in London. I may go and live with my grandparents for a couple of years. I won't be able to come back until the government changes or the rules change."

"I don't qualify for a British passport; my parents are both South African," Alex grunted without lifting his head.

This started a conversation amongst the friends. Some were conscripted and would be going in the next year or two, while one had a British passport. They shared horror stories about doing border duty. Insurgency raids into their neighbours were dangerous.

"One of the guys who was at Fish Hoek High about three years ago died the other day. My older brother was on a military aircraft, a C130, flying back from Grootfontein after a stint at camp. There was a young dog handler strapped to a stretcher in front of him. The poor guy was heavily sedated but still moaning in pain from his amputated right leg. His dog had apparently set off a landmine in the bush a couple of days before." One of Peter's friends recounted the horror story. They all became quiet, scared about their futures, wondering which one of them would die, be maimed, or would be lucky enough to make it back home.

"Look, even if you finished your military duty of two years, you then have to do a three-month camp every year. That really fucks with your job, man. What employer is going to put up with guys disappearing every year? I don't know if the government compensates them or not."

Peter added, "My cousin works in a bank in Pretoria, and he was telling me that a couple of weeks ago they had closed for the day, and their staff were waiting outside at the bus stop when a limpet mine went off. All four ladies suffered leg and ankle injuries."

The group of young men had clearly discussed these issues many times, with Alex finally joining up with them, having received his conscription papers. Alex had always been aware of conscription but never fully involved himself in the discussions as he had been too young. That is, until now.

"Look, the only thing you can do, Alex, is if you go to university you will be able to postpone conscription until you have finished your studies," Peter offered as a positive for Alex. "You still have to do your time afterwards, like the rest of us, and if you refuse, they will send you to a detention camp in the far Northern Transvaal."

Everyone chipped in, giving advice. "Well, you can always become a permanent student, do a masters, then a doctorate and even a PhD!" They all laughed, although it was hollow, each one of them frightened, angry and powerless about their futures.

Alex had thought coming to talk to Peter would make him feel better or give him solutions, but if anything, he felt worse. He was cornered; it was apparent that he could only delay the inevitable. He had already decided he wanted to go to university, which would postpone conscription by another three years.

The topic was heavy, and Alex found he had enough and made his excuses and went home.

As he got to his house, he saw his mother's car. At least she was home, and they could discuss what the options were for him.

They sat down at the kitchen table, eating the meal his mother had cooked. Sara noticed that Alex was quiet and preoccupied. She waited for him to tell her what was worrying him.

While his mother was making coffee, Alex spoke about the letter and what Peter and his friends had told him. Sara had been dreading this day; she had talked about conscription with lots of her friends and knew what the risks were and the limited options Alex would have.

She knew that Alex would not go in to the military. She recognised the dilemma he was in. They discussed his other options — being a conscientious-objector would involve a six-year jail sentence, which Sara knew in her heart he would rather endure than take up arms against the struggle he was committed to. Her heart sank at the thought of her son having a criminal record.

His only other option was to go to university. His grades were excellent, and he would have no difficulty with the entry criteria for Cape Town University. How long he could stay at university would depend on his course and whether he undertook any post-graduate studies. Even then, this would only delay his conscription.

But, it may allow him a better chance of obtaining a visa to another European country, Australia or America, where he could seek professional employment. The thought of her son in a faraway country, away from his family and friends filled her with trepidation.

Sara and Alex agreed that he would defer his conscription to go to university and consider the next steps later. That's all they could do for now.

# CHAPTER 19

*Hi Alex,*

*Life is busy here. I'm at school in the week, with compulsory study time every afternoon. I usually push through to the evening, working harder, harder. When it's exams, I'm up early in the morning as well. My grades are consistently high, and I have to keep this up to qualify for the university bursary scheme run by my mum's company.*

*I go home to Alex on most weekends and enjoy seeing my family. My mum and auntie Lulama spoil me, cook me proper food and pap. School food is okay, but never like your mum makes. My uncle Sipho and I spend Sunday mornings playing chess. He's so good, but I think sometimes he's kind to me and lets me win!*

*My older cousins have left home to live with their "girls" but come back every day to the house as they pretty much run my uncle's business now. He still drives taxis sometimes, checking out the existing routes, improving them or scouting for new ones. They are busy putting the company on a better and more secure footing. They're talking to an advertising entrepreneur, and using the sides* of the taxis as advertising space. They sell the space to companies wanting to sell, for example, washing powder, maizemeal, etc. They've already got a few taxis covered, and they are using the money they make to expand the business. They have got sound business heads, and my uncle Sipho is taking a bit of a back-seat now. He likes to sit in the yard and talk to the mechanic or catch up with the drivers who come in. Nothing is going on in Jo'burg that he doesn't know about.

The world is getting more unstable, and unrest is brewing in the townships. My uncle keeps lecturing me on how to keep my eyes open, head down, and not to stand out. He doesn't want anything untoward to happen to me; he knows how outspoken I am.

I now edit the school newspaper, and I encourage other students to write articles or to tell us what's going in different parts of the country. Of course, there's a lot of sport, how the different teams are performing. Especially cricket and rugby. We add photographs at the back.

I'm playing for the first team cricket, and they want to do a summer tour at the end of the year. Kaashi and I both qualify for the team, but the school has to ask special permission for us to stay in 'white' hotels. We've both made a pact that we won't go; why should we not be able to stay in a hotel with our teammates? This is apartheid at its most pathetic. Every aspect of our lives is governed by it, no freedom of association. We're good enough to play for the first team, but not good enough to stay in hotels with our teammates! These are the same teammates we bunk up in dormitories with at school!

*Anyway, we're taking a stand and will refuse to go!! My first act of civil disobedience.*

*What you up to, bro?*

*T*


*Hi Themba,*

*Life goes on here. I still help my granny, and we take food and clothes most Fridays to the shacks in Kommetjie. We've managed to coerce a local charity to start running a creche in the settlement. It's a real eye-opener. I took a ball one day and played soccer with some of the kids on the beach. They loved it! Now I play with them each time we go. Its great fun! Reminds me of when we used to go to the cabins in Port Alfred. Good times!*

*I spend quite a lot of time at Ed's shop. He wants to expand and eventually get a bigger shop in Muizenberg, where the beach is expansive, and there are already a lot of cafés and surf shops. He says the time isn't right yet.*

*You're not going to believe this. I had to go to Ed's room behind the shop the other day. You know I told you he lives there in the week and goes to his parents when the shop is closed?*

*Well, I saw a picture of this lady and two little children next to his bed. I couldn't help myself; I was intrigued and asked Ed straight out if that was his family. He said yes, but he keeps it quiet as his wife is Cape Malay. I asked him, "His wife?" and he said yes, she is Muslim and they had a religious marriage at the mosque. Her parents run a halal butchery in Ocean View, and she lives with them with the children. Amazing! I shook his hand and said I respected how he followed his feelings for the woman he loved. His kids look adorable. Ed says they're in primary school, and he goes to stay with his wife and the kids on the days the shop is closed.*

*I feel so sad for him that he is separated from his family. Life is so cruel.*

*But what I didn't know was that he converted to Islam so he could marry his wife! Only his family knows this, and he must trust me to confide in me. Nobody around Fish Hoek knows this or a scandal would brew. He doesn't have a moustache, just a beard. I should have picked up on that! Ha, ha, joking aside, we talk about religion, and I feel that perhaps Ed is quite lonely when he's not with his family. He tells me about the Qur'an and how it's basically the old testament of the Bible. You know, bro, when you get to know people, you realise we are more the same than we are different! I wish people would understand that.*

*I have to stay focussed on my studies as well. I also get up early in the morning to catch up on any homework or revisions I didn't finish the day before. My mum is determined that I go to university, and we've already been looking at the prospectus for Cape Town University in Rondebosch. I would still be able to stay at home, so that saves money.*

*Fingers crossed that all your dreams come true. Get that entry to uni, Themba. That's our future. I think politics at uni are going to be engaging in this climate!*

*A*

# CHAPTER 20

*January 1985;*
*Themba and Alex are in their final year at school*

THEMBA WROTE TO ALEX, TELLING him he had to go to an interview with the directors at the company headquarters to update them about his studies and future at university. They will make a decision based on his exam results, reports from school and the interview, whether to grant him a bursary for university.

*Hi Alex,*

*You'll never guess what. I have to go to my mum's work to talk to some visiting Americans. I'm part of their social responsibility programme! They've been getting copies of all my reports, and now that I qualify for uni, they want to interview me and decide whether I can get a bursary.*

*On the one hand, I'm grateful. How did a little coloured boy from a Karoo farm get as far as I have, but I have also worked shit hard and had to put up with the "stick" from the other kids. I've* survived! I did what my mum and uncle said. I put my head down and worked harder than anyone else.

I just feel bad for all the other black kids who have had to fight or protest for a half-decent education. Like at the Soweto riots in '76 where black children were protesting peacefully against having to be taught in Afrikaans. The protest escalated with American newspapers saying 332 children were killed by police. This sowed the seeds of a growing tide of protest for democracy all across the country. The violence spread to other areas and townships. Tear gas and live bullets were used to disperse the crowds.

You see, Alex, it's our responsibility now to make this government realise that white minority rule is not sustainable. This unrest won't stop. My uncle says it is just going to get uglier and more people are going to die. They've declared a state of emergency, but that's the government getting more desperate to shut black voices out. They want to violently repress any resistance, with the arm of the law behind them.

When I'm home in Alexandra, I hear from underground ANC members what they are suffering. They come into my uncle's yard so that his mechanic can "fix" their cars when really, they are using it as a meeting place. People just disappear without a trace and are never heard from again. You know that the press is heavily censored and are not able to report the facts. Even the international media are sometimes stopped by police from going into areas of urban unrest. Nonetheless, some of these stories still reach us.

Alex, these are dark days, and I am anxious. I have joined the ANC Youth League, and we want to work towards the unbanning of the ANC. At Wits University, they have a policy of non-discrimination on racial grounds. I know the government is pressuring them to adhere to apartheid laws, but they are continually showing resistance. This is going to be tested over the next few years.

Well, you know I'm a "charmer." I'll put on my best private schoolboy blazer, smile, show commitment to my education, talk the talk to these American businessmen. Half the job is done, as I have been consistently getting top grades. I want to study to become a teacher. Who knows what will happen in the future?

Wish me luck, bro.

T


Alex writes back …


Themba,

Hope all goes well with your interview. I know you'll crack it! How can they resist a cute coloured guy with dimples? Good grades, excellent cricket performance—they'll fall all over you. You better explain to these Americans what a "good performance" is in cricket. Maybe relate it to baseball? Americans love baseball! You'll get the funding, bro, no doubts. Phone me as soon as you know.

Mum is applying for me to go to Cape Town uni. It's not too far from us so I can go in by train every day. I've decided, given my strength in my science subjects, to study chemical engineering. Fingers crossed. Mum kept some money from the sale of the farm to pay for uni, but I still have to work on holidays and weekends to help with costs.

*Shit man, Alexandra is a hot-bed of protest. I know we have this censorship of the newspapers. Still, they do report on Bishop Tutu, who speaks at the many funerals of protesters in Soweto and Alex. Also, Helen Suzman is the only white MP in government who speaks up and challenges the National party.*

*She has a tough time in parliament, for being Jewish and a woman! She was a lone voice until the Progressive Federal Party got more seats. She always goes and sees for herself what is going on in prisons, and then campaigns for better conditions. She read a letter in Parliament a few years ago by a man tortured and killed by the security police. How brave was that? She goes to the funerals of activists, visits squatter camps, all of which gives her evidence to publicly challenge the government. She bears personal witness by shining this massive spotlight on atrocities. Excellent work from the inside!*

*I've joined the UDF (United Democratic Front), which is a group of different trade unions, churches and civic groups that oppose the government's latest pathetic attempt to change things by including coloured and Indian representation in government. Black people have to be represented in the homelands. Reverend Alan Boesak is heading this movement in Cape Town.*

*You know me, Themba, I've always been religious, and I think religious groups also have to lead the way and pressure the government to change. Boesak is leading protest marches, and sometimes he is detained. They can't shut him up or lock him up indefinitely. He's too high profile, even internationally.*

*It's the same with Bishop Tutu – he's coming to Cape Town next year as Archbishop. Ed and I have decided we'll go to his rallies.*

*and we'll go on any marches he leads. This bloody false accusation of the "red terror"—people fighting for equality are being labelled as communists. It's a sham. America and the UK are ignoring what this government is doing as they see communism as a more significant threat, rather than racism. I spit on them. Hypocrites.*

*The shit is going to hit the fan, bro! Well, it has literally, with those bomb blasts in Pretoria.*

*Anyway, how's the cricket going? I got my first batting century! Don't know how much cricket I can play at uni. I keep up the surfing as well. I just love catching the waves and having fun with my mates on the beach.*

*A*

# CHAPTER 21

JULY 1985 SIGNALLED THE BEGINNING of the end of apartheid. Under PW Botha, the government declared a partial state of emergency, further extending it to a national emergency in 1986.

The government used the police and defence force to violently suppress any resistance to government policies and actions.

There was much resistance to the state's interventions, in the form of mass marches, sabotage, attacking power plants, the bombing of shopping centres and businesses. The townships experienced major unrest and violent protest.

The government censored the press heavily, including shutting down the *Rand Daily Mail,* which was an anti-apartheid newspaper.

Pressure from outside South Africa also escalated, with ANC leaders in exile in London giving speeches and leading the push for further sanctions against South Africa.

Margaret Thatcher and Ronald Reagan had previously labelled the ANC a "terrorist organisation," but after the waning Cold War, their message changed to international condemnation of apartheid, and sanctions against South Africa were enforced.

The South African government became more isolated with pressure from all sides, including white South Africans' disillusionment, particularly concerning forced conscription of white South African men into the armed forces. The ANC wanted to make white South Africans aware of the military repression in the townships, the escalating violence and the continued flouting of international human rights by the government. Sabotage and marches became common. The State of Emergency acted as a unifier and mobiliser of the unstoppable force of anti-apartheid resistance. This police state was increasingly seen as unsustainable in the long term.

# CHAPTER 22

*1986.*

Hey Alex,

*I'm really enjoying Wits. The campus is enormous, and I still get lost. After 3 years I'll be used to it. My bursary funding includes paying for halls of residence, and my mum gives me money for my food. I usually go back to Alexandra during holidays or the odd weekend. It's only about a fifteen-minute drive in a car, which is easier than when I was at school, to get back home.*

*My friend Kaashi has gone to study medicine in the UK. I miss his friendly face and hope he writes to me.*

*I've joined the Students Representative Council. You know me, I love a good argument. My mum keeps on at me, "Keep your head in your books, don't lose focus." She doesn't want me to get distracted. I do work hard, but I can also be an activist at the same time. I usually get up at about 5am, do some work, then go to lectures, with the rest of the day free to go to council meetings or planning protests or sit-ins. The angry youth protests in the townships with the security police are becoming worse, and more and more violent clashes take place. We regularly send out newsletters to update students, and we attend marches and funerals in the townships. Our campus protests are sometimes on the same day as the funerals. We try and show solidarity where we can.*

*I have to be careful as I need to stay on top of my studies and get good marks, or I risk losing my funding. If I don't, the Americans will be on to me. They still keep a close eye on all my exam results. I can't believe that a large American computer company has not pulled out of South Africa yet, despite people calling for sanctions. Huh? They've been here throughout the apartheid years when other companies have disinvested. Very strange! Maybe it's about the money they are making. They sell computers across Africa.*

*This government certainly has given us plenty of reasons to protest. Here at Wits, we have to stay independent of government intervention, and every time they try and put some kind of pressure on us to stick to apartheid laws, we either protest or do sit-ins. The press is not censored to report on what we do on our own site. By the time the police invade our campus, we have already told the journalists! They're waiting with their cameras. It's our protection!*

*I know the risks, and if you become an ANC youth leader, you will get noticed, and the security police will mark you, but I don't care. There is such a strong movement in everyone calling for change; it can't be stopped. I want to be a part of it. Even down in Cape Town, things seem to be heating up with the calls to make the country "ungovernable." Tell me all about it, bro. What are you up to?*

*T*

Alex was worried about Themba. He was raising his head above the parapet just like his uncle advised him not to. But Alex understood Themba's strong feelings towards injustice that he'd experienced throughout his life. Alex tried to imagine how Themba felt. As he was so close to Themba, he was very aware of what he couldn't do, alongside what Alex could do.

Alex decided not to talk to Themba about his delayed conscription; it didn't seem relevant to their relationship. It was something he had to deal with on his own. It would somehow "taint" their letters and relationship. He didn't want apartheid to affect his and Themba's feelings for each other. How could Alex hold a gun, and go and quell a march or uprising when Themba was there, fighting the just fight. Alex cringed at the thought.

Alex joined the End Conscription Campaign (ECC), which was part of the various political affiliates calling for the ending of apartheid. Many more young people avoided conscription by going absent without leave (AWOL) and getting lost in the vast administrative system. Young men wagging their fingers at the government saying, *come catch me if you can!* Alex was aware through his membership of the ECC that the number of conscripts failing to report for service was growing every year. It was estimated that nearly 8,000 young men failed to report for service, and another 7,000 were living in Europe. Alex was beginning to think this may be an option for him.


*Hi Themba*

*I've started at uni and am also enjoying it. I also find it daunting, though. I'm used to the small high school in Fish Hoek. Our*

186

*campus is in Groote Schuur, close to Rondebosch. I still live at home, as it's cheaper, and travel in by train. I can't let my mum down, and I know I have to work hard to repay her. She's gone without to make sure I get a good education. So has your mum. We can never repay them; the only thing we can do is not let them down.*

*We have about 30% of students of other races here, so we are getting there in terms of diversity! The government calls us "Moscow on the Hill," saying we are communists. I think that's their standard insult or label they apply to anyone who actively opposes apartheid, and then this justifies them cracking down hard on protesters.*

*Our chemical engineering faculty is in the old main campus on the Rhodes estate (that's at the back of Table Mountain).*

*Yes, my mum is strict as well. I work hard, but you know how I hated coming home to an empty house and used to go to my granny's café to do my homework after school? You were waiting every day for me to come in from school at Soetewater. Your mum was always in the kitchen, preparing the supper and making us a nice sandwich. We'd sit on the stoep doing our homework. It was good. I really miss those times. Well, now I usually go to the library after lectures and work there and go home later when I know mum will be back from school. I can't bear an empty house.*

*You know when I first moved here, I was miserable and kept getting into fights. My mum had to keep going to see the principal and explain what I was struggling with. You'll never guess what! She and my old principal have been seeing each other the last couple of years. They kept it quiet as other parents might have complained about me getting preferential treatment! As if …*

*Well, now I'm at uni, they feel free to be seen together in Fish Hoek. He comes round to our house, or he and my mother go out on dates. There's not much fun to be had in Fish Hoek. Did you notice on your visits there were no liquor stores? Well, some old guy left the land in his will to the local community on the condition that no alcohol would ever be sold in Fish Hoek. There you go, a local myth! There are one or two restaurants now, but mostly my mum and her boyfriend go through to Kalk Bay. There's a restaurant on the station platform, called the Brass Bell. Kalk Bay is becoming a bit up-market and artsy now. Remember we went there for fish and chips?*

*I stay out of the way and focus on my uni work and surfing. Ed's surf shop is doing really well now, and I often go and help him out on Saturdays, before going to surf. He says he still wants to expand and eventually open a bigger surf shop in Muizenberg. There are more surfers there, and you saw how expansive the beach is. It's called Sunrise Beach and is on the station-side of the bay. The waves are good there, famous amongst the surfers. More surfers means more surfboards to sell—especially all those rich Jo'burg folks who invade the Cape during the December summer holidays.*

*I've grown my hair longer now—bit more of a hippy like Ed.*

*We've got a couple of student rallies lined up, and we're going to listen to Allen Boesak giving a sermon. Ed's also joining us, even though he's secretly a Muslim. Bishop Tutu is now Archbishop of Cape Town. He is going to live in the official residence in Bishopscourt, a white area. Can you believe it? He has to ask permission from the government to live there! Wonder if he'll do that, or just take up residence. We'll wait and see. He's so well* known internationally, I bet he just goes and lives there! The government can't touch him. All they can do is take his passport away every now and again, but then that causes a stink overseas! He's calling for more sanctions. I think he realises that change is brewing, and he wants to push it along before more people die.

The press report on what he says. He's not a banned person. He wants all those who oppose apartheid to stand together, no matter what their background is.

Ed and I are going to his "enthronement" at a big open-air showground. They're expecting about 10,000 people. Can't wait. We, as white people, need to show our support for our first black Archbishop!

Keep writing!

A

~

Themba sat on the bench in the yard of Uncle Sipho's house. The mechanic was on the other side of the yard, working on an engine. Everything was quiet. There was a distant rumble of traffic and occasional shouts and children's voices in the distance. Alexandra was a busy place, never still.

Themba put Alex's letter next to him on the bench. He had the chess pieces ready for Uncle Sipho. The sun was out and he put his head back, resting against the wall. Just as he was about to close his eyes, he saw a shadow walking across the entrance to his uncle's yard. It was a young woman, with dark, curly hair in a short afro. She was tall and slender, elegant. Her slim hands held a book, with a handbag slung over her shoulder. She looked straight ahead, calm and purposeful. She knew where she was going, and it must be important, this being a Sunday morning.

Themba shook his head and looked up as Uncle Sipho joined him on the bench, the chess set between them.

"Well, are you ready to be beaten again?"

"Uncle, who's the family that lives next door?" Themba pointed to the house on the far side of the garage.

"Oh, that's a family who moved here from Soweto. Some years ago, not as long ago as when I moved here."

"I saw a girl." He described his vision to his uncle.

"Oh, that must be their niece, Nomsa! She used to live in Soweto but moved to live with her family so it would be more convenient for her to get into Jo'burg where she works. Ask your auntie if you want to know more; she's friendly with them."

The chess game started, but Themba was wholly distracted by his vision. He was going to wait outside to see if she came home later. He kept looking toward the entrance. Maybe she was going to church? That meant she will take a couple of hours before getting back. He'd wait.

Themba's patience paid off. A few more weeks of playing chess in the yard, and watching out for Nomsa, he plucked up the courage to approach her on her journey to and from church. He tried to be nonchalant and stood at the front gate, leaning against the post, at the time Nomsa usually passed by. True to form, she came out of her front yard and started to walk towards Themba. He smiled at her and greeted her in English. She returned the greeting with a smile.

"Are you off to church?" he asked.

"Yes," she replied shyly, a hymn book in her hand. She hesitated next to Themba.

"Would you like to come in for a cold drink on your way back?"

She looked at him, thinking. Her cousin had told her about the family, and she felt comfortable saying, "Yes, that would be nice. I'll be back in a while."

Themba waved to her as she set off, and then he stepped back into the yard. He pumped the air, relieved at his success. He'd never asked a girl out before. He returned to his bench in the sun, waiting for Uncle Sipho.

He made sure the game with his uncle finished well in time for when Nomsa was due to return home. He went inside and asked Auntie Lulama if he could have some cold drinks for Nomsa and himself. She smiled at him, knowingly. Her neighbour and friend knew about Themba and Buhle since they first came to live in Alex.

Themba went to stand at the gate, waiting. Eventually, he saw Nomsa walking a calm and steady pace back home. She arrived. They went and sat under the tree in the shade, out of earshot of the family.

They exchanged pleasantries, drinking their cool drinks in the shade, and shared their family stories. Nomsa was born in Natal, in a rural area. Her family eventually moved to Soweto to get better employment. Her parents still lived in Soweto, but she had come to live with her cousin in Alex as it was easier to get into Jo'burg for work and study. She was studying computer programming while working in IT for a national bank in the city centre.

191

They spent the day together, comfortable and sharing their thoughts with each other. Themba loved to watch Nomsa talk; her voice was soft and gentle, and her smile was broad with perfect white teeth. She talked with her hands, which were elegant with long fingers. He thought of a model's hands you would see in a magazine. He was transfixed by them.

The sun started to set, and the sky darkened. Nomsa said she had to go home to have supper and to get ready for work tomorrow. She was usually up early to study before taking a taxi to the city. They stood up, and she was the same height as Themba, maybe just a fraction taller than him. He leaned over and kissed her on the cheek. She didn't mind and smiled at him. They arranged to meet up the next weekend that Themba was home from uni.

# CHAPTER 23

*December 1986*

ALEX CLIMBED DOWN THE STEEP stairs of the railway carriage at Johannesburg station. This was his first visit to the city. He realised now how Themba felt when he came down to Cape Town. It had been a long twenty-four-hour train journey with some very dull stretches through the Free State. He strained his neck, looking out for Frik.

He started walking to the main concourse and saw Frik in the distance. His dark hair was short, combed back and he wore a charcoal pin-striped suit and tie. He was a bit in awe. Frik saw him, waved and headed towards him.

They embraced, laughed and joked with each other.

"You've grown, cuz. You're not a lanky teenager anymore! Look at that hair, typical student!"

"Yeah, I'm a real student now."

Frik took him by the arm and led him out of the station towards his car.

"Shoo, very nice, a BMW," said Alex, admiring Frik's car gleaming. The blue body shimmered and sparkled in the harsh light.

"Yeah, you know, I've got to impress the ladies!" Frik laughed and opened the boot to put Alex's bag in. They drove off, towards Houghton where Frik lived. Frik pointed out the landmarks in Johannesburg, the TV tower, Ponty City, the leading general hospital on the hill, and then he drove down towards the leafy suburb of Houghton. Alex took in his surroundings: broad streets, tree-lined, with large luxurious houses behind high fences. Not at all like their little house in Fish Hoek, which only had a low brick wall in the front that he usually jumped over.

"You live here, Frik?"

"Yes, don't be taken in by all this. One of the partners in the law firm retired and sold me his ramshackle old house at a rock-bottom price. Mind you, typical old folk, the house had gone to rack and ruin. Liwa and I gave it a coat of paint and fitted new carpets throughout. That's all I can afford for now."

Alex nodded, taking it all in.

They pulled into the yard of the house. Large windows looked out onto an immaculate lawn and mature border shrubs.

Frik took him inside a rather spartan-looking interior. It was a typical bachelor's pad. Few furnishings, with just the essentials: a sofa, TV and coffee table. Frik showed him the bedroom he would share with Themba.

"Liwa should be back shortly. He's gone to Alexandra to fetch Themba. Things are a bit chaotic there; you never know if there is a protest or police invasions of the township. They may take a while. We mustn't worry and be patient."

Frik went to change as he'd been in court all day. Soon they were both in their shorts, bare feet, and sitting on the front lawn when a dilapidated old Toyota pulled up. They saw Liwa's big smile behind the steering wheel.

The car sputtered to a standstill, and Themba jumped out. The brothers greeted each other hesitantly at first, but they quickly laughed and embraced. Liwa brought Themba's bag out of the car, and they went and greeted Frik.

"That's a bit of a banger you have there, Liwa. Not tempted to drive the BMW then?" asked Alex.

"Christ, no man, can you imagine a handsome black guy like me in the BMW. Chicks would be all over me, man. But the cops, they'd stop me and slap some handcuffs on me, before you could say, 'Excuse me.' They can lock me up and throw away the key. Na, I can get about without drawing attention when I'm in the old Toyota. Don't be misled; under the bonnet, it's an excellent engine. Sometimes I do a bit of gardening out front, for the benefit of the neighbours and any police watching. Here in upper-class Houghton, I'm the official 'gardener.'" Liwa laughed and threw his arms out, directing their gaze to the immaculate lawn.

Alex showed Themba the room they were sharing, and they quickly went back outside. Liwa was getting a fire going, and they were having a *braai* on the built-in grill. Frik brought out ice-cold beers, and they sat around a table, catching up.

"What do you actually do, Liwa? Other than gardening, that is," asked Themba. He first asked in isiXhosa, but Liwa switched to English.

"Well, a bit of this and a bit of that, you know."

"Come on, man," Frik cut in. "You're my 'fixer.'" They all laughed.

"No actually, officially he's my clerk, you're the man who gets things done. Seriously, families come to me when someone disappears without a trace. Sometimes Helen Suzman contacts me to follow up a disappearance. Once I know the outcome, I pass it back to her, and she follows it up in parliament, particularly if we have strong evidence. These 'missing people' are usually in police custody. The police can do this without a warrant with the accused having no automatic access to a lawyer. We have to trawl around some of the police stations to find their loved ones. Liwa often carries messages from me to my clients who are perhaps in jail, or in hiding from the police. It's easier for him to get into places I can't. Liwa also fetches my clients and brings them to my office for consultations. I don't trust using the telephone, as I don't know if the secret police have me bugged. Times are rough, you don't know who to trust. Liwa has got my back. He speaks isiZulu now as well. Needs must."

"Shit! That's four languages," Themba and Alex say in unison, looking at each other, impressed.

"I'm a marked man, boys," said Frik. "I've joined the National Association of Democratic Lawyers, which was founded by Justice Langa. Yes, before you ask, we do have a black judge! Don't be surprised. This country needs lawyers to pressure the government into accepting that apartheid is dead. They need to move to unban the ANC, and other political organisations, or this violence will only get worse. People have had enough!"

Liwa went inside and got some steaks and sausages to cook. The smell of meat on the coals, sizzling with fat spitting out of the sausages, made Alex and Themba's mouths water. Liwa had prepared some *stywe pap* as well.

Liwa cooked the meat on the grill, turning with the tongs in one hand, and a cold beer in the other.

The evening was warm and dry. Once the four young men finished eating, Liwa stoked the coals and made a fire with some dry logs. He watched the wood catch and seemed transfixed by the flames. This was like the days when they were all younger, sitting around the fire in Port Alfred on an evening. The only thing missing was the sound of the crashing waves.

He started humming softly. Liwa then slowly started singing in his baritone voice,

*Nkosi Sikelel' iAfrika,*

*Maluphakanyisw' uphondo lwayo,*

*God bless Africa,*

*May her spirit be lifted high,*

*Hear Thou our prayers, and bless us.*

Frik joined in with his tenor voice, the two men each in their own worlds, singing the ANC anthem in whispered tones. Themba and Alex listened to the 100-year-old isiXhosa hymn, joining in the chorus.

After the singing, it took a while for the four men to come out of their reverie. The sky was black, with stars blinking in the night sky. The flames flickered across the four men's faces—a familiar scene from their childhood.

They sat talking about Themba and Alex's university lives, the new friends they had made, and some girls!

Themba told them he had met a girl, who lives with her cousin, next door to his aunt and uncle. She's a computer programmer studying and working at the same time. Her name is Nomsa, and her family were initially from Natal. A place called Valley of a Thousand Hills. Themba told them he's trying to learn isiZulu. Nomsa was helping him; the language seemed to be similar to isiXhosa.

As the evening wore on, the talk shifted to sharing their memories of summers at Port Alfred and inevitably on to cricket. Alex and Themba started to jibe at each other, quoting their performances on the pitch.

"Well, my bowling speed I reckon, is 120 kilometres per hour, at least," said Alex.

"My best score is eighty runs. I even got a hattrick of catches behind the stumps," said Themba.

"Aw c'mon, I don't think you can bowl at that speed!" They cried in unison, looking at Alex in disbelief.

"Of course, I can. Have you got a tennis ball and cricket bat, Frik?"

Frik went inside to get a bat and ball and switched on the bright outdoor light.

Alex walked to the far end of the garden, having paced out a cricket crease, with Themba positioning his bat, ready to face the ball. Alex ran in, brought his arm up and over. The ball hit Themba's shin.

"I didn't even see that!" said Themba jumping around on one leg, nursing his shin.

"I told you I'm fast. Do you believe me now?" said Alex, hands on his hips, laughing at Themba hopping around on one leg.

Themba nodded and laughed, rubbing his leg. Frik and Liwa joined in, and the four of them knocked about with the bat and ball. Frik's garden suffered a bit of damage, but fortunately, he wasn't one for flowers.

The four young men had reverted to their childhood relationships, the things they did automatically when they were together. Old rivalries, comradeship, teasing and one-upmanship. Their bond had stood the test of time, and seeing each other was like only a day had passed since they were last together at the cabins.

Eventually, they went back to sit by the fire. Alex was feeling exhausted, and his eyes soon closed; his head fell over to one side like a rag doll. The others laughed at him, finishing their beers. Much later, Themba woke Alex, and they went to bed. Liwa and Frik stayed by the fire, eventually crawling into bed in the early hours of the morning. Fortunately, it was Saturday morning, and they could all sleep off their excesses.

Liwa slept in the old servant's quarters at the back of the house. It had been repainted and modernised. Liwa was quite happy there. He had his privacy and could invite friends around or even a lady friend.

~

Alex stretched and yawned. The sun reflected through the curtains, and the day was quickly warming up. Themba's bed was empty. He looked at his watch. He couldn't believe it was nearly midday already. He put on some shorts and made his way through to the kitchen. Liwa and Frik were busy cooking bacon and eggs. The smell permeated through the house. He couldn't believe how hungry he was. Alex helped by cutting thick slices of fresh white bread, buttering it ready for the bacon topped off with the eggs.

After they had eaten and cleared the dishes, Frik announced in his booming lawyer's voice, "Guys, I'm furthering your education later today. Have you heard of a musician Johnny Clegg and his new band Savuka?"

"Of course, yes," they said in unison.

"He also went to Wits Uni where he studied anthropology. I bought some tapes of his music off this street seller in Alex," said Themba. Themba told them that he and Nomsa liked to listen to Jaluka, or as they are now called, Savuka.

"Yes, that's right. You know Johnny Clegg is an anti-apartheid activist as well. He says he's not a member of a party, so he is only standing up for human rights. He's been arrested many times by the police for violating the apartheid laws, writing songs about it, and mixing with black musicians. The security police are still investigating him, but it doesn't stop him.

"He used to go to the miner's hostel in the south of Jo'burg when he was about fourteen, and would spend time with them, all Zulu's and learn about their dancing and their culture. He ended up speaking isiZulu fluently and immersed himself in African vibe and the beat of their music.

"Anyway, he's playing tonight at the Market Theatre in Hillbrow. The show is based on his new album *Third World Child*. Hillbrow is a cosmopolitan part of Jo'burg, and it often happens that the police may try and break up his concert. I've managed to get us four tickets for tonight. Next to the theatre, tucked in a narrow alleyway, is a tiny restaurant, where we'll go for some pizzas after. They're the best Italian pizzas in town. They've got these stone ovens in the back yard, with a couple of tables and chairs inside. Beers are ice cold. It's run by a client of mine, Luigi."

~

The police did not spoil the concert this night, and they all laughed and drank beer, swaying and dancing to the African rhythm. There were no neat rows of seats at the Market Theatre, just standing room all crammed close together in the old building. They had managed to get there early enough to get standing space at the front. Alex and Themba could not get their eyes off the stage. Black and white musicians played together. The music was so loud, it rolled through their bodies, the beat swaying them, always a beer in hand. They were lost in time, mesmerised by the fusion of African and European music.

The band members broke into a spontaneous dance. The white Zulu and his black friend, thumping their feet, lifting their bent legs up high, thumping down again, swivelling from side to side, sliding down on their haunches, in perfect harmony. Singing their hit song *"Scatterlings of Africa"* ... The poignant words depicting the fractured relationships, scattered outlaws roaming the country, each trying in vain to seek sanctuary in a dangerous world.

The rest of the musicians and audience joined in the chorus … the road leading into the future uncertain.

The well-known song resonated across the theatre, capturing everyone's hearts, a unified African sound, the sound of their soul, nearly breaking under strain. Johnny Clegg knew no boundaries between himself and his brothers; they were joined as one in the music. They danced, calling out in a mixture of isiZulu and English, jumping in unison to the drumbeats.

When Johnny Clegg announced to the audience that he was shortly embarking on a tour to Europe, where his latest album had already broken sales records, the crowd roared; the band played on into the night. The French fans called him the "white Zulu." South Africa had its own superstar! The police wouldn't be able to touch him now!

This was the first time Themba and Alex had ever experienced anything like this together. This night ignited their commitment to life as they knew it should be. Apartheid had always permeated their lives, trying to prevent them from sharing all their life's experiences together, as brothers. This had to change! Johnny Clegg and his band members had laid the gauntlet out; they had to follow.

# CHAPTER 24

*1987*

THEMBA AND ALEX SETTLED INTO their second year at university, having passed the first with flying colours. The competition between the brothers spurred them on. Determined to do well against the odds, they had each made a commitment to not disappoint their mothers. Themba knew of the harm his mother had suffered, and he would honour her. She had told him the truth about who his biological father was. Themba knew that everything he now had in life was due to his mother's tenacity and strength. He would not let her down. Buhle had told Themba of the circumstances surrounding his conception and birth. Themba saw this white man who had harmed his mother, as a stranger. His birth was a matter of biology, not love. He would never acknowledge the man.

～

Alex continued with his well-established pattern of going to the library to study every day. He still didn't like getting home before his mother, preferring the soft murmurings of other students in the library while he studied or read.

He usually sat in the corner, with the large windows overlooking the gardens below, to his right. He put his books around him and started working his way through the reading work he had been given that morning.

The library was quiet as usual. The librarian was a dragon, and would inevitably look up over her large thick-rimmed black glasses and frown on any culprit who made a noise in her library.

There were students scattered around at the different tables. Alex didn't take much notice.

The person in front of him let out a loud sneeze.

"Bloody hell," he said involuntarily, having just got the fright of his life. A petite young woman in front had let out this almighty sneeze. He couldn't believe such a small thing could make such a big noise.

Predictably, the librarian looked their way, frowning disapproval. "Quiet!"

"Bless you!" he said to her back. She had tightly curled dark brown hair that fell to below her narrow shoulders in a floral dress. Brown arms over her books. She turned back to face him and thanked him softly.

She had a lovely broad smile, pearl white teeth, big dark eyes with soft curling eyelashes—a dark brown face, delicate hands with silver rings on her fingers.

Alex's mouth dropped open; he was embarrassed, and quietly stuttered, "You're welcome!"

That was it, he was totally distracted by her. She faced for-
wards to carry on studying, and he pretended as if his books were
fascinating. Her bracelets would jingle every time she turned a
page of her textbook. He could hear every sound in the room: the
murmurs and the occasional stifled giggle.

After about an hour, she started to pack up her books and put
them in her large linen bag. Alex quickly started packing his books
to put in his leather satchel. He wasn't going to miss this opportunity.

He followed her out of the library.

"Excuse me," he called out, not wanting to look like he was
following or stalking her, or frighten her away.

She turned and smiled at him.

"Um, my name's Alex. Would you like to go for a coffee at the
canteen?"

"Yes, that would be nice. I'm Alicia," she said, looking down at
her sandals.

They made their way down the path, through the garden, to
the canteen.

Lots of students were milling about, and a white boy with a
*coloured* girl didn't stand out at all. Alex offered to get their coffees
if she wanted to choose somewhere to sit.

She said her name was Alicia Williams and she was of Cape
Malay heritage. Her family originally lived in District Six but were
forcibly removed ten years ago to the Mitchells Plain township,
about 25km from Cape Town. Her father had owned a fabric shop
in the heart of the district and had been quite comfortably off. The

government moved them, but never redeveloped the district despite saying it was now a 'white' area.

Her family was hoping that in the future they could return there. Her father now ran a large fabric-stall at the Cape Town market. They were doing okay, but they were now getting older, and Alicia worried about their future.

"I live in student accommodation and go and help them at the stall on Saturdays and usually spend the weekend with them," she told him.

Alex told Alicia about his life on the farm, his father's death and their move to Fish Hoek. How his brother Themba had to move to Alexandra as well.

Eventually, he managed to tell her what he was studying, and she said that she was in her third year studying medicine. She had another four gruelling years to go. She wanted to eventually move into research medicine at Groote Schuur Hospital next to their campus.

The two young people shared their stories, their families and their journey through life thus far. Perhaps the journey had taken another turn, one they could explore together.

Alicia and Alex regularly met up at the library to study together and go to the campus café for coffee afterwards. Socialising, as a mixed-race couple, was done in a relaxed and open way on campus. The difficulties would arise when they were off-campus.

≈

Alex wanted to share with Themba his story about Alicia. He was in love and knew Themba would want to know all about her.

Hi Themba,

What you up to, bro?

I've met this wonderful girl, Alicia. She's a medical student at uni, and we met in the library. We meet up on campus; it's easier as she is "coloured." Crazy, this apartheid continues to invade our personal lives. I wish we could all just have the freedom to be with whom we want. These rules have no bearing on the reality of our lives.

Alicia and I have to be careful where we meet. We can't go to a restaurant or the movies together.

My mum has bought a new car and handed me her old VW beetle. It's excellent. I have a roof-rack and put my surfboard on the top. I usually surf when Alicia is working at the hospital or helping her parents at their market stall in Cape Town.

Her dad is a musician. He plays the saxophone, and sometimes his friends come to his house on the weekend, and they jam together. I am going through to Mitchells Plain to meet her parents for the first time. They are hosting a braai, and hopefully, I can hear the music man playing.

Alicia tells me her grandparents had been slaves in southeast Asia and east Africa and were brought to Cape Town by the Dutch. Everybody in this country has a story to tell about how they came to be in South Africa, and then how apartheid ripped their lives apart. So, it goes on.

I feel quite down about it all, but Alicia always lifts me up. A bit like you used to do, bro. I miss you loads and hope that uni is going *well. Please be careful; you know the wolves are watching and are ready to pounce!*

*How's your family doing?*

*A*

Themba read the letter and felt sad and happy for Alex at the same time. He replied.

*Hey, bro,*

*Don't lose heart, man. We must keep the pressure on the government. So many people have suffered over so many years; we can't fail them now. We must push to the bitter end.*

*I'm now a member of the Students Representative Council. We need to monitor police activities. If we hold a rally, we always put out a press release at the same time. That seems to curtail the police's enthusiasm to shut us down.*

*I suppose it's easier for Nomsa and me to meet up as boyfriend and girlfriend as we both live in Alexandra and are considered 'non-white.' We do socialise mostly in our homes, but sometimes we go to Vilikazi Street in Soweto to listen to music and hang out with our friends.*

*I try to get home to Alex most weekends, as long as we don't have any student action going on.*

*My family is great. My aunt and my mum still work together. My mum isn't interested in any relationship; she's just happy to be working and saving money. She enjoys my aunt's company, and they have lots of friends locally.*

*My uncle's taxi business is doing well with my cousins running the show. Uncle Sipho tries to keep his hand in and even still drives some of the routes. My auntie gets a bit worried sometimes, as the taxi ranks can be busy and the police keep a close eye on everyone there. Yeah, sometimes there are some wars between the taxi associations. It happens quite often. Turf warfare! It's usually over one taxi driver trying to take over someone else's route. My uncle has been in business so long, they all know not to mess with him! Uncle Sipho always says, "You keep the keys to your taxis in one hand and carry a gun in the other." I've never seen Uncle Sipho with a gun; maybe he hides it from me?*

*Take care, bro.*

*T*

# CHAPTER 25

ALEX DROVE CAREFULLY THROUGH THE busy main street leading to Kenilworth before turning off for Philippi and eventually entering Mitchells Plain. The road was narrow, cars were parked on both sides, and people were going about their Saturday morning shopping. He had to concentrate as he had not driven this way before. Alicia was composed next to him and giving him directions as they went.

He was feeling nervous as Alicia's parents had invited him to their home so they could meet him for the first time. He's sure he would be under their microscope, making sure he was right for their daughter.

They eventually turned off the main street and took a side-road into the township. Alicia and Alex meandered down winding roads until they got to a typical single-storey house with a front yard and garage. There was a row of barbed wire over their front gate. Alex got the feeling that the crime rate may be quite high in this area.

"It's because my parents keep their fabric stock in the garage, so they take extra precautions. They've had people try and set fire to their garage before. Just press the car's hooter, and my brother will come out and open the gate for us."

Alex did as he was told, and a teenager came to open the gates for them. He could see the resemblance to Alicia immediately, and he gave them a big smile as they drove in. He carefully closed up again.

Alex and Alicia walked to the front door, which was open, and her mother was standing and waiting for them. She was a small woman, with dark hair under a loose-fitting headscarf and colourful clothes.

"Good morning, Mrs. Williams, nice to meet you," Alex said, shaking her hand.

"Nice to meet you too, young man, come inside." She led the way into the house. Alicia and Alex helped her mum to get drinks and made small talk and follow-up introductions. Alicia introduced her brother, Philemon.

Philemon smiled broadly and asked Alex to come outside, and he'd introduce him to his father.

Alex noticed the back yard was covered in a grass lawn, newly mowed. There were neat borders around the edges with some herbs growing. Alex introduced himself to Mr Williams, who shook his hand.

He was busy lighting a fire and getting the coals ready for a *braai*. "Hope you like a chicken braai, son."

"Yes, I'm not fussy, sir. I grew up on a farm and eat anything that is put in front of me." Alex was trying to sound nonchalant but was struggling. Alicia's father noticed this and tried to make him feel more comfortable by asking him about his family and his university course. These were things that Alex felt comfortable talking about, and he started relaxing and started cracking jokes at his own expense.

Eventually, Philemon came outside and offered Alex a beer, which he accepted. Alicia and her mum joined them too, bringing the meat ready to *braai*. Alex started to feel more at home with Alicia sitting next to him and busy with his second beer.

"Dad, I hope you aren't interrogating Alex?" she jokingly asked her father. Alicia's mother took her turn to question Alex and asked about his family. Alex felt he should share everything with them, as they clearly were protective of their daughter and wanted to know more about him. He knew there was a lot at stake, with Alicia committing to a seven-year medical degree and he was white.

Mr. Williams cooked the meat, and they all shared the food, sitting under a grapevine, threaded across to form a natural sunshade. Alex was relaxed and enjoyed their company and the family meal. He was not used to this anymore. Usually, it was just him and his mum.

The shared meal gave the family time to get to know Alex and observe the interaction between him and Alicia. They were in love; they held hands and talked to each other with smiles on their faces.

Mr. Williams was relieved to meet Alex, but he still remained concerned. When everyone was clearing away, he and Alex stayed outside on their own. Alex felt this was perhaps deliberate.

"Alex, I can see you and my daughter are fond of each other, but I feel I must raise something sooner rather than later. You know I am one of five brothers, and my wife is one of seven."

"No sir, I knew you were both from large families but didn't know the details," Alex replied.

"Yes, we could all see from a young age that Alicia is gifted, particularly in science and mathematics. We all decided that we would jointly fund her university education. We are not wealthy people, but everyone chips into a pot of money to pay for university. My wife and I make sure everything is accounted for and work hard to ensure Alicia does not have to worry or even work part-time while at university. Alicia helps us on a Saturday at the stall when she does not have a shift at the hospital, but we do not put pressure on her to do this for us.

"Son, you know that the teenage pregnancy rate among coloured girls is notoriously high, and the fathers do not always stick around, leaving the girl as a single parent without a job prospect. The girl remains in a cycle of poverty that she's unable to get out of. We do not want this for Alicia. Do you understand what I'm saying?"

"Yes, sir," Alex gulped.

"I'm going to be blunt. We do not want Alicia to fall pregnant, and equally, if you're serious about her, that's fine, but don't walk away from your responsibility. You are a white man and could quite easily ignore Alicia and leave her life in ruins. There are no repercussions for you, but there are for Alicia," Mr. Williams said sternly.

Alex hesitated, knowing he had to tread carefully and say the right thing.

"Mr. Williams, I have deep feelings for your daughter, and I would not be irresponsible with her future. I want to finish my degree as well, and my mother has worked hard to fund my university studies. She is very strict with me, and I am not allowed to fail, as there is no money for any re-takes.

"My respect for Alicia is for who she is, not because of the colour of her skin. I know the law does not sanction our relationship, but this will not stop me from being committed to your daughter, if that's what she wants from me. This, with all due respect, is not a casual relationship, sir."

Mr. Williams nodded wisely, liking what he was hearing. He knew that Alicia and Alex could not marry in this current political climate, but the future was also unclear, and nobody could predict what would happen about apartheid.

With that awkward conversation out of the way, Mr. Williams said, "You can call me Abdallah, son."

Alex smiled, knowing he must be at least initially accepted by Alicia's father.

The group enjoyed the sunshine and started to relax in each other's company. Alicia had a shift at the hospital on Sunday, so she and Alex left later in the afternoon. Alex remembered his manners that his mother taught him and thanked them for their hospitality.

Once in the car, driving back to Alicia's student residence, Alex let out a big sigh of relief.

"Shoo, I think your dad has provisionally accepted me!"

Alicia squeezed his thigh and nodded, leaving her hand on his leg. "Of course he has. I knew they'd like you."

Alicia invited him in for a coffee before he had to return home to Fish Hoek.

"My roommate has gone home for the weekend," she said while she boiled the kettle in the corner of the large room. "We have the place to ourselves."

Alex was not sure what was going to happen; he'd let Alicia take the lead. They sat on the bed, drinking their coffee. He was acutely aware of Alicia sitting close to him. He smelled her soapy freshness and turned to face her. She looked up at him expectantly; her smile was welcoming. The room had a large window, letting in the soft early evening light. Her shoulders were glowing brown in the sleeveless summer dress she was wearing, and her legs were folded under the soft fall of the fabric.

He leaned over and cupped her face in his hands and met her lips. They were soft, moist and enticing. Very soon, they were enveloped in each other's arms, with a promise of things to come.

Suddenly, Alex heard Mr. Williams' voice in his head. He broke away.

"What's wrong?"

"Your dad gave me a clear message that you should not fall pregnant, that the whole family is making sacrifices to fund your place at university. I can't jeopardise that!"

Alex looked so worried. Alicia giggled and ran her fingers through his hair, teasing him.

"You silly man. I'm a medical student; I know how contraception works."

She couldn't help but find it funny; his face was scrunched up and so serious. "Alex, I'm taking the contraceptive pill, and you will not be the first man I have slept with in my life. Enough of my past, come here, so I can kiss you to death." With that, she put her slim fingers through his hair to the back of his head and pulled his face close to hers, giving him a long lingering kiss. She wrapped her legs around his waist and slowly, his lips moved down to her neck and shoulder until her sleeveless dress dropped down further. They had both reached a point of no return.

"That's better," she said, arching her back and letting him take over.

# CHAPTER 26

*1988*

*Hi, Alex,*

*That's it, now it's head down for the final year at uni. It's been a battle with my studies, girlfriend and political activities. My mother keeps pressing me, making sure I keep up and do well with my uni work. My uncle keeps his ear to the ground, making sure he keeps us all safe. If I am at any risk, he'll be the first to know.*

*I've been elected president of the student's council, so I have a lot more responsibilities and strategic planning for our programme of activism.*

*I just feel there is increasing tension in the country now, things are going MAD! This bloody apartheid government has to concede and admit that apartheid is no longer viable. Sorry, sounds like I'm writing one of my political speeches for a rally.*

*What is worrying is the government's incursions into Botswana and Mozambique, killing ANC leaders who are exiled in our neighbouring countries. Six ANC members were recently killed in a bomb blast in Bulawayo, Zimbabwe.*

*All around us in Jo'burg, there are bomb blasts and consequent police raids. You openly read about it in the newspapers now. There are some ANC attacks on military personnel and buildings also. Then the army retaliates and kills activists in Northern Transvaal. The killings carry on, too many to mention. I've lost count as to how many people have been killed on both sides.*

*This worries me much, but the longer the government keeps apartheid alive, the worse it's going to get.*

*I see things in Cape Town have also been unsettled; this unrest has also spread to places like East London and the homelands like Ciskei.*

*My life is quite conflicted at the moment. I'm studying hard, but I'm also working on political activism. I won't tell you anymore, but I'm convinced the secret police are following me. They seem to know where I'm going; I'm not stupid, and I can pick up when someone is following me. I was followed by two white guys when I went to meet Nomsa in town. We deliberately went to the park where there are fewer people, and these guys blatantly kept following us. I'm worried about Nomsa now, and we've arranged to only meet up in Alexandra on the weekend.*

*She's such a beautiful girl, and I love her so much. I couldn't bear anything happening to her. I need to keep her safe. Fortunately, she lives next door to me in Alex, but I can't go through every weekend as I've got meetings, etc., to go to on campus. I must keep seeing her; she's become my life. I want to marry her when I've finished my studies.*

*Life is just about studies, political meetings and spending time with Nomsa, at the moment. I can't slip back with my studies, or my sponsors will be all over me. They're not particularly interested in what I'm doing, as long as my grades are good. They're about to pay my final year's fees, so soon I'll be okay. I'm not ungrateful, I would never have been able to study without my bursary. But I want all black kids to have the opportunity to go to a half-decent school, and maybe even university or undertake apprenticeships. We need mechanics and doctors!*

*My dream is to be part of the future that reshapes this education system we have, for everyone. It will be a long struggle, even if the ANC is unbanned and forms part of a future government.*

*Well, Alex, I hope you are keeping safe, and I wish I could see you and explain my feelings to you. You're my bro, nothing will ever change that.*

*T*

*PS. Remember what I said years ago? Make sure you burn my letters.*

Alex read Themba's letter. It was unusually long and mirrored what he was learning from the newspapers. He read them in the library after lectures or in his granny's café on the weekend

The situation worried Alex as well, and he felt Themba has taken his political activism a step further, putting himself out there as president of the student council of what was seen by the government as a radical university.

Although Cape Town University was seen as left-wing by the government, they had mostly been left to their own devices. There had recently been incidents when the police had followed protesting students and beaten them as a way of getting them to break up a protest.

It took Alex a while to respond, as there was so much he wanted to talk to Themba about and wished he could do it face to face. They were both in their final year, and their whole future depended on how well they did. His marks were good, and he wanted to aim for a distinction this year; even if he didn't achieve this goal, he'd still have a good degree. He thought he may just ignore his 'call-up' papers and carry on with his life.

Alex was due to start an internship at an oil refinery just outside Cape Town, as part of his final for his chemical engineering degree. Uni holidays would be busy at the refinery and studying. Alicia was now in her fourth year and needed to spend more time at Groote Schuur Hospital. She also had seminars on campus, and on those days, they grabbed precious time together at the library and the campus cafeteria.

Alex put pen to paper.

*Hi, Themba,*

*I keep up with the newspapers every day and am worried as you seem to be in a hotbed of unrest. Please, please be careful. Just write to me, even if it's short letters so that I know you're safe. Remember, Frik's there if you need him!*

*Bishop Tutu got permission for a protest march in Cape Town. Pressure, pressure on the government, it has to be relentless. I went with Ed, Alicia and a couple of other students from uni. You won't believe it, the press reported that 30,000 people were attending. We marched through Cape Town. It was peaceful. Bishop Tutu has that effect on people; they follow his lead. He calls for peaceful protest and talks bluntly to the government about change that is needed. He cries for the bloodshed of the children of this country. Bombs are going off; people are killed in roadblocks, raids and attacks on government installations. The police seem to have a campaign of harassing him at every event.*

*We all feel that things are a tinder box; just one spark can lead to an almighty explosion. We surely can't get to the point when the whole country is at war with each other. What will our children's futures be like?*

*We're going to set up another high-profile event, to protest against segregation on the beaches. It's symbolic of all the other areas of society where discrimination is in your face. Those signs outside public buildings with separate entrances. Alicia and I, if we had to go into the municipal offices, would have to go in separate entrances. We could never go to the beaches together.*

*I want to marry her, but I can't even ask her as it's against the law! I could get ill and go to the hospital, and she could treat me, but I can't marry her or live with her.*

*I've met her family, and they seem to have accepted me, even though they had doubts initially. I go through to Mitchell's Plain often and enjoy their company. Her dad sometimes has some musician friends over, and they jam together. He plays the saxophone and is an outstanding jazz musician.*

*The political situation is so unsettled, where will it end? I get so angry at the injustices and killings. I can understand why people have resorted to violence as a means of protest. Violence is not the answer, but what else is there? I don't know, this government needs to sit up and take note of the demons they have unleashed. It's their fault, they should have dismantled apartheid decades ago. They know what the rest of the world thinks. It's not just, and it's not Christian!! They claim to be Christians, but they are anything but …*

*I'm going to end off now, have to get a dissertation finished and get ready to go to work. Ed sends his regards by the way!*

*Be careful, brother. Wish I could be with you.*

*A*

∽

Sara was in the kitchen, cooking a meal for the three of them. Alicia was slowly becoming part of their lives, and Sara felt that she was the daughter that she and Dan never had. But in a sense, she was more of a daughter-in-law given the romantic relationship she had with Alex.

Sara felt that Alicia was going to be in their lives for many years to come. Was it wishful thinking on her part? The apartheid laws prevented this young couple from getting married, and once again, Sara felt that segregation would deny her son happiness.

Looking through the kitchen window at the young couple sitting side by side on the patio, engrossed in each other, talking and laughing, she prayed they wouldn't be harmed. Alex didn't say much to her, but his actions spoke loudly.

She thought about Alex's relationship with Themba. Their love and affection for each other were born out of two personalities that fit together. Themba's belief that Alex saved him from drowning in the river cemented their commitment to each other even further. They were now like a hand and a glove. Their skin colour never came into the dynamic other than through the external restrictions apartheid placed on them. Removing those shackles seemed to be something both of them were fighting for.

As in his relationship with Themba, Alex's relationship with Alicia was without any racial bias or boundary. In Sara's mind, they had a right to that relationship, to live together and even to have children. The injustice of it all saddened Sara and tore at her heart. She wanted to protect them, but she couldn't. This was beyond her control.

If Alicia and Alex ever felt that they needed to put their relationship above their family and their country, and move abroad, she would understand, even though it would deeply sadden her. How they would do this, she did not know. They would both have professional qualifications so they may be entitled to some kind of visa. She doesn't want to put ideas into their heads but was sure that was what a lot of young people were thinking of doing.

# CHAPTER 27

THEMBA FELT ALEX'S ANGUISH OVER his relationship with Alicia, as well as the political climate, becoming more and more volatile and dangerous for both of them. He was finishing his final teaching placement at Alexandra High School. It was the same school where he had first started when he and Buhle arrived in Alexandra. He enjoyed teaching, and his mentor at the school was inspiring.

Themba had managed to buy a bicycle and would ride from his aunt and uncle's house to the school every day. When he got home, he spent time marking homework and preparing for the next day's teaching. Once Nomsa was back from work, she would either join him, or he would visit her at her aunt's next door, having their evening meal together.

Themba discussed with Nomsa the dangers they were all under, the threats they faced. Nomsa wanted Themba to be safe and with her, but she also accepted his need to be part of the activism against apartheid. During their private moments together, they agreed that if the dangers to Themba became acute, he would have to lay low and maybe not tell Nomsa where he was in order to protect her. They agreed that only Frik was to know where he was and to help him if he was arrested.

Once a week, Themba took the minibus into university for lectures. On Friday, he had finished his lectures and was walking towards the taxi rank in central Johannesburg. He stopped at a café to buy a cold drink and noticed two white guys leaning against a wall across the road, watching him. Two white guys at a taxi rank, no chance of blending into the crowd there!

He knew the café owner, and sat and enjoyed his drink. "Si, have you noticed those two white guys before?" he asked in isiXhosa, nodding at the two men outside.

Si shook his head, *no.* Themba finished his drink and left the café, walking towards the taxis. He opened the minibus door and glanced over his shoulder as he climbed in. The two guys had disappeared, but he was feeling very uncomfortable. He knew he had to trust his gut instinct. He spoke to the taxi driver and asked him to keep an eye out for them following the taxi.

"Don't worry, I know how to lose those guys," the taxi driver said. Once all the passengers were in, the taxi took off with the spinning of wheels. Taxi drivers were notorious for their ability to nudge between traffic, ramp pavements, cut corners, take shortcuts, all to shorten the journey. The more trips, the more money they made. This taxi driver was no exception.

Themba had climbed into the back of the taxi so that he could see out the rear window. First, he saw a dirty red car, he thought it was a Toyota, follow them, but the ducking and diving by the taxi driver soon left them behind. Themba could relax even though he was beginning to feel sick from the bumpy ride at the back.

These incidents of being followed left him feeling very uncomfortable. He and Nomsa were due to attend an event next weekend in Soweto. It was a funeral at the Regina Mundi church, for some activists recently killed in a police raid in Soweto. He'd better watch his back. He checked with Uncle Sipho whether there were any murmurings about any police raids in Soweto.

The dusty parking area was filled with cars and taxis by the time Themba and Nomsa arrived in their taxi at Regina Mundi Catholic Church in Soweto. Pedestrians were threading their way in between the vehicles towards the church entrance. Their route had been from Alexandra to Johannesburg, and then another taxi out to Soweto. Themba did not notice if the two men were following him again. He was not in his usual routine on a Saturday, but nonetheless, he was careful. He made sure they were always in a group of people and boarded the Soweto bound taxi without any hitches. People were thronging the taxi rank, most of whom were going to the funeral. They got lost in the crowd.

Themba was not particularly religious but wanted to show respect for the dead comrades. Nomsa and his other activist friends wanted to show solidarity with the people in Soweto. The church had a long history of sheltering activists and was often a place of safety.

Themba and Nomsa found a space on a bench at the back of the church. The organist was playing quietly while people filed in. Nomsa whispered to Themba that students during the 1976 uprising had run into the church to shelter from police bullets. She pointed to the damage in the ceiling and the marble stand at the altar. It was peppered with bullet holes—a reminder of a bloody past.

The service was sombre but also became uplifting when hymns were sung. The congregation gathered outside for refreshments after the service. People used the opportunity to speak to each other and to pay their respects to the families.

Themba sighed with relief when he and Nomsa got back home to Alexandra. He did not notice if anyone had followed them. Themba did not want to worry Nomsa, so he didn't say anything.

Monday, it was back to teaching. Themba was finishing off his placement and had a meeting with his mentor. They went through his portfolio of work, which Themba handed in. His mentor would mark it and pass his report to Themba's university tutor. Themba could finally relax.

He left the school gates behind him, on his bicycle through the bustling streets of Alex back home. Alex was a busy township, and Themba didn't notice a dirty red car following him. He happily peddled along the dusty road, enjoying the exercise and freedom. Themba worked hard on the uphill, but once at the top, it was downhill to home. He free-wheeled but didn't see the red car nudge his back wheel until it was too late. Themba flew over his handle-bars, tumbled and fell with a loud thud on the ground.

The car blew its hooter. "Hey kaffir, fuckin' watch where you're going, man!" Themba looked up and saw the two white guys who had been following him before, shouting at him. They accelerated and took off into the distance. His body ached, his head throbbed, and now he started to shake all over. His bike was a mangled mess. He slowly got up, picked up his bag, which had spewed papers all over the pavement. They must have been following him from school. The roads were always busy in Alex, with cars hooting and drivers noisily gesticulating at each other. He kicked himself for not being vigilant. He had become complacent after the uneventful trip to Soweto.

Was this a warning? Now he was scared. They could have "accidentally" killed him, and nobody would have known who was responsible. Just another road traffic accident statistic. Those two guys deliberately made sure he had seen them in the car. They wanted him to know they were following him. *Shit, what now?*

Themba slowly pushed his mangled bike down the hill and walked into the yard. Uncle Sipho was talking to the mechanic when he looked up and saw Themba, all dusty, dirty, blood running down his temple. Bike wrecked.

Uncle Sipho tutted and walked towards Themba. "Come inside, boy, tell me what happened. Let's clean you up before your auntie and mum get home!"

While drinking a strong tea with plenty of sugar, Themba told his uncle what had happened. They drew up a plan together. Themba only had one more week at the school, and his uncle would transport him each day. Themba could then use the taxis to get into university from the following week.

Themba felt he needed to be more alert, watch those around him, and keep himself safe. Once he was on campus, he would be fine, it's just the journeys or any excursions in or out of university that could cause a problem. Sipho would speak to all his drivers, ask them to be alert to anyone following them or Themba.

The last week at the school went without incident, and Themba felt relieved. His mind became pre-occupied with his final studies in preparation for his end-of-year exams and the dissertations he needed to complete.

The secret police who had been following Themba, took on a more sophisticated strategy. They had achieved their desired objective of flagging up that they were watching him. Now they had two teams, alternating, watching him travel to Wits University and every time he went outside campus, they followed him. The consequence of this tactic was that Themba was not always aware of being followed.

Themba noticed them sometimes following his taxi into Jo'burg, but they remained mostly undetectable. When he went through to Soweto, unbeknown to him, they followed him as well. He's started to feel hemmed-in; it was a sixth-sense kind of feeling, like when hairs stand up on your head, but you don't know why. Were they building a dossier on him, like Frik told him they do? When were they going to close in and pounce and arrest him when he least expected it? Would his vigilance be good enough to protect him? Would he disappear into a black hole like everyone else?

All these thoughts and fears rolled around in Themba's head. Was he paranoid or were his fears a reflexive flight response to danger? On balance, Themba felt he needed to follow his instincts.

# CHAPTER 28

THE MONTHS WENT BY. MAY, June, and July, but Alex did not hear from Themba. He wrote him a few short letters, urging him to let him know he's okay. Alex phoned Buhle, but she said she hadn't seen him. He hadn't been home for a few weeks, which was not unusual. She knew he had a lot of university work due after his teaching placement in Alexandra and also some meetings on campus.

Alex got the feeling that Buhle did not know the extent of Themba's political activism. He didn't want to alarm her, so he kept the discussion brief and light-hearted.

Alex didn't have Nomsa's contact details, so he couldn't speak to her either. Alex knew Themba had been followed by the secret police, but not whether that had continued or whether Themba had curtailed his political protests. Knowing Themba, he thought that was unlikely. He was unflinchingly committed to the cause.

After another month, he was struggling to contain himself, and he was in a continual state of heightened anxiety. He didn't tell his mother; he knew she would start worrying as well. He was not sure what to do. Should he wait it out, or should he go looking for Themba? Would it be possible to find him?

He's been keeping count through the newspapers of the number of bombs or limpet mines that had recently exploded. He'd counted thirty-five already this year; they seemed to be increasing in the last eight weeks. This was without taking into account the shootings, stabbings and violent raids and attacks all over the country. The situation was a powder keg being ignited and ready to be blown up at any moment.

Alex couldn't sleep at night; he didn't know where or what Themba was doing. Was he safe? Had he been detained and tortured? Had he been killed and his body dumped in some piece of earth nobody knew where? He had vivid dreams of Themba's body being dumped in a hole, or of him hanging from a tree, his body swinging in the wind. He woke up in a sweat, not sure where he was. He couldn't talk to anyone about it.

The not knowing was eating at Alex's insides. He couldn't control it, and it was affecting every waking moment of the day. He felt compounded to go and look for Themba himself, to make sure he was okay. Was Themba alive? He needed to do something; he needed to fix this. He knew there were actions he could take. He had lots of contacts in the media, through journalist student friends at university. He knew he could contact his liberal political connections, and if need be, he'd go higher up, even to Bishop Tutu or Helen Suzman themselves. Helen Suzman was the MP for Houghton, where Frik lived. She had many times spoken up on behalf of people being detained. He felt there were options, but it was up to him to initiate them. This drive to find Themba became all-consuming. Life went by in a blur.

Alex went into the main campus and made his way to his faculty head's office. He went down a dark corridor until he got to the door marked *Professor Ibrahim.* Alex knocked on the door and waited. He heard a voice say, "Come in."

The professor was sitting behind his desk with piles of papers in front of him and on the chairs. He jumped up quickly and made space on a chair for Alex and motioned for him to sit.

Alex didn't know where to start; he said how he was worried about his brother who was at Wits University. He hadn't heard from him in months, and it was now July.

Professor Ibrahim looked at him above his silver spectacles, which sat on the lower end of his nose. He didn't say a word throughout Alex's speech. He nodded wisely, saying, "You must be anxious; these are extremely volatile times. You must be careful in trying to look for him; don't be a bull in a china shop. You have to tread cautiously. Is there anyone you can confide in, who can discreetly find out what has happened to him or what his whereabouts are?"

Alex told his tutor about Frik, and how maybe he or Liwa would be able to help him find Themba. It's what they'd done many times for other families. Liwa was a master of wheeling and dealing and finding people. He felt the only way was to go and see Frik and Liwa and to see if they could help him find Themba. They may not even have realised he was missing.

Alex arranged with Professor Ibrahim to have a week's compassionate leave with the possibility of more, if needed. Professor

Ibrahim reminded Alex of the importance of his studies. This was his final year, and there was much at stake.

Alex considered his tutor's wisdom and went home to make arrangements.

Alex phoned Frik, not saying much, but he arranged for Frik to collect him from Johannesburg station on Friday.

The long train journey from Cape Town to Johannesburg seemed to be taking forever for Alex. The long stretches across semi-desert areas, the Karoo, the place where he and Themba's bond was formed.... He started reminiscing in his semi-conscious state.

He closes his eyes and could see the Fish River where they used to go swimming, sliding down the boulders behind the farm-house, and going to the cabins in the summer. Buhle cooking in the kitchen.... He smiles, remembering her reading mistakes when cooking from a recipe book, the laughter at the odd tastes. Buhle was the heart of their home, his and Themba's. She cooked for them, washed their clothes, cleaned their homes, and was always a constant in their lives. His mother checked on their homework, made sure they worked hard. Two mothers, two different sets of skills, both equally important to Themba and Alex.

Alex remembered the brotherly love that developed between him and Themba. Two farm boys, loving the outdoors, squabbling and making up with each other, heads down and doing their home-work together every day. He felt this foundation was part of who he was as a man today. Did Themba feel the same way? It was difficult for Alex to understand it from a black person's perspective. Alex knew he, as a white person, did not suffer the same discrimination that Themba encountered. Alex tried not to take this advantage for granted. He tried to align his political thinking with his Christian values. God wants us to love our brothers, Jesus did not discriminate, he washed the feet of all his disciples, he loved even those who had "sinned." God loves us all. Alex believes that with all his heart.

Now, as an adult, he knew his love for Alicia was based on who she was. She was beautiful, funny, intelligent, and understood him without saying anything. She sensed his mood, gave him time and slowly and gently eased him out of a melancholy dip. A bit like Themba did. Themba was the bubbly, glass half-full kind of person. Alex was reflexive about his own behaviours and recognised that he was often impulsive, but sometimes it had served him well. Look how, after that first sneeze of Alicia's, he got up without thinking about it and approached her.

Slowly, slowly, the train made its way through the Free State and barren flatlands, not like the Karoo at all. Red dust everywhere, just the odd small town station for the train to stop at. He knew Winnie Mandela, wife of Nelson Mandela, was put under house arrest in Brandfort, which was 58km north-west of Bloemfontein, the capital of the Free State. What must that have done to her? Leaving her isolated in a God-forsaken wilderness, her children removed from her care, her husband in prison? It could drive you mad. How could a person cope without anywhere to escape to? If you tried to get on a train at a station, the whole town would know it was you and police would stop you or pick you up at the next station stop. The police knew what they were doing by putting her in the Free State. A bit ironic, that provincial name; she wasn't free and never would be. Her past tortured her. The victim becoming the perpetrator of violence and instigator of terror on her own people in Soweto. Her followers would "necklace" people they felt were informants. Her speeches were fiery and involved inciting her followers to violence. Violence begets violence, and so the cycle of deaths and injuries continued.

Eventually, they pulled into Johannesburg station where Frik was waiting for him. This time, the newness and lustre of Johannesburg passed Alex by. Frik tried to make conversation but eventually gave up. They continued their journey in silence.

They arrived in Houghton. Frik told him he was staying in the same room that he and Themba shared. Alex put his bag away and went outside, waiting for Frik to join him.

"So," said Frik, "to what do I have the honour of this visit? Look, I'm always happy to see you, Alex, but I hope this is not affecting your studies?"

Alex let out a long slow breath as he gave Frik the last letter he had from Themba.

"Frik, he always writes to me, even if it takes a couple of weeks. He's always responded. I've written him about four short letters, asking him where he is, is he upset with me, did I do something wrong? No replies. His family are not aware of where he is, but I don't want to scare them by continually asking after him."

Frik sat quietly, his hands forming a steeple in front of his face. He was in lawyer mode. "Alex, you have to understand that South Africa is currently going through a tough period. There are a lot of protests, and violence is ongoing. Bombs going off, people disappearing, raids, shootings, stabbings. Lots of people have been killed or injured. Believe me, I've been so busy trying to find some of these people. I try to keep them safe, but these times are volatile, and nothing is predictable. Nobody is safe, including you and me. I'm going to tell you something the general public doesn't know. There are some third-party, highly influential people, not politicians, who are currently facilitating a meeting with some members of the government and the ANC, outside of South Africa.

De Klerk has just taken over from Botha, as State President. White voters expect that De Klerk will carry on the apartheid government. What people don't know is that he now realises things cannot go on as they are; the violence, as bad as it is, will only escalate. He has told this third party, let's call them 'influencers' from the business world, that he wishes to de-escalate the tensions by talking to ANC leaders. He's privately agreed to meet Bishop Tutu and several intermediaries to look at a peaceful way forward.

Alex, you have to promise me that none of this goes out of my home. You cannot talk to your activist friends, nor any of your journalist contacts. If this gets out, there will be hell to pay. Remember, some right-wingers are armed and willing to continue fighting for apartheid. Their guns are loaded! This is a very precarious situation; we're on a knife's edge. De Klerk knows that with the fall of Marxism, there is no longer a valid argument to be had by the government that the ANC will be manipulated by them. He's planning to meet Nelson Mandela and discuss a peaceful way forward.

Alex, please keep quiet, and don't try and look for Themba."

Alex thought about what Frik had just said but remained worried. "I think he's been killed, and nobody will admit it. You know he was being followed. The secret negotiations are not going to stop people on the ground from carrying on the way they always have.

Maybe something has already happened to him. I don't think the violence will immediately stop until there is a clear sign that apartheid is well and truly dead!"

"You're right, Alex, but that's why I'm telling you not to make waves and go looking for Themba. I know how hard this is for you, but looking for him will put everyone around him in danger and alert everyone that he has disappeared. Do you trust me when I'm giving you advice?"

Alex nodded, trying to hold back the tears and anxiety wrenching his stomach. He felt like he was going to be sick.

"Well, you must blindly trust me because you're my family and Themba is like my family. I wouldn't let anything happen to him if I could prevent it. You and I will have a nice quiet weekend together. We'll do ordinary things. We'll go to the movies, go for something to eat. Have a *braai* together, before you go back on the train to Cape Town on Monday. I'm also being watched, and I know the secret police have a dossier on me. One of the anti-apartheid lawyers, Albie Sachs, was recently in Maputo, Mozambique and had a bomb planted under his car. We think it was put there by the South African secret police. Fortunately, he was only injured when it went off. Believe me, I know the risks, and I try and keep myself and everyone around me safe."

Alex felt deflated, worried and anxious for Themba. He still didn't know the truth, and his heart ached for Themba. How could he protect him if he didn't know where he was? He promised Frik he wouldn't do anything impulsive or stupid.

Frik got the fire going, and asked Alex to get some steaks out of the fridge.

237

He went back outside where they sat quietly, drinking a beer, watching the fire until it was the right temperature for the steaks.

"Where's Liwa, Frik?"

"Oh, most probably visiting some chick he's got on the go. He's a real Casanova, loves the ladies, in case you haven't noticed. He doesn't tell me where he goes on the weekends. I leave him to it; he needs down-time on the weekend. He'll be back at work on Monday, but I think you'll miss him this visit."

When it got too chilly, they went inside to eat and watch TV.

Saturday, they enjoyed the day together and went to the movies. Their familiar and gentle camaraderie settled Alex's anxiety somewhat. It took Alex's mind off Themba's dilemma. Afterwards, they went to the Spur restaurant, for smoky chicken and spare ribs. Alex had started to unwind a bit and even laughed at Frik's jokes.

Frik enjoyed Alex's visit, even if it was under stressful conditions. He felt guilty about not telling Alex the truth about Themba's disappearance but knew that the only way he could keep them all safe was to never inadvertently let slip that they knew where Themba was. He was willing to carry the burden until circumstances changed.

Sunday went by uneventfully. Frik took Alex on a tour of Johannesburg, and they were early to bed for a five o'clock start on Monday morning. Frik had to be in court, and Alex was due to catch a train back to Cape Town.

# CHAPTER 29

ALICIA WAS WORRIED ABOUT ALEX. She'd noticed how withdrawn he had been since coming back from visiting his cousin in Jo'burg. His natural melancholy had deepened. It was as if he'd fallen into a deep, dark hole, and she couldn't help him out. She knew how much he loved Themba, and his disappearance was affecting him significantly.

She tried to distract him, but it didn't always work. They planned for the demonstration at the beaches, and they produced pamphlets for other marches. She was feeling pressure with her studies, combined with helping her parents at their market stall on Saturdays. She was finding it hard work to keep Alex afloat. She'd have to speak to Sara, see if she could also keep an eye on him.

This weekend they were due to visit her parents. Alex usually fetched her in his old Beetle, drove to Mitchell's Plain and stayed overnight. Her parents had accepted him as another son, and he got on well with her younger brother.

They'd have a *braai*. Alicia's father had invited some of his jazz band friends to come over, and there would be a bit of their regular jamming session. Alex always enjoyed these. She was hopeful that it may, at best, distract him.

# CHAPTER 30

AUGUST. WINTER. THE ANGRY WAVES crashed against the shoreline, digging up the seabed and spewing it out again. The wind howled, the trees creaked and swayed almost to breaking point against the relentless gales. The white sand was kicked up and stung your eyes and any exposed part of your body as you walked along the expansive stretch of beach. A beach that stretched to eternity.

Liwa put the ladder against the cabin's back wall. He climbed up with his tools on a belt. He was inspecting the roof and nailing down any loose sheets of corrugated iron so the wind wouldn't blow it away. Some parts of the roof were leaking, and he had to fix them so the cabin remained water-tight.

It was also an opportunity for him to keep an eye on the track leading to the cabins. It was difficult to hear a car approaching as the crashing of the waves and high winds muffled every other sound.

He'd been here for over two months now. Nobody had come to check on who was working at the cabins. That was not unusual. The farmer was quite elderly now and did not venture this far out.

He knew that the Smit family kept the cabins in good repair and only came every summer Christmas holiday. He never checked during winter, but despite this, Liwa wanted to make sure nobody was aware of him being here.

He finished his work for the morning and carefully negotiated down the ladder. He didn't want to injure himself, that would be stupid. He didn't like heights, so he needed to tread cautiously.

He entered the cabin via the back door. The figure in shadows was bent over the open books on the kitchen table. He looked up as Liwa came inside. They spoke in isiXhosa.

"You hungry yet?" he asked.

"Mmm, yes, just need to finish off reading this bit," was Themba's reply. There were deadlines to meet, and distraction must be avoided.

Liwa pottered about in the kitchen, slicing bread and cutting cheese and salami. He boiled the kettle on the gas stove.

Eventually, Themba closed his book and looked up. "I'm hungry now."

He made space for the food on the table.

"It's still all quiet around here now," said Liwa. "I've kept a lookout every day from the roofs, but nobody is about. It's unlikely anyone will come down here in winter. Frik was right, we're well hidden. When do you think you'll finish writing that piece of work?"

"In about two days," Themba replied. He looked out through the windows, at the crashing waves and remembered times gone by. He felt disconnected with the past and his future. Where was this path leading him? Had he jeopardised all his hard work throughout high school and university just to fail at the final hurdle? His political beliefs and actions were at the heart of who he is. He could not stand back from the steps he had taken; he had no regrets other than the pain and worry it had caused those who love him.

Themba read the newspapers that Liwa brought him after every trip into town for provisions. The violence and bombings were not abating. If anything, they were getting worse. He read about the "Cradock Four," who were young ANC activists who left Cradock to go to a political meeting but never arrived. They disappeared into thin air. This made Themba nervous; the danger was all around them, even in faraway places like Cradock. It was creeping closer and closer, like a madman in the night, stalking them, ready to pounce at any moment.

Their routine was for Liwa to go into town to post off Themba's assignments to Frik, who handed them to Themba's tutor, keeping to his deadlines as they had arranged. His final exams for his degree were a looming challenge for Themba. Had he prepared enough? Would he even be able to sit them in safety with the knowledge that he wouldn't be arrested as soon as he returned to university? Working and studying on his own was difficult; he was not sure his judgements on which part of the coursework to focus on were accurate. He wished he had guidance. He would have to work through all the course work and hope for the best.

Themba and Liwa had driven down to the cabins in the middle of the night, laden with Themba's books and some clothes. The secret police's tactics in following Themba had gotten more intense and blatant over the last week before they left. Themba knew instinctively that his freedom was limited and they were about to pounce. He confided in his uncle Sipho, who agreed and warned him that it was now the time to take drastic measures. He drove Themba in the middle of the night to Frik's house.

The nights were getting cold when Sipho turned into the familiar driveway in Houghton. Frik was expecting them and opened the back door for them to come in without being seen. All the house lights were off. They sat in the dark with Frik and Liwa, discussing the options for Themba. The cumulative effect of all his political actions and solidarity with others who were protesting in Soweto and other large towns was making the secret police nervous. They had the power to arrest him without a warrant and could detain him indefinitely without charging him with an offence. Once he was in their hands and under their control, there was little or nothing anyone could do. Themba's life was in danger, and the potential for his family to be harassed was high.

They decided that it would be the safest for Themba to hide out at the cabins in Port Alfred. Liwa would drive him there, and Frik would make arrangements for all Themba's coursework to get to his tutor for marking. Liwa would post the work in from Port Alfred.

They packed Themba into Liwa's car, and set off before the sun had a chance to rise.

"I think this is the best plan. The secret police will not know of the cabins in Port Alfred, and certainly would not be able to find them," Frik said to a nervous Sipho. Sipho knew he had to keep the family calm and would play down the dangers, saying Themba was staying at the university campus.

Uncle Sipho told Buhle and Nomsa that Themba was focussed and working at the university until he was ready to write his exams.

They must not worry about him; he was safe and protected on campus. They were satisfied and knew there was nothing they could do but wait. Nomsa felt uncomfortable with all this. She knew Themba was in danger. She daren't even think about where he actually was. Even though she doubted he was on campus, she would never say so. Hopefully, their ignorance would be their protection if the secret police ever interviewed them.

~

Uncle Sipho enjoyed sitting in the sun on the bench where he and Themba used to play their chess games. He could see who came into his yard. He knew what was wrong with any of his vehicles by the sound of the engine, and what his mechanic needed to do to repair them. He ordered and purchased the spare parts himself. He liked to keep his hand on the tiller even though his sons were the ones driving the business forward.

His eyes were closed, head back against the wall, the winter sun on his face. Uncle Sipho heard an unfamiliar car pull into his yard. It was a red car, with two white guys in it. He continued sitting where he was, eyes half-closed, pretending to doze. He heard them getting out of the car, doors slamming shut.

"Hey, Grandpa, we're looking for Themba Dlomo. Have you seen him?" they asked in Afrikaans, standing in front of Uncle Sipho, hands in their jacket pockets.

Calmly, he replied, "I don't speak Afrikaans," he replied in English, determined to make them feel as uncomfortable as possible. Keep them on their back feet. Some of these guys never spoke anything other than Afrikaans.

245

They asked him the same question, slowly, but in heavily accented English.

"No, he's not here. He's at Wits getting ready for his exams. Haven't seen him for weeks." This was true, Sipho hadn't seen him for weeks.

The two white guys grunted, turned and walked to their cars. "Fuckin' kaffir, bloody lazy sitting in the sun sleeping. He knows fuck-all, we're wasting our time here," they commented to each other in Afrikaans, shrugging their shoulders and returning to their car.

"Fucking Umlungu, white scum, stupid idiots. Think I'd tell them anything," Uncle Sipho whispered to himself in isiXhosa.

The driver of the red car reversed and spun out the yard in a cloud of dust.

Alex continued with his studies, trying to concentrate. Once his mind was set on his work, he got better at compartmentalising his thoughts and focussing. Professor Ibrahim always had a listening ear, and when he felt overwhelmed, Alex went to chat with him in his office. They had coffee together and talked about everything and anything. This relaxed environment, talking about everyday things, brought Alex's level of anxiety down. It was as if Professor Ibrahim, in his calm manner, absorbed Alex's fears like a sponge. Sharing his problems made them seem less threatening.

Professor Ibrahim was Muslim, and Alex enjoyed discussing politics, but also their religions. Alex gained a better understanding of Islam as the professor read him excerpts of the Qur'an. They were familiar tales from the Christian Bible with Moses leading his people; Jesus was also seen as one of the prophets.

"Alex, people who become Muslim do not abandon Jesus but return to his original teachings. Islam sees Jesus as a prophet, from a long line of prophets like Moses and Abraham, Peace be Upon Them. As Christians, you believe in the Holy Trinity, but in Islam, there is only One God. That, Alex, is the fundamental difference."

Alex was amazed by all the similarities between the two religions. Their philosophical debates stimulated Alex's mind, giving him a broader sense of the place of religion in his life. His respect for Islam grew as his relationship with the professor deepened. Alex considered the belief of the Holy Trinity, which he had always struggled with, but in Islam, there was One God. Alex wanted to have a religious conviction based on sound knowledge rather than blind following.

Alex's relationship with Professor Ibrahim was one he cherished. The professor was generous with his time and his wisdom. He was like a father-figure to him, one who guided and challenged him to evaluate his own beliefs. Professor Ibrahim gave Alex a copy of the Qur'an, which he placed alongside his Holy Bible in his bedroom. Alex found these two holy books a source of solace and a challenge to his own belief systems. Alex knew the studying of both religions would be part of his future development. Alex thought to himself, *What if we can accept each other's ethnic diversity and our religious diversity as well?* Alex knew the current struggle was for racial equality, but the need for a broader debate on religious and other diversity struggles would surface in the future.

Alex left the campus and made the regular train journey home from Rondebosch. He had made this journey for three years now and could rattle the names of each station off in his mind. Alex knew the rhythm and the sounds on the track. He always looked at the fishing boats when he went past Kalk Bay station and tried to pick out the colourful boats of any of his friends who were back from a day's fishing. Sometimes, he hopped off the train and went to chat with them and buy a *snoek* for his mum. It was a relief to talk to them; their routines continued no matter the politics in the land. Fish were caught. Fish were sold. They went home to their families with money in their pockets. It was a good life. This predictable rhythm was hypnotic and took him away from the tumult of his family worries. He was clutching at mechanisms to keep himself from drowning. He knew what worked and regularly talked to Alicia about his fears - she was a calming influence on him and always gave him wise advice.

Alex got off at Fish Hoek station, walked through the underground subway towards the exit. He continued walking home. It was still light enough for the street lights to be off, and slowly, he made the journey back in automatic mode. When he turned the corner of their street, he noticed a red car parked outside his house with two figures sitting in it. This was unusual; his mother rarely has visitors in the week.

He walked up to his house and noticed two men in the red car. As they saw him enter his driveway, they got out and called out to him.

"Mr. Smit!"

Alex turned and nodded in their direction. He noticed the crumpled ties and ill-fitting jackets. He'd never seen them before. Were they armed undercover police?

248

Alex faced them, the front door still shut, and put his hands in his jeans pockets to stop them from shaking.

"Ah, Mr. Smit, we're from the police, and we want to ask you a few questions. Can we come in." They asked in Afrikaans, all smiles and friendly.

Alex replied in English. "No, you can't, unless you have some kind of warrant. You can ask your questions here."

"Might not be a good idea, sir. What will your neighbours think?" they commented in broken, heavily accented English.

"I don't care what they think. I don't know you; you're not showing me any official document or badge, so we will talk out here."

The two men looked at each other and dropped the false smiles. Alex was tall, powerfully built, confident, and white. They couldn't terrorise or intimidate him into supplying them with answers. They'd have to try the nice-guy approach.

"We're trying to locate Mr. Themba Dlomo. Do you know him and when did you last see him?" they asked in serious, dull tones.

"I know him; we grew up together on our family farm in the Karoo. I haven't seen him for ages. He lives in Jo'burg."

"Are you sure? He's not in trouble; we just want to ask him to help us with some enquiries we have." They said this as if Alex would feel placated by their need to be asking Themba to "help" them.

"Yes, I'm sure. I haven't seen him for a long time. Now if you'll get off my property, or I'll have to get the local police to show you off my front garden."

The two men looked at each other and shrugged, not sure what to do next but needing to have the last say in the most threatening way possible.

"Play it your way. We'll be back, and the next time we'll have a warrant to search your property, and if you don't cooperate, we'll arrest you for withholding information!"

With that, the men turned and walked slowly back to their car.

Alex muttered to himself in English, "Well fuck off then assholes!" There, that made him feel better. He let himself in, locked and chained the door and leaned with his back against it, closing his eyes. Danger averted. Hopefully, for now, they were satisfied. He dreaded that they may come back and become more heavy-handed with him or his mother.

Alex made himself a strong coffee, grateful he had warded them off and stopped them from searching the house, which would really have upset his mother. He hadn't burnt Themba's letters, but they were in a metal box, buried in the ground behind some bushes in the back garden. Alex knew he should have destroyed them, but he just couldn't bring himself to do it. It was Themba's voice, his jokes, his stories, their lives lived apart. No, the letters were safe. He could never deny their relationship. How could you deny you had a brother? Impossible! He felt those childish writings and shared experiences were somehow sacred to him.

~

Frik was managing his role as the agreed go-between for handing Themba's work to his university tutor so that he could still sit his exams later this year. He'd managed this well, sometimes using

250

one of his secretaries to take the envelope with Themba's written work through to the tutor at Wits University. He tried alternating different people to make the drop-off. Thankfully, this had worked so far. The tutor had given feedback that Themba's work was remaining at a high standard, and he was satisfied that he would be able to sit his upcoming exams with some degree of success.

Liwa did their shopping in town at the same time as doing the postal run. They agreed that Liwa wouldn't phone Frik unnecessarily in case the phones were tapped. He wouldn't contact Nomsa or Alex either. It was too risky; the police might be watching all of them.

They'd been there for three months now. It was freezing in the cabins in the dead of winter, but there was a small gas heater, which they sat around at night. They daren't light a fire in case any wanderers spotted the smoke and assumed someone was at the cabins. There was no electricity, which was fine if you were only there in the summer. Now in the winter months, Themba and Liwa used a gas lamp at night. The cabin had an eerie feel to it, with ghostly voices playing on their minds. Their shadows dancing against the walls. Their heightened level of anxiety and fear was causing them to imagine sounds in the darkness of night. The creaking trees, the stormy seas.

They talked it through with each other, and tried to make jokes about it. Themba had even taught Liwa how to play chess. His uncle Sipho had thoughtfully packed the chess set for him and Liwa to while away the long cold nights.

It was agreed that Liwa would ring Frik after three months, to find out if it was safe for Themba to return to Johannesburg just before he was due to write his final exams. Just a few more weeks to go. Both men were feeling the strain but tried to keep each other's spirits up with happy memories and heated chess games.

Themba felt guilty about not being able to tell Alex that he was safe, but he couldn't jeopardise his friends, his family or Nomsa's safety. He couldn't tell Nomsa where he was going either, just that he needed to lay low for a while.

Another four weeks went by. Themba was getting anxious about preparing for exams and he felt he was working blindly without his tutor to give him guidance. He also missed Nomsa and his mum. He knew Alex would be worrying about him too. He was feeling helpless, and if it wasn't for Liwa's company and protection, he knew he would not have stayed in hiding for this long. Frik must have guessed this, which is why he'd asked Liwa to bring him to the cabins and to hide out with him. Liwa had nerves of steel and was not easily frightened or intimidated by circumstances or people.

Liwa and Themba agreed it is time to make the phone call to Frik to find out if it was safe to return to Johannesburg. Frik and Liwa had agreed to speak isiXhosa using a code they had pre-arranged. If it wasn't safe, Frik would tell him he couldn't have visitors as he was going to Cape Town. If Frik said to him, "It's about bloody time he came home instead of spending all his time with his girlfriend," then this would be the green light code for them to return to Jo'burg.

This was, hopefully, the final trip in to Port Alfred for Liwa. He posted off Themba's work and used the pay phone at the post office to call Frik.

The phone rang, and rang. Eventually Frik picked up. "Hi, it's Liwa", he greeted Frik in isiXhosa. "How's things?"

"Hey man, what you up to?" Frik asked, "it's about bloody time you came home instead of lazing about with your girlfriend."

Liwa continued speaking to Frik in isiXhosa, "she's dumped me so I had better come home. See you next week." After that brief exchange, Liwa knew it was time to go back to Johannesburg. Relieved, he climbed in to his car and made the journey back to the cabins.

Frik and Liwa had agreed that they would have to stay at Frik's on their return, to be on the safe side. Liwa just wanted to go home. Themba absorbed Liwa's news, sighing with the release of the tension, holding his head in his hands, shaking with fear and glad the long isolation was over. He felt for those people in prison, isolated and not seeing their families. His relatively comfortable stay in Port Alfred was nothing compared to what other activists had to tolerate. He felt grateful and hoped he would be safe when he returned.

Liwa and Themba packed everything away and tidied the cabin as if they had never been there. They began the long road journey back to Johannesburg, with Liwa whistling a tune under his breath. Life could now go back to normal.

# CHAPTER 31

THE SHRILL RINGING OF THE phone woke Alex up. He lifted himself up on one arm and glanced at his watch. *Bloody hell, it's 6am on a Saturday.* He dragged himself out of bed as the phone carried on ringing. He picked it up.

"Hello?"

Sara came out of her bedroom into the hallway where the phone was, tying her dressing gown around her waist. She was frightened; early morning phone-calls usually brought bad news. Sara saw Alex pick up the phone, and then he froze, not a word. She could see his hand shaking. She walked towards him. Alex had his back to the wall and slowly slid down until he was sitting on the floor. He was pale with tears rolling down his cheeks, his hair all matted from sleep. He was shaking so much he couldn't say anything.

All he could say was, "Themba."

Sara took the phone from Alex as he rolled over into a ball. She listened.

"Hi, Themba, how are you my boy?" she asked, tears rolling down her cheeks as well. She struggled to stay calm and listen to what Themba had to say. Themba was crying as well, babbling in isiXhosa. Frik took over the phone and told Sara that Themba was staying with him at the moment; he'd come out of hiding and he was okay. She told him Alex was in shock and unable to talk. Frik said if he wanted, he could ring Themba later when he felt up to it. Sara agreed and gently put the phone back on the cradle.

She got down on the floor next to Alex and held him in her arms. His body was shaking uncontrollably, but she held him tight to her. She stroked his hair. "It's okay, it's okay, Themba is safe, he's with Frik." Eventually, what she'd repeated permeated his fuzzy brain. He started to calm down, and his breathing became regular. His emotions had been building up over the months, and now culminated in the utter relief he felt that Themba was alive and well. Alex had been fearful every time the telephone rang. *Would it be bad news, was Themba alive or dead?* The waiting had been unbearable.

"Come, let's go have a coffee." Sara got up, held Alex by the hand and they went to sit at the table in the kitchen. She boiled the kettle.

Eventually, he said, "I can't believe it, Mum, he's been missing nearly five months. I thought he was dead and buried in some obscure unmarked place that we would never find."

"I know, but Frik says they had no choice; he couldn't tell anyone, so they arranged for Liwa to take him down to the cabins in Port Alfred where he could hide. You know nobody ever goes there in the winter. Themba carried on with his uni work, and Liwa would post it to Frik to hand in to his tutor. He's come back because he needs to sit his final exams. Frik also says it's going to be announced on Monday that the ANC and the other political affiliates are to be unbanned."

Alex lifted his head, looked at his mother and slowly, a smile started to form on his face. This was the news they had all hoped and prayed for. Relief at last. All the hard work and suffering over so many years by so many, was leading to this.

"Hallelujah!" Alex shouted, waving both arms up in the air. He grabbed his mother, lifted her up off her feet, laughing and crying at the same it. They collapsed on the sofa.

"When you've caught your breath and had a coffee, phone Themba back. He's at Frik's for now."

~

After he put the phone down, Themba looked over at Nomsa, who was watching him, not sure how he was going to respond. Themba walked towards her and put his arms around her and started shaking.

"I'm so sorry, I'm so sorry," he kept repeating, his whole body going into a spasm. Nomsa held him tight to her so he could hear her regular heart-beat and breathing, hoping their interlocked bodies would calm him down. His breathing eventually returned to normal, and he loosened their embrace to look at her. He cupped her face in his hands.

"Nomsa, I'm so sorry for what I've put you all through. I never thought that all my activism would affect my family. I suppose I was arrogant, thinking I was invincible. The great Themba, afraid of nobody! It was so close to me being sacrificed for the cause. It's made me realise how important you and my family are to me."

Nomsa took his hand, and they went and sat on the sofa. "Themba, you were fighting a just cause as best as you knew how. I do believe God was guiding you on behalf of us all. We could not all do what you did. You supported, you challenged, and you helped to shine a light on injustice. I think you were very brave. I am also relieved that you are now safe."

When Themba had returned to Houghton, Liwa had gone through to Alexandra to tell his family he was back and that he was safe. They were so relieved. They hugged Liwa, thanking him for looking after their son. Buhle cried; she had not wanted to believe he was in danger, but the risk was always at the back of her mind; uncertainty that she had to live with every day. Now that he was back in Johannesburg, she was relieved.

Liwa had explained that Themba should remain in Houghton with Frik until the following week when it was going to be announced that the ANC was to be unbanned. The secret police would no longer be a threat, and Themba had finally been able to come home and prepare for his exams.

The family danced with joy, praising the Lord and hugging each other. They never believed they would see this day, but here it was. It was like having a far-fetched dream, that in your heart you knew would never be fulfilled, finally come true.

Liwa went to see Nomsa next door to give her the good news. The family spent some time together asking Liwa many questions. Liwa asked Nomsa if she wanted to go back to Houghton with him to spend the weekend with Themba. She didn't hesitate, grabbed an overnight bag from home and made the journey to Houghton and Themba.

# CHAPTER 32

ALEX AND THEMBA FINISHED THEIR final exams and waited eagerly for their results. Themba returned to Alexandra to be reunited with his family and Nomsa. They celebrated in the best way they knew how, with Uncle Sipho making a *shishinyama* in the yard. Celebrations were for the joy they felt at Themba returning home safely, and for the unbanning of the ANC, which meant their lives were no longer at risk and they didn't have to worry about Themba "disappearing" and never being found. Their worst fears did not come true.

Alex, his family and friends also celebrated Themba's safety and the beginning of the road to equality for all. Alex went through to Mitchell's Plain with Alicia and celebrated with her family. He asked her to marry him as soon as they could, and the family celebrated their engagement in true South African style with a *braai*.

The summer warmth lifted everyone's spirits; people could not believe this was actually happening. The newspapers reported that Nelson Mandela was being released after twenty-seven long years of incarceration. He was staying temporarily in the prison governor's home, and arrangements were being made for his future. Other ANC prisoners were also being released.

The world watched as he finally walked out of Victor Verster Prison, holding his wife's hand. He raised his fist. This was the first time that South Africans saw him or heard his voice.

After thirty-five years, Archbishop Tutu welcomed Nelson and Winnie Mandela into his home in Bishopscourt.

Archbishop Tutu and other religious and political leaders called for an end to sanctions, now that the dismantling of apartheid was irreversible. The ANC and other anti-apartheid groups ended their use of the armed struggle for freedom. There were rumblings of violence in Natal between the Zulu leaders and Umkhontu we Sizwe, the armed wing of the ANC. They only disbanded once the transfer of political power had taken place. The country was still on a knife-edge of anger and revenge, with the potential to escalate into uncontrollable violence between the different political factions.

The road to tenuous peace awaited.

# CHAPTER 33

ALEX STARTED WORK AT THE oil refinery in Cape Town. He and Alicia were wrapped up in their joy and preparations for their future together. Their families were relieved that the young couple could finally be together without continually looking over their shoulders. Alex and Alicia had to wait for the law to change repealing the legal segregation of races. He made plans to buy a house in the Bokaap of District Six. It was a small house, and Alex also arranged to rent the house next door for Alicia's parents. He wanted to gift them their dream of returning to District Six. On a practical level, it was close to Groote Schuur where Alicia would be doing medical research, and it was accessible for him to the refinery.

The conscription of white South African young men had not been rigorously enforced since the breaking up of apartheid. Alex could finally move on with his life.

Themba was undertaking post-graduate studies part-time while working with the department of education during the transition period and consulting with the ANC leadership on the road forward, following his dream of a standard policy of educating all children in

South Africa. Themba was now part of the team focusing on building that future. He and Nomsa bought a house in Kempton Park.
They were one of the first black families to purchase property in
what was traditionally a white area. Buhle joined them.

Frik started his pupillage and was a junior member of the legal
team supporting the process of drawing up the new constitution.
He was hoping to work with Justice Pius Langa and Justice Ismael
Mahomed, to eventually finalise and implement the Constitutional
Court of South Africa.

# CHAPTER 34

*December 1991*

ALEX WAITED IN THE ARRIVALS area at Cape Town Airport. Common symbols of the apartheid past, like Johannesburg International Airport being renamed Oliver Tambo Airport which reflected the new South Africa. The flight from Johannesburg was announced as having landed. He had never flown in an aeroplane, and neither had Themba. This would be a new experience for them both. Alex paced along the barriers looking out for his brother. Eventually, he saw him coming through the exit doors, smiling broadly.

"Hey, bro," Themba greeted him with a wave. They hugged and slapped each other on the back. Alex took Themba's bag, and they went to an airport café for coffee.

"Phew man," said Themba, "that was exciting. Never done this before. As the plane takes off, you're thrown back in your seat. The nose of the plane goes up, and you're up, up, up in the sky." He laughed.

Alex smiled at him. He couldn't believe he was there, finally. It felt relaxed and casual; socialising in a café together was so comfortable and natural for them. The world, as they knew it, had changed for the better.

They had so much to share with each other since their graduation and settling into the new South Africa. Alex knew Themba was working for the Department for Education and was now a legitimate party member of the ANC. This was now grown-up mainstream politics, not activism.

Themba explained that the conference he was attending next week was to form a consensus on education and how the future would look, and his remit was to focus on education in the rural areas. This had always been his passion, and Alex saw the fervour and vision in Themba's face. His whole life had been leading to this moment in time when all children would have access to a good education. Alex shook his head and thought, *the country's children are in good hands.*

"So, how's your job, Alex?" Themba eventually asked.

"Good, I'm enjoying my work and of course the salary! I'm busy buying a house as soon as my trust money comes through. My Pa left me a small amount of money for when I turn twenty-one. I'm using it to put down a deposit for a house in the Bokaap that Alicia and I like; it survived the demolition of its neighbour District Six area of Cape Town. I've asked Alicia to marry me as soon as the segregation laws are repealed. She said yes." Alex was still surprised, happy, euphoric, and unbelieving that Alicia wanted to be his wife.

Once they'd finished their coffees, they headed off to find Alex's car for their journey to Fish Hoek. It was Friday afternoon, and Alex wanted to get out of Cape Town before the afternoon traffic on the highway.

They got to the car, and Themba let out a breath. "Hey man, where's the Beetle you had?"

Alex smiled. "Well, this is an upgraded VW; it's called a Jetta and part of my employment package. A company car." They put Themba's bags in the boot and made their way out of the airport.

Themba had never been this side of Cape Town. They passed the townships of Langa and Nyanga. It was an expansive area covering many townships—a maze of shacks and occasional brick houses and makeshift huts. Poverty was all around; you could not escape it. Themba had seen the sprawling mass of shacks from the aeroplane window. You could not get a sense of the vastness of poverty other than from the air, looking down.

Themba wondered how long it would take to uplift people's lives to the basics of having electricity and running water. The sheer amount of effort, money and government commitment was mind-blowing. Was it even possible to achieve the impossible? How would they satisfy millions of people's expectations?

Eventually, they got on to the highway, and Alex pointed out Rondebosch and his old university. They made their way towards Muizenberg, and the coastal route that Themba knew that lead towards Fish Hoek.

Sara heard the car pull up on the drive, and she ran outside to greet them. She saw Themba, all man now, with his big smile with the dimples on either side. His hair was short, not like the wild afro he used to have as a student. They smiled at each other then reached out and clasped one another; each could hear the other's familiar breath and heartbeat.

"Let me look at you, son," said Sara, holding him at arms-length. "Gosh, I've forgotten how handsome you are." Themba smiled in response, gripping Sara's hand tightly, not knowing what to say.

Alex got Themba's bag out of the car boot, and they went inside.

Sara made them a cold drink, and they sat outside on the patio that Themba and Alex had built when they were teenagers. Peaceful sounds surrounded them in the garden. She caught up with Themba's news about his work at the Department of Education. He told them that he'd been offered a government sponsorship for a two-year part-time post-graduate business master's degree. He knew it was a lot of work to do part-time and also work full time, but he'd manage.

"How's your mum, Themba?"

"She's good, still working. Nomsa and I have bought a house in Kempton Park, just outside Jo'burg. We want to get married, but it will have to wait until I've finished my master's degree. It's going to be a big Zulu wedding, a week-long celebration. I hope you'll all come?"

"Of course, we wouldn't miss it for the world," said Sara, and Alex was grinning and nodding as well. What a fantastic celebration it would be for them all.

Themba looked down at his hands shyly, and softly gave them the best news. "Nomsa is expecting." He looked up at them both in turn. "I'm going to be a dad!"

Alex stood up and grabbed Themba by the hand. "Fantastic news, a free South African rainbow baby. Congratulations, man!"

"Yeah, my mum is going to come and live with us to help us look after the baby so that Nomsa can go back to work after maternity leave. It's going to be a hectic time, but we'll manage."

Sara got up and went inside. She came back out with a tray with glasses and champagne. "I just had a feeling we were going to be celebrating something momentous." Alex shook the bottle, building up the gas inside, and when he popped the cork, he sprayed it all over Themba. They all laughed and cheered, eventually pouring the left-overs in the glasses.

Themba and Alex built a fire, ready to have a *braai*. Their relationship was so intimate that they didn't have to speak to each other while getting everything ready. They settled into the familiar, comfortable camaraderie of preparing a meal.

They sat up late into the night next to the fire, talking about their future and their dreams, just like they used to do when they were children.

The morning sun was warming up the house; time to start the day. Alex and Themba shared the outside bedroom like old times. Sara made them breakfast, and they had already decided they would head down to the beach for a surf. The wind was up today.

Alex took Themba to see his granny, Eileen. He pushed the café's door open. His granny looked up, knowing it was her grandson

266

coming through the doorway. She saw Themba and came across to give him a hug. She invited them back for something to eat and drink when they had finished swimming and surfing.

Alex had two boards strapped to the top of his car, ready for them both.

"Ed has moved to Muizenberg now. He's got a much bigger shop, and he has a large flat above it where he lives with his family. We'll pop in to see him tomorrow on our way to Newlands." Alex had bought tickets to the one-day cricket test match between South Africa and India, the first international tour since the dismantling of apartheid.

~

It was to be a weekend of "firsts." A chance for Themba and Alex to do what all young people do: surf, swim, go to a café and sit together to have lunch. Go to a sporting match and cheer on their national side, sitting in a crowd of supporters of all colours. Go to a pub afterwards to enjoy a beer. Visit friends, no matter what the colour of their skin, cultural or belief systems were. To enjoy each other's company and enrich each other's lives with friendship and love.

The weekend was strange, yet at the same time, it was typical for them. This was a world that Themba and Alex had always wished and dreamed about. To have those everyday freedoms, to not have to plan ahead or think what they were going to do together. Just to do things on impulse without external restrictions inhibiting them. Experience things, just like brothers do.

# CHAPTER 35

SUNDAY LANDED ON THEIR DOORSTEP before they knew it. They dropped in to see Ed in Muizenberg, on their way to the cricket match in Newlands. The shop was much bigger than his one in Fish Hoek. He had a much more extensive range of boards, both those that Ed had built and some top brands, ready for tourists in the holiday season. Ed sold swimming costumes, wet suits and various paraphernalia for all ages needed for swimming and surfing. His business appeared to be thriving. Holiday makers and surfers were browsing and shopping.

Ed's wife was helping him in the shop, and his children came to greet Themba and Alex. The children told them about their school in Muizenberg and their friends they played with.

The family seemed content, happy and settled.

The international cricket ban against South Africa had been in place since 1970 and was now lifted. The World Cup was to be held in Australia in 1992, and this Indian Friendship tour was the first in the new age of the Rainbow Nation.

Alex and Themba took their seats in the Newlands grounds. They looked up at the spectacular Table Mountain and Devil's Peak, setting a dramatic backdrop to a momentous occasion. This had to be one of the best cricket grounds in the world, they commented to each other. Alex had managed to get seats close to the pitch, just a couple of rows back. They had a view of the crease, running left and right of their line of sight.

The India captain, Mohammad Azharuddin, and the South Africa captain, Kepler Wessels, tossed a coin. India won and chose to bat first.

Themba and Alex had a programme each, noting the players and their scores as the game progressed. The best Indian batsman was Jadega on 48 runs off 69 balls. They enjoyed rattling off the players, Kirsten, Tendulkar, and the man of the match, Hansie Cronje. These were names they would remember for the World Cup the following year.

South Africa won by six wickets with three balls remaining. Themba and Alex enjoyed the match, not because it was the most exciting, but because they were able to experience it together, enjoying their love of the game as brothers.

The game was not without some controversy. The South African captain, Kepler Wessels, had played for Australia during apartheid—a professional sportsman pursuing his dreams in an imperfect situation.

They went to Forrester's Arms pub in Newlands after the match, mixing with all the other cricket fans. There were black, white, Indian, and coloured and many languages spoken, adding to the buzz and atmosphere. Although the game was thought by everyone to be mediocre, it was the fact that it was actually taking place that was the source of celebration. Everyone was speculating about the team for next year's World Cup in Australia. Did South Africa stand a chance? Should the team include a more culturally diverse group as a priority rather than merely focussing on winning in the short term? Big questions to come, and equally big decisions to be made by the South African Cricket board.

After the festivities, they headed off for Kalk Bay to the Brass Bell restaurant on the station overlooking the harbour.

Again, a familiar place for Themba, one he'd experienced before, but now an added experience, going with Alex to the restaurant.

They ordered a feast of crayfish and fish and chips, and they washed their meal down with an ice-cold beer. They raised their glasses to each other. They couldn't believe they had made it this far, to this place. They reflected on their day, their enjoyment watching their favourite sport, drinking a beer in a pub together with other cricket fans. This was the stuff their childhood dreams were made of.

They finished their meal and had a coffee, watching the waves splashing against the windows of the restaurant. Their mood turned to introspection. It was dark outside and the evening turned cool, with the waves crashing so near to them it felt like they were sitting on the rocks.

Alex felt it was the right time to talk about something sensitive with Themba.

"I know about your birth father and who he is. He's the farmer of Kasteel."

Themba nodded. "I want nothing to do with him; he's just a biological factor in my life. He doesn't mean anything to me. My mother is the one who suffered and brought me up to be the man I am today. I owe her everything."

Alex acknowledged this but felt there was an outcome that Themba should know about.

"My mother has kept in touch with some of her friends at the school where she taught in Cradock. For years after we left Cradock, Klaas Senior's drinking got way out of control. He became a chronic alcoholic, and even the church minister couldn't ignore it anymore and stripped him of being a deacon in the church. This sent him into a spiral with him losing 'face' and 'status' in the community, all at once. It became common knowledge that he took this rejection out on his farm workers, and also on his family. Even his wife and children could not escape his brutality."

Themba looked intently at Alex, absorbing everything that he was hearing.

"His farm was due to be repossessed as well, which only increased his dependency on alcohol. One evening, he was driving his tractor in a field that he was trying to plough. Why, nobody knows, as it's not something he would typically do. Anyway, the plough at the back got stuck, and his tractor would not go forward. He got out of the driver's seat to go and try and fix the problem."

Alex took a deep breath and continued.

"He must have been blind drunk because his whole arm got stuck under the plough-blades and was severed. He lay there overnight and bled to death. Nobody had missed him or came to look for him until the next day. His wife was used to him 'disappearing' overnight so hadn't sounded the alarm. One of the workers found him the following morning, lying on the ground in a pool of blood with the tractor engine still running."

Themba absorbed all this, let out a sigh and shrugged. "Well, he got what he deserved, an undignified and lonely death."

"Yes, apparently the funeral was a rather small and sad affair. Klaas's wife immediately sold the farm and moved to Port Elizabeth."

They both looked out of the restaurant windows, the inky darkness with the waves lashing against them. They shivered and decided it was time to go home.

When they got back to Fish Hoek, they went to sit outside on the patio to finish their day off with a final beer together.

"What does the future hold for us? Do you think we'll be able to pull ourselves up and out of the grasp of discrimination and oppression? Will people be able to change their behaviour?" Themba thought out loud. Alex hesitated, not sure. These were such big questions.

"Bro, we don't know. I wish we had a crystal ball to see into the future and prevent ourselves from making mistakes. Things had to change; the way forward may be rocky and steep, but we must persevere. The next few years of transition towards the elections are critical. I pray it will be a peaceful process. It may only be with time that we unravel and realise the full extent of the damage apartheid has done over so many generations."

"Yes, you're right." Themba looked at his brother; they were the future. They had to believe they could work it all out for the sake of their children. "My biggest concern is that the removal of the cancer of apartheid will leave us with permanent damage—damage we may struggle with for years to come."

# EPILOGUE

THE RELEASE OF NELSON MANDELA and his fellow political prisoners was followed by a transition period to free and fair elections. These were held in 1994 with Themba, Alex, and their families jointly exercising their right to vote for the first time.

Helen Suzman was appointed by Nelson Mandela to head the first electoral commission, which oversaw the elections.

Nelson Mandela was inaugurated as President in May 1994. His wish was to unite the country, where the victims and perpetrators of human rights abuses had to learn to live alongside each other.

The South African Constitution was drawn up, and the Constitutional Court was established in 1994, coming into effect in 1997.

In 1995, the Truth and Reconciliation Commission was set up by Nelson Mandela and chaired by the newly retired Bishop Desmond Tutu. The Commission determined that apartheid was a crime against humanity and that the liberation movements were conducting a just war. The political affiliation of a victim or perpetrator of crimes was irrelevant to the determination of whether the offence was a gross violation or not.

Statements were taken and oral testimony given in person throughout the country over eighteen months. All oral evidence was recorded, and hour-long summary episodes broadcast weekly on national television. The real horror of the human rights abuses, which had not been fully reported in the media during apartheid, were finally laid bare for all to witness.

The Commission made recommendations to the government, with some perpetrators being granted amnesty after full disclosure for politically motivated crimes. Limited reparation was awarded to victims, for example, the funding of a gravestone for a loved one.

The Commission identified more than 19,050 victims of gross human rights violations. Amnesty was granted to only 849 of the 7,111 applications received.

It was felt that this traumatised country needed to lay bare the past's dark truths and lay ghosts to rest to contribute to national healing. The Commission heard formal evidence covering a thirty-four-year mandate period.

The Commission heard moving testimony by family members who had suffered traumatic losses, police brutality and intimidation. The years of dehumanising injustice and oppression served to highlight their resilience in dealing with such adversity. The victim's ability to forgive was humbling, their search for the truth about the circumstances of a loved one's 'disappearance' was moving. The Commission hoped that following forgiveness and reconciliation that national healing would begin.

There was some criticism regarding the Truth and Reconciliation Commission's *restorative justice* approach rather than following a path of *retributive justice.* Following a further study in 1998, it was felt that reconciliation had not been fully achieved, with those seeking justice subsequently taking cases to the South African and US courts.

Given the scale of the scourge of apartheid and the attempts at reconciliation, the country's future still looks turbulent. New generations are born, old injustices fester, and poverty, corruption and unemployment remain barriers to a brighter future for some. But there is a robust and progressive constitution and freedom of speech in place. These are the tools for future generations to build on and attempt to repair the long-lasting damage caused by apartheid.

# ACKNOWLEDGEMENTS

AS A WHITE CHILD GROWING up in the apartheid era, I was aware of the segregation markers, like the signs outside public buildings and beaches.

The South African black voice, other than that of black religious leaders, was absent or silenced. Those contributing to the political struggle tried to challenge and highlight the inhumanity of apartheid. Removing it was torturous, and it left scarring and damage for a lifetime.

I made a promise to my eighteen-year-old self never to vote in an election until all South Africans had universal suffrage. That day of voting in 1994, queuing up with South Africans of all colours, aged thirty-six, was also my first voting experience. I was living in Durban at the time, and I brought my young son in his pushchair and took my turn at the kiosk. The queues were long, people were chatting, and the atmosphere felt historic, momentous and peaceful all at the same time.

I moved to the United Kingdom in 1998 with my English husband and two young sons. My beliefs in politics, free speech, and the right to vote are imbedded in my early life in South Africa. I have always voted in the United Kingdom and always encourage my sons to vote, citing Nelson Mandela's lengthy incarceration and life's work in fighting apartheid to achieve every citizen's right to vote.

I must thank certain people whom I have not met. I trained as a social worker in the United Kingdom with local government support. For that, I'm genuinely grateful. The work of Jane Elliott, the US educator and anti-racist activist, shaped my thinking as a student. I developed this further in my academic studies and ultimately, as a university lecturer myself. My earlier voluntary work in South Africa and my social work with disadvantaged children and their families of all ages and backgrounds in the United Kingdom were based on a robust anti-discriminatory belief system.

I thank the talented, funny and insightful Trevor Noah. His book, *Born a Crime*, was an inspiration, especially regarding my lack of knowledge of the Alexandra township. Although I had worked alongside the township, i.e., in Sandton, I never ventured inside it. He also gave me insight into what it felt like to be a "coloured" child and man in South Africa.

The work of Sizwe Mpofu-Walsh, in his book, *Democracy and Delusion, 10 Myths in South African Politics*, gave me insight as to the effects of the history of South Africa on the present day. Also, his experience of the privileged private school system in South Africa. Thank you.

While this book is a work of fiction, I have attempted to be as accurate as possible with the real events in South Africa. If there are any mistakes, they are mine.

Finally, thank you to my family and friends for listening to me talk about this book over many months, and for their helpful input when my memory failed me. Their constructive criticism has allowed me to improve the story, and their belief in me kept me going.

Thanks to my knowledgeable older brother, Piet, who knew how to build the "wire cars" when we were children. He helped remind me of our shared memories of our visits to Cradock to our grandparents throughout our childhood. He had been a keen surfer in his youth and also experienced compulsory conscription. His memories and experiences have been woven into this story.

Thank you to my husband, sons and daughter-in-law, who have been hugely supportive. Their love of South Africa is shared with me.

Lastly, dear reader, I hope you have enjoyed this snapshot into the somewhat turbulent history of South Africa. If it has uplifted you, I hope you will be inspired to visit South Africa. If you feel able, a review of this book would be most welcome.

If you would like to be updated about my upcoming projects,
please contact me via my website — https://randlezone.wixsite.com/mysite

The lyrics of Scatterlings of Africa can be found in —
www.johnnyclegg.com